...ories in her third-gra... ...ver since. After publishing poetry at university, she ...rned to novels. Her Regency historical romances ...ve won or been placed in contests by the Romance ...riters of America, *Romantic Times* magazine, National ...eaders' Choice and the Daphne du Maurier Award. She ...ves with her husband in Texas. For news and contests, ...sit juliajustiss.com.

Also by Julia Justiss

Sisters of Scandal miniseries

A Most Unsuitable Match
The Earl's Inconvenient Wife

The Cinderella Spinsters miniseries

The Awakening of Miss Henley
The Tempting of the Governess
The Enticing of Miss Standish

Heirs in Waiting miniseries

The Bluestocking Duchess
The Railway Countess

Look out for the next book, coming soon!

Discover more at millsandboon.co.uk.

THE RAILWAY
COUNTESS

Julia Justiss

MILLS & BOON

First Published in Great Britain 2021
by Mills & Boon, an imprint of HarperCollins*Publishers* Ltd,
1 London Bridge Street, London, SE1 9GF

www.harpercollins.co.uk

HarperCollins*Publishers*
1st Floor, Watermarque Building,
Ringsend Road, Dublin 4, Ireland

The Railway Countess © 2021 Janet Justiss

ISBN: 978-0-263-28405-8

06/21

Printed and bound in Spain
by CPI, Barcelona

To my darling granddaughters
Anna, Samantha and Bennett.

May you fly as high as your wings will carry you.

Chapter One

~~~~~~~~~~

Bristol, England—March 1834

'If it *can* be done, it will certainly be a magnificent achievement,' Crispin d'Aubignon murmured to himself as he stood reviewing his notes outside the office of Richard Cranmore, the engineer surveying the final leg of the proposed Great Western Railway.

With the substantial return he'd earned on his investment in the Liverpool & Manchester, he was always looking for other promising railway ventures. If he received the answers he anticipated from the engineering assistant he would be consulting in just a few moments, he'd be ready to sink some money into this new scheme.

Review completed, he walked in to find the bare outer office deserted. Not surprising, since the firm's main headquarters was back in London and this suite of rooms had been rented only for the duration of the local survey. But the front door had been left unlocked, which indicated there should be someone on the premises.

Proceeding towards the inner office, he called out, 'Hello! Is anyone here?'

He'd been about to add his name and the reason for his visit when he reached the doorway and stopped short.

Seated behind the desk of the inner office was a woman. Not just a woman, he realised as she looked up at him enquiringly, but a young and very attractive one.

Though her gown wasn't as outlandishly elaborate as those in the current fashion, he recognised the material as expensive and the cut and fit as expert. Glossy dark hair with glimmers of auburn glistened from the elaborate arrangement of curls pinned to her head, and the eyes turned up to him were a beautiful green, framed by long dark lashes. The pale skin of her face looked petal-soft, her nose aquiline and lovely. Lush lips and a temptingly curved figure produced an immediate jump in his pulse and a prickling awareness in the rest of his body.

No gently born woman worked, and offices employed only male clerks. So what sort of woman could she be? The *chère amie* of one of the engineers?

Before he could settle his rattled brain and produce speech, she said, 'Can I help you?'

A little embarrassed to have been caught frankly staring at her, Crispin stammered, 'Dellamont. I'm here to consult with a Mr Gilling?'

Surprise widened her eyes. 'Lord Dellamont? Excuse me, but I was expecting someone…older. Most potential investors are,' she explained. 'Austin—Mr Gilling—should arrive shortly. Indeed, when I heard someone walk in, I thought it was him.'

She rose from behind the desk, her tiny waist emphasised by the wideness of her skirts. Though she was rather tall for a woman, the top of her head should just about reach his chin, Crispin thought. He could wrap both arms almost completely around that small frame, if he were to embrace her.

And ah, would he like to embrace her! Just who was this enticingly lovely woman?

'If you'd step back into the front room, you can wait there,' she was saying. 'I apologise that our reception area is so…bare. Not expecting to be in Bristol long or to be receiving investors or clients here, my father didn't consider it worth renting the quantity of furniture and comforts we have at the London office. Would you like a cup of tea? I can send Father's assistant to the shop at the corner.'

'No, thank you.' Though the girl made to lead

him towards the outer room, Crispin lingered, compelled to find out more about this lovely creature.

Then the significance of what she'd just said registered. 'Your father?' he repeated. 'You are... Richard Cranmore's daughter?'

'Yes. Since there is no one to perform proper introductions, I'll introduce myself. Marcella Cranmore, my lord.' She gave him a curtsy that was long on grace and exaggerated deference.

If she were truly the respected engineer's unmarried daughter, that would make her a member of the rising merchant elite—who were known for their strait-laced morals. No chance of a casual, pleasurable encounter with a woman of that background, regrettably. The price of getting to know this young woman better would be marriage—which should prompt him to terminate the conversation immediately.

Just then, the outer door opened and a young man of about his own age bustled in. 'Ah, Austin, there you are,' the young woman said, gifting the newcomer with a dazzling smile.

The engineer returned a fond one of his own. After sparing Crispin only a cursory glance, he said, 'Sorry I'm late, Marcella. Some problems with the equipment at the site—it's rather hard to access. But your father was insistent that I return as soon as possible, since he was expecting a visit by some fancy nob who's already dropped a pile of blunt buying shares in other railway ventures.'

The lady's smile wavered. 'Viscount Dellamont?'

'Yes, that was the name.'

She inclined her head towards Crispin. 'He's already arrived.'

Gilling turned towards him, as if seeing him for the first time. 'Lord Dellamont?'

'I have that honour,' Crispin said drily.

Though the young man's face coloured, he gave Crispin a quick bow. 'Pleased to meet you, my lord. Austin Gilling, Mr Cranmore's assistant chief engineer. No offence meant, I assure you.'

'None taken.'

'If you would be gracious enough to wait a few minutes longer, I need to have Miss Cranmore record some of the measurements we've just taken. After that, I will be happy to answer any questions you might have.'

'Let me send for that tea, my lord. We'll make you as comfortable as possible while you wait, and then Mr Gilling will give you his full attention,' Miss Cranmore said, giving him a placating smile—as if he were a querulous child who needed soothing.

'If Mr Gilling is going to be giving you pertinent figures about the approach slope, I'd like to sit in on the discussion.'

'The figures are of a highly technical nature. We wouldn't want to waste your valuable time, boring you with mathematical details,' she replied.

'Whose significance I couldn't possibly comprehend?' he suggested, not sure whether he was more amused or offended by her treating him like a rich, self-important, clueless dolt.

Her overly gracious demeanour slipped a bit. 'Are you a trained engineer then, my lord?' she asked with some asperity.

'No. But since I have…er…dropped a good deal of blunt in several other railway ventures, I've made it my business to become more acquainted with some of the technical issues involved with constructing them.'

'I really can't see why—' Gilling said, but Miss Cranmore waved a hand, motioning him to silence.

'If it would please you to know the figures, you are certainly quite welcome to listen. We have no objection to our investors becoming more knowledgeable about the technical aspects of our engineering projects. It can only increase their appreciation and admiration for the work my father's engineers accomplish.'

Giving Gilling a warning look, as if to remind

him he was dealing with an investor whose plump pockets might fund the project that paid his salary, she said, 'Do step back into the office, then. Mr Gilling, will you bring another chair? And please let me send Timmons for that tea, my lord.'

'If you wish to have some,' Crispin said, curious about what was going to happen next.

And even more curious about why the daughter of a successful, well-known engineer would be sitting at a desk in his temporary office. Her father, he knew, had made a comfortable fortune building railways and bridges. Even were it not highly unusual to have a female clerk in their office, the family was certainly well enough off that his daughter need do nothing more taxing than help her mother run the household, visit friends, and spend her father's blunt on clothes and fripperies while her parents lined up prospective suitors.

The tea order dispatched to the assistant who ducked in when Miss Cranmore called him and an extra chair brought by Gilling to the desk, Miss Cranmore resumed her seat behind it, Gilling taking the one he pulled up beside her. While she extracted a notebook from the desk drawer, the engineer pulled a pad from his waistcoat pocket. Once she had taken out her nib pen and opened the inkwell lid, she nodded to Gilling.

'Have you and Father finished all the measurements of the slope leading up from the river?' she asked.

'We have one more section to complete—the slope is rather steep there, so the work goes slowly. We're having to break the hundred-foot segments into many smaller increments for the forward tape man to be able to keep it level at his chest. Are you ready for the numbers?'

She dipped her nib in the ink. 'Ready.'

For the next few minutes, Gilling read off a list of lengths while Miss Cranmore copied them into her logbook.

'That's all I have for now,' Gilling said. 'After I speak with Lord Dellamont, I'll head back out to rejoin Mr Cranmore. We hope to finish the rest of the measurements today and then can begin figuring the angles necessary to construct the grade.'

The assistant arrived with tea, Miss Cranmore pouring while Gilling put away his notebook. 'So, my lord, what would you like to know?' he asked.

'The countryside immediately outside London is flat enough, but as one journeys westwards, especially after Chippenham, the land becomes increasingly hilly, with several rivers and a canal to cross. How do the engineers propose to deal with these?'

Gilling angled a look at him. 'You are familiar with the terrain?'

'I'm not a professional surveyor, of course, but

before investing in any venture, I prefer to ride the route myself. Evaluating the difficulties it may pose and therefore the chances of it being successfully completed. I have to admit, when I first looked it over, I was rather sceptical.'

'And are you still sceptical?' Miss Cranmore asked.

'That's why I wanted to talk with Mr Gilling.'

'The route is challenging,' Gilling admitted. 'The stations at both Temple Meads and Bath will be elevated and require the construction of viaducts. In addition to bridges crossing smaller waterways, there will be a major bridge to carry the track over the River Avon. The Kennet and Avon canal will have to be diverted, and one major tunnel constructed through Box Hill outside Corsham, on the highest point of the route.'

'Which, I understand, will be the longest tunnel ever attempted?' Crispin said.

'True. But the engineer in overall charge of the project, Mr Brunel, worked on tunnels with his father, also a superior engineer. No one in England has more experience.'

'How steep will the gradient be?'

'For the majority of the line, no more than one in one thousand. The Box Hill tunnel will be steeper, of course, but manageable.'

'What about the stone underlying the tunnel?

Will it be able to support having so long a cavern carved out of it?'

'Mr Brunel believes so. He intends to sink shafts along the route to examine the geology of the rock, of course, before the construction begins.'

'How about curves going up and down the grades?'

'No angles more acute than ten degrees, except perhaps in steeper areas where switchbacks will be necessary. But the engine's speed will be slow enough in those instances not to pose a danger.'

Crispin nodded, satisfied. 'I think that alleviates most of my concerns.' He ought to head out himself, but he couldn't quite master his desire to chat further with the intriguingly accomplished Miss Cranmore.

Giving in to that impulse, he said, 'I know you're anxious to get back and complete your work, Mr Gilling, so don't let me keep you any longer.'

Gilling nodded back. 'The Great Western will be a boon for its investors, I assure you, Lord Dellamont. Mr Brunel intends to create not only a direct link between London and Bristol, but by constructing of a fleet of fast, transatlantic iron ships, to New York as well.'

If Brunel were successful in doing all of that,

an investor's return on this venture could be huge, Crispin thought. 'Thank you, Mr Gilling. I shall keep it all in mind.'

'Will you be back in the office later, Mr Gilling?' Miss Cranmore asked as the engineer put his teacup back on the tray and then rose from his chair.

'I don't know. It depends on how long the final measurements take.' Dragging his chair back against the wall, he added, 'Your father said not to wait here for him, that he'd meet you back at your lodgings.'

'Perhaps you will join us for dinner, then?' she suggested, giving the engineer another of her lovely smiles.

'I would like that,' he replied, returning another smile of his own. 'But I'll need to make calculations on the data we collected today so I can recommend to your father the best way to proceed along the final approach while keeping the angle of rise within acceptable limits.'

'Father and I will be working on the figures as well. We could compare notes,' Miss Cranmore said.

He nodded, as if it were a common occurrence to have a lady figuring angles and slopes. 'Thank you for the invitation. I shall certainly join you if I can.' Turning to Crispin with a bow, he said, 'Thank you for coming by, Lord Dellamont. Mr

Cranmore is gratified by your interest in our project, as I'm sure Mr Brunel will be also. My lord, Miss Cranmore.'

Giving them another bow, the engineer walked out. Miss Cranmore, Crispin noted, followed the engineer's progress out of the office with a wistful look on her face.

Crispin found himself unaccountably annoyed—and a little bit jealous—of the engineer for the favour with which he was treated by this lovely young woman. Which made no sense. They were in no way competing for Miss Cranmore's attentions. After this one meeting, he would never see her again.

But because of that fact, he meant to take advantage of this opportunity to find out what inspired a girl of her beauty to spend her evening solving geometric equations with her father.

'You needn't rush, my lord,' she said, at last turning her attention back to him. 'Please, finish your tea.'

'Thank you, I shall.'

'You seem…rather well versed in angles and gradients. Have you studied them?'

Crispin smiled. 'My classics education at Oxford didn't prepare me to evaluate the nuts and bolts of technological advances like railway engines—but the machines fascinate me. I'm convinced the new industrial age represents the future of wealth and economic expansion, and railways the future of transportation.'

'And so you are eager to invest in them.'

'I was fortunate enough to have a great-aunt who left me a small bequest. After I left university, I travelled to the north to investigate the companies beginning the transition from using horse-drawn vehicles on rails to harnessing the new steam engines designed by Mr Stephenson for the Stockton and Darlington. My modest investments in that and several similar ventures were rewarded. So I now follow rather closely the bills introduced into Parliament for the construction of new lines, riding the countryside myself to evaluate the proposed routes.'

'I have to admit, you seem much more knowledgeable than most of our aristocratic investors.' Her face blushing a little, she added, 'I'm afraid I may have been…rather too dismissive upon first meeting you.'

'Thinking I was a useless fribble with more money than comprehension?'

'A dandy, anyway,' she added, her flush deepening. 'If I gave the impression that my opinion of you was derogatory, I do apologise.'

Crispin suppressed a smile. She'd made it rather obvious that was indeed her opinion of him, but he wouldn't embarrass her further by pointing that out—and risk having her speedily dismiss him. Because he was even more curious about her now than he'd been upon first meeting her, and wanted to know more.

For how long would he be able to lure her into talking with him?

Chapter Two

'If it won't be interrupting your work too much, I think I'd like another cup of tea,' Crispin said, testing the waters.

An annoyed expression briefly crossed her face before she summoned another smile. 'Of course, my lord. Let me pour for you.'

She was obviously eager to get back to her calculations. But, as he'd hoped, the need to humour a potential investor won out over her desire to resume her work.

Which would be…calculating angles and slopes. How unusual was that? He couldn't wait to learn more.

'Apology accepted. But if you don't mind my asking—what are you doing here, copying down measurements in your father's office? Your mother must be unusually tolerant to allow her daughter to work somewhere outside her home.

And you seem to know a fair amount about angles and elevations yourself.'

Her flush deepened. 'If you must know, Mother doesn't know I do that. She allows me to go into Papa's London office—she thinks just to fetch him tea and bring him supper when he works late. And she allowed me to accompany him to Bristol to make sure he ate properly and didn't work too hard while he was surveying the route. To be honest, she'd have palpitations if she knew I spoke with engineers and met with prospective investors.'

'Without a chaperon, too!' Crispin added with a smile, enchanted by her wide-eyed honesty.

'Not entirely!' she protested. 'My maid attends me at the hotel and if I go out in town. But the poor dear is bored to death at the office, so by mutual agreement, when I come here, she cedes her duty of watching over me to Papa's long-time assistant. Timmons worked for my grandfather before he came to Papa, and has known me since I was a child.'

'You must have a pretty firm grasp of geometry and natural science, if you do calculations.'

She nodded. 'If you think Papa overindulgent, I must confess I took shameless advantage of his grief. He intended to train my brother to succeed him, you see. But my brother Richard died of a sudden fever when he was twelve. I was ten years old then, and at first, I just wanted to console my father, since he seemed to find my presence comforting. But I've always been as fascinated by technical details as you seem to be, and gradually, when I asked him questions about his drawings, he began explaining them and showing me the mathematical principles involved in creating them.

'I lost a year with him when Mama insisted on sending me away to a fancy female academy— where I learned nothing at all useful—but fortunately, after I escaped from that, I was able to wheedle my way back into Papa's office and quietly slip back into consulting with him.'

'And do you consult with engineers and investors in the London office?' he asked, fascinated.

'I serve them tea sometimes, if they call when I'm there to help Papa. He says I can help charm investors. But there are too many people coming and going in the London office, so I can't get away with staying there all day. Mama would object anyway, as she likes me to accompany her on her shopping and visiting. Such a boring waste of time! Which is why I love being in the country!' she added with a radiant smile. 'I've been able to have dinner with Papa and go over the figures every day.'

Crispin tried to imagine his sisters, his mother— or indeed, any female of his acquaintance—looking so enraptured at the idea of spending the evening with her father, solving geometry problems. And failed utterly.

'How I wish Papa would allow me to accompany him to the job sites—but even he isn't indulgent enough to do that,' she continued. 'Oh, if only females were allowed to study at university! Papa could have trained me to become a professional engineer...if I'd only been a son,' she ended on a wistful note.

'I'm sure your parents felt blessed to have such a helpful daughter.'

Instead of appreciating the compliment, her eyes flashed. 'Blessed that I am a female, useful only for directing a household and looking ornamental? I'm sorry, but I'm afraid I cannot agree.'

She fell silent, obviously struggling to get her anger under control. After blowing out a breath, she smiled again. 'What of your family?' she asked, redirecting the conversation. 'You're a...' she checked the notepad on her desk '...a viscount, are you not? Does your family appreciate your interest in railways?'

With a bitter smile, Crispin heard in his ear the contemptuous voice of his father stating his opinion of this new project—an echo of his views about all the others. 'Not in the least,' he said drily.

At his tone, she angled her head at him. 'Ah.

So, like so many of the gentry, they feel investing in commercial projects should be beneath you? Although if you are a viscount in your own right you can please yourself, whatever your family might think.'

'It's a courtesy title,' Crispin admitted. 'My father, the Earl of Comeryn, is…not indulgent. And you've summed up rather neatly his opinion of my activities.'

After enduring years of family brangling, his frustration at his father's unwillingness to cede to his heir any meaningful control over the estate he'd one day inherit—and the Earl's constant criticism and interference in the few areas he had allowed Crispin to participate—had finally propelled him to quit Montwell Glen and strike out on his own after leaving university.

'He should at least be pleased that you made good investments. If you invested with the Stockton and Darlington, you should have had an excellent return.'

Crispin hesitated, needing to choose his words with care. He couldn't tell her that instead of being pleased and proud when his son doubled or tripled his initial investments, the Earl had declared himself embarrassed. Because, the Earl proclaimed, regarding his son disapprovingly, a *gentleman* earned his living from the land—not from trading with 'a handful of vulgar, nouveau riche commoners'.

He suspected his father would be not so secretly pleased if this next venture failed. Every time he pressed Crispin for details about his proposed investments, the Earl confidently predicted that *this* time, his disgrace of a son would lose his capital and be forced to come back, cap in hand, to beg for the support of his long-suffering family.

He also suspected much of his father's ire derived from his inability to keep his wayward son firmly under his control. The Earl resented that Crispin had been able, not just to escape the family, but to remain financially independent, disproving his father's predictions of his failure.

'So he doesn't approve,' Miss Cranmore said when Crispin remained silent. 'That's foolish as well as unfortunate. But at least you *are* independent and able to do what you wish, regardless of your father's views. Not hampered on every side by the restrictions of gender that prevent you from doing anything useful.'

'Truly? I thought most women believed having a home, a husband and a family to raise was the best use of their time.'

'I'd rather have mathematics,' she said bluntly.

Surprised and rather amused by her answer, he said, 'I expect your mother, if not your father, has a different view of the matter.'

Miss Cranmore sighed. 'I shall stave off marriage as long as I possibly can, despite Mama's urging and her lofty expectations.'

He could certainly relate to that desire, Crispin thought, repressing a grimace. He, too, intended to delay as long as possible setting up a household. Duty required him to marry a woman society considered suitable to become the next countess, the same requirement that had led his father into the disaster of his parents' union. Having only recently escaped the tension, tears, and continual upheaval of his familial home, he hoped for a good many years of calm and quiet before he was forced to give up the independence and serenity he so valued and become saddled with a wife.

'I can't blame you there,' he said wryly. 'Being pushed into marriage to gratify a family's desire for wealth and prestige is detestable. Are you certain that's what your mother wants?'

'I'm afraid so. Whereas I have no interest in attaining an "elevated" status. Or in wedding at all, really, unless…' Her voice trailed off, her eyes taking on a faraway look.

Crispin remembered her longing gaze following Mr Gilling.

'Unless it's to the right gentleman?'

Her face flushed again, letting him know he'd hit his mark. When she looked up, lips parted to reply, her gaze met his and something potent and physically charged flashed between them.

It startled her as much as it did him, for she continued silently staring at him. For a long moment, the air between them almost shimmered.

Ah, what a treasure she would be...for the right man, he thought, mesmerised.

Before he could think what to say next, a shuttered look replaced her earlier delightfully candid expression.

Setting down her cup, she said, 'Thank you for taking the time to chat, my lord. Technology *is* the way of the future, and railways *are* the future of transportation. You are wise to have recognised that, and you won't be sorry you invested in it. Especially not this project. Father would not have undertaken it if he hadn't believed wholeheartedly in Mr Brunel's vision. If you speak to the solicitor at Papa's London office, he'll be happy to assist you in buying shares. Now, I'm sure you have many demands on your time, and I won't hold you any longer.'

Standing, she put her cup back on the tray, which meant he had to rise as well. He tried to think of another angle of discussion that might prolong the conversation, but she was already walking towards the office's back door. 'We've finished, Timmons,' she called into the back room. 'You may collect the tray.'

Turning back to him—and remaining by the doorway, a safe distance away—she said, 'I hope you *will* invest in the venture, my lord. Papa's company will not disappoint you.'

With no excuse to linger, he had to give her a bow. 'Thank you for your time, Miss Cranmore. You've provided me with a wealth of interesting detail. It was a pleasure to meet you.'

'And you, my lord. Good day.' She made him a curtsy.

Then, as he resigned himself to leaving, she unexpectedly gifted him with a mischievous grin. 'You're not nearly as useless as I thought when I first saw you.'

Before he could reply, she slipped out the back door. Chuckling, Crispin walked out.

Still not sure what had happened between them—that sudden flash of physical intensity that had startled them both—but disappointed to quit her presence, Crispin headed back to his hotel.

She was definitely unusual. Not only more candid and forthcoming with a stranger than he'd have expected, but absolutely unimpressed by his title and position. An indifference that in his experience was exceptional.

He'd certainly never encountered such obvious disdain from any gently born female on the few occasions when he'd been dragged to some *ton* entertainment. Instead, he recalled with distaste, the active pursuit by maidens or their mothers eager to capture the favour of a future earl had driven him to escape as quickly as possible.

That fact alone had been enough to pique him into trying to learn more about Miss Cranmore. Her obvious delight—and unexpected competence—in matters of geometry and mathematics only deepened her appeal.

And if he were nakedly honest, he'd been absurdly gratified that what had, in the end, raised her opinion of him hadn't been his title or pedigree, but the knowledge about railway engineering for which his own father so often denigrated him. Something, unlike the status he'd been born to, that he'd accomplished solely through his own efforts.

Unfortunately, as lovely, unusual and intriguing as she was, there was no possibility of any relationship between them going forward, even if he were interested in wedlock, the only association her family would permit. Though her father's income probably exceeded the yearly amount earned by his father's agricultural properties, a Miss Cranmore and a Viscount Dellamont did not travel in the same social circles.

For a virtuous young maiden, friendship with an unrelated male was as impossible as the more intimate but less formal liaison her beauty and uniqueness inspired him to desire.

He would just have to count his meeting Miss Cranmore as an unexpected delight of this investment trip and put her out of mind.

Once back at his lodgings, he packed his belongings, intending on an early departure the following morning. Fortunately, his mother's birthday was still a month away, so he could put off stopping by Montwell Glen and inviting another tirade from his father. He'd return directly to London instead and check on the progress of the bill approving the Great Western.

And catch up with his best friends from Oxford, Gregory Lattimar and Alex Cheverton—if the former weren't in Northumberland tending to the family estate he would one day inherit and the latter at Edge Hall, the vast pile in Sussex he managed for his distant cousin, the Duke of Farisdeen.

When he himself inherited, thanks to his father, he might not have as great a command of the essentials of managing a large estate as an heir should. But, he'd promised himself, he would have amassed a reserve of ready cash to buttress the continuing declines in agricultural revenue.

That fact in itself should make his father furious.

If only he wouldn't also inherit the Earl's duty to provide heirs to the title—which meant acquiring a wife to go along with the estate, he thought with a sigh.

Thrusting away the unhappy memories the very idea of matrimony always invoked, he turned his thoughts back to the more pleasant matters he would need to attend to once back in London. First among them would be a stop at Cranmore's London office so he might speak to the solicitor about investing in the Great Western.

If he put off that task for a bit, might he catch another glimpse of Miss Cranmore at her father's office?

The instant flare of interest that possibility generated should warn him such a meeting wouldn't be a good idea. Miss Cranmore, he reminded himself, could become neither his friend nor his mistress, the only two roles he would be interested in having her fill. No matter how fascinating she might be, he had no desire to pursue the sole permissible option—making *her* that obligatory wife.

Despite those facts, he found himself strangely reluctant to forget her. But, he reassured himself, since it was highly unlikely that he'd ever see her again, as time passed and the strong impression she'd made faded, following that prudent course of action would become easier.

Chapter Three

A week later, in the sumptuous family town house on Tavistock Square in London, Marcella Cranmore stood stoically while her maid fussed with adjusting the final details of her dinner dress. It would please Mama to have her wear the fashionable new gown that had just been delivered, she told herself, trying to curb her impatience. She might as well look her best, since there was always the chance her father might bring someone interesting home to dine with them.

Not, sadly, Austin Gilling, whom she knew was still slowly making his way back from Bristol, rechecking measurements for the most challenging aspects of the Great Western project, the tunnel at Box Hill and the bridge over the Avon.

The image of another 'interesting' gentleman popped into her mind before she could prevent it. Drat, why could she not banish for good the memory of the most unusual investor she'd ever met?

Of course, it didn't help that Viscount Della-mont was also perhaps the handsomest man she'd ever met, with his wavy dark hair, deep brown eyes sparkling with intelligence, and tall, wiry frame that exuded energy. She'd been astounded at the depth of his understanding of the engineering challenges of the Great Western project. And later, when she had time to review their exchange, she'd become guiltily aware of how forbearing he'd been of her initially treating him exactly as he'd described—as 'a useless fribble with more money than comprehension'.

The few other aristocratic investors she'd met by chance at her father's London office either ignored the young woman who served them tea as a servant far beneath their notice, or gave her a considering glance that sized up her feminine charms before realising the engineer's daughter was unavailable, upon which they, too, ignored her. Investors from her father's own merchant or business class treated her with avuncular indulgence, as a pretty little thing who brightened her father's office.

Not one of them—and if she were truly honest, not even Austin—had ever expressed a particle of curiosity about her fascination with mathematics.

When she recalled the singular conversation she'd had with Dellamont—in which she'd imparted more information about what mattered to her than to anyone but her father—she had to laugh at the absurdity of it.

Perhaps it *was* the absurdity of Miss Marcella Cranmore exchanging personal information with someone she'd only just met—and a high-ranking aristocratic someone to boot—that had made the whole exchange possible. She'd probably not have been as candid with someone from her own world, someone she might encounter again.

An odd little wave of disappointment went through her at acknowledging that fact, as it had each time she recalled their meeting—which she did far too often. The disappointment, probably, of knowing she'd not be able to further an acquaintance with the one gentleman who seemed to find her odd and unfeminine interest in mathematics intriguing and her ability to figure geometric problems admirable, rather than simply strange.

And then there'd been that...flash of attraction between them at the end, warning her it was past time to terminate their discussion.

Before she could mull over the implications of those unexpected feelings, a knock at the door, followed by her mother's entrance, put an end to her recollections.

'How lovely you look!' Mrs Cranmore exclaimed. 'Didn't I tell you that deep bronze satin would be a wonderful foil for your eyes and hair?

And your hair so cleverly arranged, with the curls on top and to the sides.'

'The gown is very pretty, Mama. I'm glad you are pleased.'

'Especially pleased to have you looking so fine when we are having an important guest to-night!'

A shock of excitement zinged through her, quickly suppressed. It wouldn't be *him*. It could never be him. 'Who, Mama?'

'Your papa had to work late again, unfortunately, but your grandda just arrived in town and will be able to join us.'

'Grandda?' Marcella repeated, delighted. 'How wonderful! I haven't seen him in ever so long.'

'Well, you know he doesn't like London. Give him the good country air at Tynemouth.'

Marcella laughed. 'Since he spent most of his youth down in the smoke and ash of the mines, I don't see how he could complain about the air in London!'

'That's why he prizes fresh air so highly,' her mother responded. 'I'm glad you are eager to see him. You do love him, don't you?'

'Of course! Oh, I know he can be all brusque and blustery on the outside, but he's a darling underneath. As you very well know, Mama.'

Her mother sighed. 'Indeed I do. He worked hard so Ma, God rest her soul, and I could have all the luxuries he never did. You do want to make him happy, don't you?'

A vague apprehension tempered Marcella's enthusiasm. 'Of course I do. Why do you ask?'

'Oh, no reason. I'm just…making sure. You get so involved in your figures and daydreams sometimes, I worry that you lose sight of anything else.'

Marcella felt a pang of guilt. Her mother was a sweet darling, too, entirely content to immerse herself in furnishing and running her household, purchasing fashionable clothing, and visiting and gossiping with her friends. She'd never understood her odd duck of a daughter who preferred learning about mathematics and geometry and natural sciences rather than being schooled by her mother in household management, stitchery, and fashion.

She knew it hurt her mother when she escaped from those endeavours to join her father in his office, fascinated by his drawings and eager to discuss engines and mechanics.

Father had been so encouraging, she'd once hoped he'd allow her to take her elder brother's place. But though he'd consoled his grief by permitting her presence and indulged her eager interest in his profession, by now she'd realised that, though he would let her peek in on the periphery of his work, he would eventually turn over the operations of his firm to one of his apprentices, many of whom he'd tutored and then assisted on to distinguished engineering careers of their own.

Turn the business over not to her, but to someone like Austin Gilling.

Trapped into the traditional female role, one day she'd have to marry. Were she to marry a businessman or tradesman, she'd swiftly find herself relegated to caring for the household and the eventual children.

The thought was unendurable.

To have any chance of hanging on to some involvement in the mechanical world that fascinated her, she would have to marry an engineer.

Someone like Austin Gilling.

Despite, she thought with a sigh, the fact that though he treated with avuncular affection, he hadn't yet seemed to notice that she was no longer a child.

Having been father's apprentice, then assistant, for many years, he seemed to still see her as the little girl in braids who'd sat at her father's knee to console him after the death of his son.

He'd consoled her then, too—igniting a gratitude and appreciation that had turned from a child's hero worship into a deep affection that convinced her, once she gave in to the necessity of marriage, she would prefer him over all others.

She just needed to make him see she was now a

woman grown. A woman whose familiarity with her father's business would be a considerable advantage, were he eventually to take it over. She'd need to work harder at opening his eyes, because time was running out. In another year or two at most, both her mother *and* her father would expect her to marry.

'Have you heard a word I've said?' her mother's exasperated tones recalled her.

'Sorry, Mama. But honestly, when I'm dressed in such a gorgeous gown, as if I truly were a princess, I have trouble stringing two thoughts together!'

Fortunately, that response mollified her mother. 'I can well imagine! Come along then, Princess! My da is waiting.'

Putting worries about matrimony from her mind, determined for this evening just to enjoy this rare visit from her grandfather, Marcella took her mother's hand and followed her out of the room.

Although her father didn't return in time to join them, dinner with her grandfather was still a merry affair, with him teasing both his daughter and his granddaughter. But after the meal had been cleared away and Marcella escorted him to his favourite chair in the parlour to enjoy his after-dinner cigar, he clasped her hand, halting her beside him.

'I'd have a word with ye, missy.'

'Of course, Grandda. What did you want to say?' she asked, seating herself beside her mother on the sofa by his chair.

'Ye know I'm not like to drag my weary bones to London for no good purpose.'

'No. But if you'd make the journey on one of Papa's railways, your old bones would be much more comfortable.'

'Cheeky lass,' he reproved with a smile, chucking her under the chin. 'I prefer a strong horse under me, and well ye know it. And there's no' of yer father's railroads from Newcastle to London anyway.'

'Maybe not yet. But there will be.'

'That's as may be. What I really want to see before I die is my only grandchild safe and settled.'

A frisson of alarm trickled through her. Hoping he wasn't going to press her about what she feared he was, she said, 'I am safe and settled, Grandda. You don't need to worry about me.'

'Nay, lass, ye know what I mean. I want to see ye married to a good man, established in yer own house, and bringing up babes of yer own.'

'There's still plenty of time for that,' she replied. 'I'm not past my last prayers yet.'

'Ye're a beauty still, and well I know it. But

that's no reason to dally. Ye're one and twenty now, lass! When yer ma was that age, yer brother Dickie, God rest his soul, was five years old, and ye a feisty three-year-old. I want to dandle my great-grandbabes on my knee afore I turn up me toes.'

'Don't even talk about that!' Marcella cried, squeezing her grandfather's hand. 'We want you with us for years yet.'

'Aye, and so I will be, God willing. Still, I'd like to know a fine man had taken over caring for ye well before that. It's yer ma's fondest wish as well, something she's been hoping for these last five years and more,' he added, nodding at her mother.

'I never wanted to press you, darling. But I do think it's time,' her mother said.

'I…I know you've been urging me. So…what do you both want me to do? Start attending the assembly in Newcastle?' She hated the idea of leaving London, but there were a number of engineering firms in the northern cities. Attending cotillions in Newcastle might introduce her to other candidates, if she failed to secure Austin Gilling's regard.

After a glance at her mother, her grandfather said, 'I'd have better than that for my darling girl. Yer pa's done well by my one chick; she lacks for nothing. It's ye that will inherit all that's mine, child. Newcastle isn't a grand enough stage for the granddaughter of the "Factory King". Ye'll be a prize worth winning, even in London.'

Marcella knew her grandfather was wealthy— one of the leading developers of the factory system, as a boy he'd turned his mechanical aptitude into designing machines to streamline first the mining, then the weaving industries. But she'd had no idea he intended to make her his sole heiress.

So shocked was she by the news, it took a moment for the significance of the rest of his words to penetrate. 'A prize worth winning in London?' she repeated. 'Are you saying you want me to enter society *here*? You're joking, surely!'

'And why not? I hadn't yet the wealth to make yer ma's dream of wedding a lord come true, but I have it now, and plenty besides. Why else do ye think I accepted the baronetcy? Not that I care two flicks of my finger for being called Sir Thomas, but the nobs value it. Ye're every bit the equal of any lady born. And all those fine gentlemen will fight to win the hand of Sir Thomas Webbingdon's heiress!'

'You needn't worry that you won't fit in,' her mother inserted earnestly. 'That's why I insisted you attend Miss Axminster's School for Young Ladies! There's not a trace of North Country left in your speech, your manners are as fine as any lady's, and you're more beautiful than all those gentlemen's daughters put together.'

The memories of her miserable sojourn at boarding school returned in a rush. Yes, she'd managed to shed her regional accent, but that had hardly made her accepted. She recalled the slights, the snide remarks, the condescension. The loneliness.

The very idea of trying to force her way into association with the girls who had snubbed and ridiculed her filled her with revulsion.

'Mama, just because I can speak and act like one of them, I assure you, I will never be accepted by society. Even if I wanted to be, which I certainly do not! How can you believe I'd even be invited to any *ton* parties? Only those born into that class are admitted to Almack's and society balls!'

Her grandfather shook his head. 'Money still talks. And ye'd be admitted sure enough, as long as ye have the right sponsor. And ye will.'

'A sponsor?' she echoed. 'What society lady would sponsor me?'

'A baron's wife,' her mother broke in excitedly. 'Da told me before dinner this evening that Lady Arlsley agreed to sponsor you for this Season!'

A rapid search of her memory produced no recognition of that name associated with her society classmates—not that she would have expected someone related to any of them to take on such a role. 'Who is Lady Arlsley, and why would she agree to sponsor me?'

Her grandfather chuckled. 'Lord Arlsley rowed himself rather far up the River Tick a few years ago. Came cap in hand to my bank, wanting a loan on the quiet to pay back the moneylenders that were threatening him. I told him I'd lend him the money, nothing said to no one, and for simple return of principal with no interest, if he'd agree one day to do me a favour. He couldn't wait to snap up the bargain. And now his lady wife will honour it.'

A cold shudder went through Marcella. She could well believe Arlsley had consented on such favourable terms—and was now relieved to pass the burden of fulfilling the deal on to his wife. His wife, who had almost certainly been coerced into agreeing, and would bitterly resent the embarrassing burden she'd been shackled with.

It would be Miss Axminster's all over again, only worse.

While she sat speechless, horror-struck, her grandfather reached down to pat her knee. 'It will be just fine, chick, ye'll see. Now, we know not to aim for a duke or an earl or a viscount, someone that high in the instep. But a baron or baronet— that'd be enough to win ye the title of Lady and make all yer ma's dreams come true. And win ye a well-placed husband in the bargain.'

'Oh, Marcella, can't you just see it?' her mother exclaimed. 'When I read in the newspapers about all the glittering balls and dinners and routs, I'll be able to picture *you* there, beautifully gowned, with handsome and elegant young men vying for your attention!'

Her mother might believe in that fantasy, but Marcella knew better. 'It sounds lovely, Mama, but I truly think I would have a better chance of finding a responsible, caring husband from among our own class. Surely you wouldn't want me to wed someone who courts me merely for my dowry?'

Which, she was pretty sure, would be the only kind of aristocratic gentlemen interested in wedding the daughter of an engineer and the granddaughter of a man who'd begun his life working in a coal mine.

'Don't sell yerself short, lass,' her grandfather said. 'I'm not saying ye have to wed some nob just for the sake of it, but there's no harm in looking about. Not when doing it will delight yer ma. And give Lord Arlsley the chance to redeem his promise. If there's no one to yer liking, ye can be finished with it, and no harm done.'

The fact that she wouldn't be pressured into marriage made her feel a bit better. But she still couldn't view the prospect of a Season with less than revulsion.

She had no doubt whatsoever that she would end the Season unwed. And by wasting several months attending society events, she'd lose not just time working with her father, but also the opportunities coming into Papa's office would offer her to entice Austin Gilling into seeing her as the eligible young woman she now was.

'Now, lass, ye're not going to kick over the traces and disappoint yer ma, are ye? Not when it would be such a simple thing to make her and yer old grandda happy. All ye'd have to do would be buy lots of pretty gowns and go to parties. How hard would that be?'

Marcella looked from her grandfather's entreating expression to her mother's exuberant, excited face. Both of them had done nothing their whole lives but protect and indulge her. Knowing she had the final choice, could she be selfish enough to deny them what would obviously delight them both?

Pushing the memories of Miss Axminster's out of her mind, she said, 'Would it really make the two of you that happy?'

Her mother reached over to hug her. 'It would be a dream come true, my darling!'

'Aye, a dream come true for yer grandda, too, to see his only chick so thrilled. Only wish my dear Nan would be able to see it, too.'

'She will, Da—from Heaven,' her mother said.

Dismay welled up in her. She couldn't quite force herself to agree—but neither could she find it within her to disappoint them. 'I… I'll consider it,' she said at last.

'Wonderful!' her mother said, leaning over again to hug her fiercely. 'Oh, my sweet, you will be a triumph!'

A disaster, more like, Marcella thought glumly. *If* she agreed to do this. Although she'd only said she'd 'consider' the possibility, Mama was already acting as if she'd given her wholehearted consent.

Just then, the sound of the front door closing and booted feet on the stairs caught her ear. Eager for an excuse that would send her away from any further entreaties, she jumped up.

'That must be Papa arriving! Mama, why don't you get Grandda his pipe? I'll meet Papa and arrange for his dinner.'

Nodding, that beaming smile still on her face, her mother went over to fetch her grandfather's pipe and tobacco. 'Oh, Da, thank you!' she heard her mother exclaim as she walked out of the room. 'I'll see my little girl elevated where she belongs at last!'

Trying to still the trepidation that made her heart race and her palms sweat, Marcella met her father halfway up the stairs. 'Welcome home,' she said, leaning up on tiptoe to give him a kiss. 'Grandda's here. Shall I have Cook bring you

some dinner in your office before you go in to
see him and Mama?'

After getting home late, her father normally
preferred taking a tray in his office rather than
inconveniencing the staff by eating at the dining room table that had already been cleared and
reset. 'Yes, dear, that would be fine.'

'Go wash up, and I'll bring dinner in to your
office in a trice.' Giving her father a hug, Marcella headed down the stairs.

A half-hour later, Marcella sat at the chair in
front of her father's desk, sipping tea while he
ate his cold meat and cheese. After he'd wolfed
down some sustenance, she said, 'Do you know
why Grandda came to London?'

Pausing, her father set down his fork. 'Yes.
Your mother long ago confided her hopes to me,
you know.'

'Oh, Papa, I really don't want to do it!' she burst
out. 'You know how I was treated at school! Belittled, slighted. I hate the idea of going through that
again—and you know that's what would happen.'

Her father nodded. 'True, it might happen
again. It's also possible that, with the support of
an aristocratic sponsor who, one assumes, would
not introduce you to anyone she thought would
treat you disrespectfully, your time in society
would be much more pleasant. Balls and danc-

ing and dinners! You'll never know unless you try. And it will make your mother and grandfather so happy if you do.'

If even her father sided with them—how was she to resist?

'What if it is awful?'

'Would you let a pack of arrogant, self-important gentry scare you away? Or goad you into acting less than the true lady you are?'

Smiling as she recalled the investors she'd humoured, she said, 'I've never yet worried about aristocratic opinions.'

'There you have it. If you truly find it unbearable, you can give it up. I'll intervene to placate your mother. I promise you will not be pushed into wedding some gentleman just because he owns a title. But there's always the chance you might meet one who values you for who you are, whom you find appealing, too.'

The image of Lord Dellamont's face flashed briefly before her eyes. If she did go into society, might she meet him again? That possibility was almost enough to make her agree on the spot.

She still didn't know quite what to make of him. He'd been neither high in the instep nor condescending. He hadn't seemed to expect to be catered to and flattered—indeed, he'd seemed offended when she'd done that. Most surprising, he'd been shockingly knowledgeable about the technical business of building a railway and appreciative of the skill and expertise necessary.

Though a beneficiary of the old system of landed wealth, he pronounced himself looking forward to a future based on wealth earned in a very different way.

Was he a visionary? An opportunist?

It seemed they just might share the same outlook about the future.

Plus, he was handsome and appealing enough to make her heart flutter. Which was ridiculous, when he was so far out of her sphere, he might as well inhabit the moon.

Lady Arlsley might have enough influence to force Marcella's way into society. But she was unlikely to have enough clout to foist her charge high enough to encounter socially the son of an earl.

And what if she did?

A viscount might have found it amusing to chat with Miss Marcella Cranmore, engineer's daughter, while discussing the railroad investment he was considering. But that didn't guarantee he'd not give her the cut direct if she were to intrude herself into the select society to which he belonged by birth.

Would he snub her there—or not?

It might be worth going, just to find out.

But society was composed of many large gatherings. And if Dellamont spent much of his time outside the city, investigating potential investments, she could commit herself to this enterprise and not encounter him at all.

Her father patted her hand, recalling her. 'So, what do you think? Can you tolerate giving it a go? For your grandda and mama's sake?'

'I can leave if it becomes unbearable?'

'Absolutely.'

'And you'll let me come back and work with you in the office once it's over?'

Her father sighed. 'Honestly, my dear, I'd really prefer to have you find a fine man and marry him. I'm not getting any younger, and I'll not be around to watch out for you for ever. Much as I love having you there, I don't want you to waste your youth and beauty hanging about my office. There's so much more a husband can offer that a father can't—if you know what I mean.'

'Papa!' she said, blushing. A blush that deepened when she recalled the rush of attraction she'd felt when Lord Dellamont gazed at her.

What would it be like to have a husband who could appreciate her mind—and her body?

If she *were* to discover such a combination it would certainly not be found in Lord Dellamont, she told herself stoutly.

Still…

'Very well, Papa, I'll agree. But I shall hold

you to your promise of letting me return to your office when all of this is over!'

Chuckling, her father patted her hand. 'It's a bargain. But I shall be very surprised if some wise young gentleman doesn't lure you away from me first.'

Marcella was rather convinced of the opposite. But she might be able to salvage something positive from this unappealing course of action.

Being introduced into society might prompt Austin Gilling into finally realising that she was now a desirable woman. Knowing other men were courting her might just shock him into deciding to try to claim her for himself.

Chapter Four

$\sim\!\!\sim\!\!\sim\!\!\infty$

A week later, on the other side of town, Crispin took a hackney back to his modest rooms on Jasmin Street after an evening spent following the debate in Parliament on another proposed rail venture. After paying off the jarvey, he walked up the front steps, intending to change and head to his club for dinner.

He smiled, recalling the convivial evening he'd spent with his two good friends a week ago. Not much had changed in their worlds—Gregory Lattimar still bemoaned his father's lack of involvement in the family estate that left him responsible for running it without having the full legal authority to do so, while Alex Cheverton had provided an amusing account of the meeting with his distant cousin and employer, the Duke of Farisdeen. Between his description of the austere, monosyllabic Duke and his mimicking of the Duke's son, who never lost a chance to treat him like the employee he was, Alex had kept them both laughing over dinner.

Unfortunately, Alex had returned to Sussex and Gregory was dining with family tonight. He'd have to trade their superior company for the excellent meal provided by his club and a few hands of cards afterwards. He'd been having a string of good luck lately, which provided some always welcome additions to the cash reserve he used for new investments.

But as he walked through the front door, his valet and general manservant greeted him with a letter. 'This came for you this afternoon, my lord. The messenger had been instructed to wait for an answer, but I told him you were in consultations at the House and probably wouldn't return until mid-evening.'

'Thank you, Haines,' Crispin said, taking the note. A sense of dread filled him as he recognised his name scrawled on the outside in his father's distinctive script.

He'd hoped to avoid the Earl for at least another month. What did his father want with him now?

A quick scan of the short note left him in equal parts surprised, irritated and apprehensive. Comeryn disliked London and seldom brought his family to the capital for the Season. He often complained he'd had enough of frivolous society and his wife's extravagant spending when Crispin's oldest sister had been presented three years ago and didn't intend to have them waste another penny there until required to present Crispin's younger sister next year.

This summons to the family's London residence must mean that the Earl had made one of his infrequent visits to the city, which he occasionally did to attend the Lords. Crispin had had no idea his father planned to come, but since avoiding his father was something of a mission with him, he wouldn't have expected to.

What would the ever-disapproving Earl complain about this time?

A quick check of the mantel clock indicated it wasn't yet late enough that he could use that excuse to put off the interview. Might as well go straight away, get the unpleasantness over with and hopefully find enough congenial company at his club afterwards to dissipate the bad feelings an interview with his sire always aroused.

Or perhaps he could call on Gregory afterwards, see if his friend would be able to spend the rest of the evening with him once his family dinner concluded.

His spirits rising at that prospect, Crispin paused long enough to have his valet brush his coat and give him a general inspection to ensure his attire was in perfect form—staving off having the interview begin with one of his father's favourite sermons about his son not appearing in a style befitting his rank and breeding. Girding himself for the interview to come, he had Haines summon him a hackney.

His first surprise upon arriving at Portman Square was finding the knocker back on the door. Since Comeryn's visits were usually short, he didn't normally have the skeleton staff that manned the town house do more to accommodate his presence than remove the holland covers from his bedchamber, study and the small family dining room. His next surprise was having the door answered by Viscering, their butler, whom he would have expected to remain at Montwell Glen.

'Good evening, my lord,' the butler said, bowing him in. 'You've been keeping well, I trust? Finding some exciting new ventures, I hope?'

'I'm very well, thank you, Viscering,' he replied, warmed by affection for the man who'd been a stalwart part of his life since he was a boy. 'Always on the lookout for a new project. How are you?'

'Tolerable, my lord. Lady Comeryn would like a word before you go in to see the Earl, who is in his study.'

'Mother is here?' Crispin said, shocked.

'Yes, and your sister Lady Margaret as well.'

'A shopping trip?' Crispin guessed. Though his mother must have been unusually persuasive—or more likely, tearfully persistent—to induce his normally tight-fisted father to allow such a trip. Maybe he'd relented for her birthday—as well he ought, Crispin thought, the familiar feelings of resentment and simmering anger rising towards his imperious father and the autocratic, unbending rule he exercised over his wife and children.

After a slight pause, as if debating whether or not to say anything, Viscering said, 'I believe the Earl intends to remain for the Season.'

That was so astounding, Crispin froze in the act of handing the butler his coat, hat and cane. 'The Season? Are you sure?'

'Most of the staff accompanied us, with those remaining ordered to close up the Glen, so I believe so. I thought you…might like to know.'

'Thanks for the warning,' Crispin said. 'You'd better take me up to see Mama.'

Whatever was going on? he wondered as he followed the butler up to the small back sitting room that was his mother's private retreat. He couldn't think of a single reason why his father would ignore his oft-stated distaste for the city and gift the family with a trip to London for the whole Season, much as he knew his mother would be thrilled at the opportunity.

As he walked in, the Countess rose, her lovely

face lighting with delight. 'Crispin, my dearest!' she exclaimed, rising to hug him tightly.

He hugged her back, both revelling in her affection and feeling guilty. The impossible position he occupied, acting since boyhood as sort of buffer between his father's iron will and her gentleness, had never improved his mother's circumstances more than temporarily. But though his mother had encouraged and supported his drive for independence, leaving Montwell Glen had left her without a protector.

Even if whatever protection he offered was always short-lived.

His long-smouldering anger redoubled at his father, who had married this beautiful, shy, soft-spoken lady for her substantial dowry and never appreciated her. Cowed and belittled by her husband, she had endured by showering her children with the affection her disdainful spouse spurned.

Would her life have been better if she'd stood up to him? Crispin wondered again. Or would that have only created more of the turmoil and distress that had driven him to flee the family home after university and return as seldom as possible? A pointless conjecture—his gentle mother didn't have it in her to confront anyone.

'How have you been keeping? Sorry it's been so long since I've been home.'

She patted his hand. 'Never mind about that.

Knowing you are pursuing your own life without…interference, and happy doing so, is enough for me. Did your exploration trip go well?'

'It did. Fine weather, enjoyable rides, and excellent hostelries along the way.' He paused, tempted for a moment to tell her about meeting Miss Cranmore. But though he thought his mother would find his account of such an unusual girl amusing, mentioning the name of any single female might invite a discussion of marriage—something he knew his mother wanted for him—that he'd rather avoid.

Instead, he continued, 'The Great Western venture poses greater risks than the previous schemes I've backed, but the concept is intriguing and the possibility for return could be enormous.'

'So you've decided to invest.'

'Yes. I spoke with the firm's solicitor when I returned to London two weeks ago and arranged to purchase shares.'

He'd been excited to drop by Richard Cranmore's office. But though he'd been impressed by its tasteful opulence and treated with dignified deference by the solicitor, the owner, Mr Cranmore, had been nowhere in evidence.

Nor, alas, had his daughter.

'How are you getting on—and how is it that you look lovelier every time I see you?' For truly, his mother did look more than usually radiant.

'Thank you, kind sir!' she said, her eyes taking on a sparkle. 'It must be the excitement of being in London again. You know how much I love the city.'

'Father should bring you more often,' he said with some heat. 'Are you really going to spend the whole Season?'

To his concern, the light in her eyes dimmed. Looking troubled, she said, 'I'm afraid that depends...mostly on you.'

The feeling of trepidation that settled in his gut whenever he had to deal with his father intensified. 'How could it depend on me?'

His mother sighed. 'I'm only guessing, since as you know the Earl never informs me of anything and I might be quite wrong. You'll be talking with him shortly anyway. I... I just ask that you not immediately refuse whatever it is he means to demand of you. For my sake? You know how... unpleasant he can be when he doesn't get his way. He could well ship us back to Montwell Glen as unexpectedly as he packed us to come, and Maggie is so excited to be able to spend some time here! Even though she's not old enough yet to attend society events, I can take her to meet the ladies whose approval she must have when she's presented next year, we can visit the shops and the theatre and attend a few evening events. She's been over the moon at the prospect! I'd like to keep your father in good humour long enough for her to sample at least some of that.'

'And let you sample it, too. It's been three years since you've been in London long enough to attend social events and catch up with all your friends.'

She smiled. 'I'm not denying I'll enjoy it as much as Maggie!'

The mantel clock bonged and her smile faded, a nervous look replacing it. 'You'd better go see your father now. He'll have been informed you've arrived, and you know he can't tolerate being kept waiting.'

'Yes, far be it for me to dally for a pleasant half-hour with my mother,' he said acerbically.

'You will be...patient?'

Reining in both his anger and rising sense of dread, he kissed her hand.

'I'll be...reasonable. If at all possible, I'll do what he wants, if it means you and Maggie can enjoy the delights of London for an entire Season.'

'You won't let him set you off?' The tears he so dreaded formed in the corners of her eyes. 'You know how much it upsets me when he does,' she ended on a whisper.

As much as his mother's distress upset and angered him, he thought grimly, setting his jaw. Summoning up a smile, he said, 'I shall display the patience of Job. But you're right, I'd better go in before he can decide I'm tardy. No sense giving him a whip to whack me with before we even get started.'

'Thank you, my darling,' she said, rising to give him one last hug. 'Having time here in London, seeing you, would be the best birthday gift I could receive.'

'Don't worry,' he said, releasing her. 'I'll pacify the beast—for you.'

An uneasy mix of anger, resentment and apprehension roiling in his gut, Crispin paced out and headed for his father's study.

After a knock at the door, his father's voice bade him enter. Taking a deep breath, he walked in and made his father a bow. 'You wished to see me, sir?'

The Earl gave him a silent, head-to-toe inspection, making him grateful for Haines's diligence, before responding, 'A more dutiful son might have added *What do you wish me to do?*'

Gritting his teeth, Crispin resisted responding that by now the Earl should know better than to expect him to live up to his father's concept of 'dutiful'. Mindful of his promise to his mother, he said nothing—which was a provocation in itself, but he couldn't bring himself to utter something placating.

After a few minutes of silence, the Earl continued, 'I imagine you didn't expect to see me in

London. I certainly wasn't happy about having to come. Disappointing as your conduct often is, I'm certain that you understand you must eventually do your duty. Since I understand better than anyone how disagreeable that generally is, I've been indulgent enough to allow you to postpone it. But a situation, and an opportunity, has arisen that makes that indulgence no longer possible.'

'My duty?' Though, with a rising sense of distaste, he was pretty sure he knew what his father meant, he would have him spell it out. 'Which duty would that be, sir?'

Since learning to run the estate, deal with tenants, and manage accounts are all 'duties' you've not allowed me to carry out.

'Marriage, of course,' Comeryn returned with a frown. 'Which I'm sure you understood. Disappointing you may be, but you're not a complete dolt.'

Keeping a tight hold on his temper, Crispin said evenly, 'Why is it suddenly imperative that I perform that duty now?'

'If you spent as much time concerned about agricultural matters as you do about vulgar commercial enterprises, you'd know that the price of crops and the value of land have steadily eroded since the wars ended. Diligent as I've been to avoid it, the estate's agricultural income has gone down every year. Sooner or later, the estate will need a large infusion of cash—the sort of cash that can only be provided by a dowry as handsome as the one your mother brought. Which brings me to the opportunity I mentioned.'

The Earl paused, but Crispin knew better than to interrupt with a comment or question. That would only be tolerated once the Earl finished his speech and invited a response—or dismissed him.

'An acquaintance—Lord Arlsley—tipped me off that his wife would be sponsoring a female with the most spectacular dowry society has seen in years. She's not the sort of female I would normally countenance—her antecedents are in trade—but the grandfather for whom she is sole heiress was ennobled, which makes her at least tolerable. Arlsley assured me the chit is attractive enough and has been schooled so she won't be an embarrassment. Though, once you've married her and bred some heirs on her, if you find her intolerable, you can always ship her off to the country, go about your business and conduct your discreet liaisons elsewhere. The upshot is, you need to cease gambolling about England and remain in London for the Season. Attend society events, meet the heiress, charm her and marry her. For the good of the family and the estate.'

Bad enough to have to wed to secure the succession. The idea of marrying money and then shunting his wife aside to dally with other women was truly disgusting. Though Crispin wasn't surprised at the suggestion. He'd suspected for years that his father had kept a string of mistresses.

Stifling the immediate refusal he wanted to return, he said, 'So who is this female?'

'I don't recall the name, not that it matters. Despite your dealings with railway commerce, it's unlikely you would have encountered the grandfather, who I'm told is known as the "Factory King". Made his blunt in the mining and weaving trade, got himself knighted in the bargain. Be assured, I don't expect you to have any social dealings with him. I trust you'll know how to depress his pretensions, if he should try to hang on your sleeve.'

Ignoring that, Crispin felt emboldened to ask the only thing that really interested him. 'Just how badly dipped is the estate?'

As expected, his father immediately recoiled in anger. But, somewhat to Crispin's surprise, the Earl didn't direct at him a barrage of abuse for having the temerity to ask. 'I had to borrow the last three years to put the crops in, plus make essential repairs, and the returns haven't been good enough to repay any of the loans. The banker's been recommending that I sell off some unentailed land, the impudent upstart! Then, with her presentation next year, there's Lady Margaret's dowry to be considered.'

Things must be worse than that if his father had

chosen to disclose that information—probably with the intention of putting further pressure on Crispin to make the marriage his father wanted.

Concerned despite himself, he said, 'I thought part of Mother's settlement provided for Maggie's dowry.'

'The funds have been utilised…elsewhere,' his father said cryptically.

The estate forced to sell off land—undervalued land, with the depression in agricultural prices. His sister, her dowry funds compromised.

'If the estate is short of cash, I've built up a reserve—'

'I'll not take any money earned in trade!' his father bellowed. 'Don't insult me by suggesting it. I know my duty as a gentleman, even if you seemed to have forgotten it.'

'But you'd have me marry a tradesman's heiress?'

'That's different, and you know it. He's a baronet now, and marrying to secure a handsome dowry is a time-honoured way for a gentleman to raise the ready.'

Having nearly to bite his tongue to forestall replying that the difference between the two was so slight, it would take a magnifying glass to see it, Crispin took a long, slow breath.

He wouldn't allow his sister to suffer for his father's delicate 'gentlemanly' sensibilities. He'd make sure there was money for a dowry, whatever happened. As for the estate, that would require more finesse, since legally he couldn't intervene in its running until he actually owned it. But if it proved necessary, he would figure out how to provide an infusion of funds for that, too—later.

For now, he just needed to honour his promise to his mother. 'So I'm to meet, charm and marry this girl?'

The Earl nodded. 'That's the short of it.'

'If she's that well dowered, there will certainly be competition.'

'Not many young, attractive suitors will possess the pedigree or the title you do. If you make half an effort, I believe you have a good chance of success. You owe it to your name and your inheritance.'

Crispin burned to be able to tell his father what he could do with his sense of 'duty' to the name and title. But the image of his mother's worried face stopped his tongue.

If he wanted to spare his mother and give her the pleasure of spending the Season in London, a reward she richly deserved for enduring her bitter sham of a marriage, he couldn't defy his father outright. If he agreed to participate in society, she would have time to enjoy the city.

Otherwise, his refusal would likely set off a tirade that would unnerve his mother, sister, and everyone in the household, after which his father would pack them all up and drag them back to Montwell Glen.

He could tolerate it, he decided. At least until his father called his bluff, demanding that he marry either the heiress chit, or if he failed to impress her, some other well-dowered female, at which time he'd be forced to refuse.

It was the only birthday present his mother wanted. How could he disappoint her?

'If I agree, you'll allow Mother and Lady Margaret to remain in London for the Season?'

His father shrugged. 'I'd rather avoid the expense of maintaining them here. But you will have a better chance of success if the Countess is in London, able to access that circle of females who run society in order to secure introductions and invitations to parties at which the Heiress is going to be present.'

'And if I don't succeed in winning the chit's "affections"?' he asked, hardly able to keep the irony from his voice.

'See that you do. Or failing that, win the hand of some other female with sufficient dowry.' The Earl glanced down at his desk. 'The Sutterlings' ball is in three days. You'll arrange to be present. You've disappointed me many times. Don't fail me in this. That is all,' the Earl concluded, waving towards the door to signal the interview was over.

'Sir,' Crispin said, bowing, happy to comply.

Nothing gave him more pleasure than to quit his father's presence.

He'd stop briefly to reassure his mother, perhaps look in on his sister. Then he'd head to the Lattimar town house.

If Gregory didn't have to return immediately to Northumberland, he'd see if he could coax his friend to linger a while in London. If he were going to have to put his own priorities on hold while he endured—as long as he could stand it—the social events of the Season, having his best friend along would make the experience less dismal.

Although the end was sure. A refusal to wed, a tantrum from the Earl, and his family's immediate departure for Montwell Glen. The only way to avoid that would be a wedding.

Not even his mother's unhappiness would force him to that drastic a solution.

Chapter Five

❧∼∽❧

Three nights later, after escorting his mother to the group of friends she'd promised to meet at the Sutterlings' ball, Crispin scanned the room for Gregory Lattimar. When he'd called at his friend's home after the interview with his father, though Lattimar was due to leave shortly for Northumberland, he'd managed to convince him to attend this one ball.

Spotting Lattimar at the far side of the room where refreshments were being dispersed, Crispin went over to meet him and snag a beverage of his own.

'Good evening, Greg, and thanks for coming to help make the evening bearable. How goes it so far?'

'The food is good, the wine is superior, and no hovering mamas have coerced me into dancing with their daughters, so it's been fine. Have you met the Heiress yet?'

'No. Have you?'

'Lud, no,' he said with a shudder. 'Thankfully, I'm not in need of a fat dowry. When I finally marry, I'll be looking for a female of impeccable breeding and character to help redeem the reputation of my rakish family.'

Crispin smiled. 'I wouldn't worry about that. Just because your younger brother married a former courtesan and one twin sister married an adventurer? After all, the other twin married an earl, and your family boasts a fine pedigree. No one as swimming in blunt as the heir to the Lattimar barony needs to worry about his standing in society.'

'Maybe. But my formerly notorious mother is still not received by the highest sticklers, something I wish I could change. It makes me furious, since she's done nothing scandalous for years and the gentlemen who earned her that reputation received hardly a murmur of reproof for their parts in it. But no matter. At least, unlike you,' he added, tapping Crispin on the wrist, '*I* have no need to marry this Season.'

'I've no intention of marrying either. As you well know,' Crispin responded with some asperity. 'So you may cease ragging me.'

'I don't know. Might not be a good idea to pass up the Heiress. Her sudden appearance in society has the clubs all abuzz. There are already bets being laid on how long it will take her to snag someone and just how high she might aspire to rise. Her fortune is supposed to surpass Golden Ball's.'

Crispin was about to tell his friend—again—that despite his father's insistence, he didn't need money enough to resort to as drastic a solution as marriage when his mother came over. 'Gregory, how nice to see you again. Your family is well?'

'Very well, thank you, Lady Comeryn. You're looking radiant tonight!'

'You're very kind. I am enjoying being back in London. It is such a delight to be in company again! I'm hoping to call on your mother soon.'

'She will be happy to see you.'

'And I, her. You will give her my best?' As Gregory nodded, his mother put her hand on Crispin's arm. 'I'm afraid I must steal away my son. Unless you, too, would like an introduction to—'

'Gracious of you, Lady Comeryn, but since I'm not in need of an heiress, I'm content to leave the field to those who are. Go on,' Gregory said, grinning as he gave Crispin a little shove. 'Be your most charming.'

'Sorry,' his mother murmured as she led him away. 'But, as instructed by your father, I must present you to the Heiress. By the way, Lady Auberly assured me, with some surprise, that she is quite presentable. I think you should…give her a chance.'

'Mother…' he said in a warning tone.

'Nothing more, I assure you! I can hardly ask more, since I'm already so indebted to you for agreeing to this.'

'All for you, Mama,' he said, steeling himself to be pleasant for the decent interval he must remain conversing with the girl before he could escape. Also wondering what on earth he *would* converse about with a young female of tender years with whom he could have almost nothing in common.

As they approached the opposite side of the ballroom where a bevy of young females and their chaperons awaited the next dance, he caught a glimpse in profile of a tall, slender lady with a crown of dark curls that shimmered with auburn highlights in the candlelight. A little jolt of shock and delight went through him.

Could it really be… Miss Cranmore? What in the world would she be doing here?

Smiling, he picked up his pace. If it truly was her, maybe he could speak with her after he'd done his duty by the Heiress.

Just then, the lady turned in his direction, and he caught his breath.

It was indeed Miss Cranmore, and she looked… dazzling! The evening gown with its wide sleeves, low décolletage and narrow waist above a wide bell of skirts seemed expressly designed to display her lovely curves, while her dark eyes were as sparkling as the jewels at her neck and ears.

As if pulled by some invisible cord, he found himself walking towards her. He was about to speak to her when he suddenly realised that his mother had halted next to him. The matron beside Miss Cranmore curtsied to him, as did the young lady, her polite smile turning radiant as she recognised him.

'Lady Arlsley, Miss Cranmore,' his mother was saying, 'allow me to present my son, Viscount Dellamont.'

Confused, he frowned. Arlsley...was the name of the Baron whose wife was sponsoring the Heiress. His mother had fetched him a moment ago expressly so she might to introduce him to the Heiress.

Which meant... *Miss Cranmore* was the Factory Heiress?

He was dimly aware of bowing, his tongue automatically producing the required politeness, while shock was succeeded by disbelief, then by a dawning sense of anger...and outrage.

He'd thought her so unusual, so uninterested in the normal female activities and pretences. She'd professed a desire to stave off marriage as long as possible and a total uninterest in marrying to improve her station.

Yet bets were being placed at this very moment in all the London clubs, wagering on how soon she'd marry and how highly born a husband she'd trap.

Had she been playing him for a fool back in Bristol?

The polite society smile frozen on her face, Marcella turned to glimpse the clock on the far-away mantel and figure out just how much longer she had to remain at this accursed ball before she could insist that Lady Arlsley let her go home.

This second evening of her society debut was proceeding much like first. While it had not been quite as dreadful as she'd feared, it was unpleasant enough an echo of her time at Miss Axminster's that she wasn't sure how long going she'd be able to stand it before she held Papa to his word and insisted on being allowed to abandon the Season she'd never wanted.

The morning after her dinner with Grandda, a glacially polite Lady Arlsley had received her. The following two afternoons, she'd taken Marcella calling on aristocratic ladies who woodenly acknowledged her chaperon's thanks for inviting her to their entertainments, those ladies looking no more enthused about the prospect than her sponsor. While so far no one had openly cut her at the two events she'd attended, few beyond the immediate circle of Lady Arlsley's acquaintances had deigned speak with her and the other young ladies making their debuts had pointedly ignored her. Mercifully, she hadn't yet encountered any of her tormentors from her time at Miss Axminster's.

The coolness of her reception by the feminine contingent was in sharp contrast to the abject flattery she'd received from the smattering of gentlemen who had asked to be presented. All of them, she was certain, must in such urgent need of her dowry that they were prepared to overlook her lack of family and breeding. Not one of those desperate gentlemen interested her in slightest—and one she already held in aversion.

Lord Hoddleston had seemed to sense the dislike beneath her politeness. For some reason she couldn't fathom, her inadequately concealed distaste seemed to amuse and pique his interest rather than discourage him. She'd actually had to resort to visiting the ladies' retiring room to escape his persistent attentions at last night's rout.

Fortunately, she hadn't encountered him yet this evening and could only hope that good luck would hold. Since he was a baron of ancient lineage, the fact that she found him distasteful was unlikely to persuade Lady Arlsley to allow her to avoid him. Her sponsor would probably jump at the chance to marry her off to the first available candidate and be rid of a charge she'd been no more eager to take on than Marcella had been to agree to this worthless endeavour.

Her fixed gaze not prompting the hands of that mantel clock to circle any faster, she turned back towards the ballroom…and saw *him* approaching. Shock, delight and nervousness rushed through her in rapid succession.

Though she'd known there was a chance she might encounter Viscount Dellamont at some society event, she hadn't really believed it would happen. But as he continued to walk right towards her, it became apparent that she was indeed going to meet him again.

He'd been arrestingly handsome that day in his well-tailored jacket, breeches and dusty riding boots. He looked even taller and more commanding in formal black evening wear. A riot of dark curls shadowing his forehead, his square-jawed face with its intense, intelligent eyes compelling above an intricate white neckcloth, he all but took her breath away.

How would he react to her being here, invading his realm? Would she sense between them the same heady spark of attraction she'd felt in Bristol?

Nearly dizzy with anticipation, her spirits soared at the possibility of speaking with, perhaps even dancing with, someone who knew the real person behind the 'Factory Heiress', the hated moniker with which society had saddled her.

Then he was at her side, the lady who must be his mother presenting him. She tried to order her scrambled wits to respond with the appropriate phrases while her pulse pounded in her ears and a nervous eagerness made swallows swoop and dive in her stomach.

She was dimly aware that the musicians were tuning up to resume the dancing when Lady Arlsley said, 'So good to see you again, Lord Dellamont. I believe that's a waltz I hear? I'm sure Miss Cranmore would be delighted to dance it with you.'

Would he be delighted to dance with her? After Lady Arlsley's leading comment, it would be awkward for him to refuse.

And he didn't. Bowing, so she couldn't really see his face to gauge his reaction, he held out his arm. 'If you would do me the honour, Miss Cranmore?'

'Of course, my lord.' She placed her hand on his sleeve, a tingle running up her arm as he led her on to the floor.

As the music began and he placed one hand at her waist and took her hand with the other, the rush of pleasurable sensations coursing through her body once again momentarily paralysed all thought. They'd taken several turns around the floor before she recovered wit enough to look up at his face.

With a frisson of alarm, she noted the rigid jaw, the expressionless face, and the gaze that looked not at, but through her.

Her excitement vanished as swiftly as it had arisen. If he hadn't wished to acknowledge her, why had he consented to be presented?

Maybe she was wrong to assume he'd danced with her unwillingly. Either way, she simply had to know for sure.

Gathering up her courage, she said, 'It was a pleasant and unexpected surprise to see you here tonight, my lord. I know you are frequently out of London.'

'It was a surprise to see you as well. More of a shock, actually.'

She couldn't really tell anything from his tone. 'A shock to me, too. I certainly hadn't intended to be here.'

'So you said earlier. I seem to remember you telling me something about your *mother's* aspirations. How you yourself had no interest in attaining an "elevated status" and preferred mathematics to marriage?' He gave a short, bitter laugh. 'You certainly took me in, didn't you? Or was all that palaver just a ploy to intrigue me, knowing you were going to meet me again in London?'

She gasped with outrage. 'You think...you think I *deliberately* misled you?'

'You're here, aren't you? Swanning about at a society ball surrounded by company a good deal more elevated than can be found in an engineering office. With all of them knowing your goal is to trade your vast dowry for as high a title as it will buy.'

'You think I intend to sell myself for a title?' she asked, truly enraged now. 'I'll have you know I had absolutely no desire to be here in this so-called "elevated" company! And what about you?' she asked, suddenly struck. 'The only titled men who've sought introductions to me have been fortune hunters. Yet I seem to recall you pronouncing how "detestable" it would be to marry for wealth or advantage. Or were you trying to "intrigue" me, too, back in Bristol?'

She was furious—and much more hurt than she should be. She'd always known that meeting in Bristol was singular, that if he were to encounter her somewhere else, there was a good chance he'd cut her. It was because he'd induced her to hope for more from him that she was so disappointed now.

She felt a rising sense of outrage that he'd led her to talk about herself and what she found important, made her think he shared her views on industry and progress. When at heart, he'd just shown himself as cold, calculating and arrogantly dismissive as all the other aristocrats she'd ever encountered.

The fact that she'd been completely bamboozled by his charm cut her to the quick. Feeling suddenly unable to endure another moment of his traitorous hands touching her, she pulled away from him and stopped short, compelling him to halt also. 'You will return me to my chaperon now.'

'That would suit me perfectly,' he said icily.

Ignoring the exclamations of annoyance and distress of the other couples who had to swerve to avoid them, he offered his arm. She could barely bring herself to place her hand on it, but did, holding her head high, willing the tears that threatened not to fall while he escorted her off the dance floor, more or less shoved her towards her chaperon, gave her a stiff bow, and stalked off.

'What have you done? Everyone in the ballroom is staring at us!' Lady Arlsley hissed.

The hurt and disappointment layered on top of the strain of the last few days was finally just too much. If she had to remain in this room one more minute, she would suffocate. 'Let them look,' she cried. 'I... I must go to the ladies' retiring room.'

Breaking away from her chaperon, she hurried towards the exit of the ballroom.

Only to halt as she reached the door. She might

find solitude in the retiring room—or she might encounter a clutch of disdainful females who'd delight in ignoring her or offering more of the slyly insulting compliments she'd received so often these last two nights.

Worse, as soon as the dance ended, the room would probably fill with ladies eager to gossip about her sudden departure in the middle of the waltz.

She couldn't endure that.

Suddenly her gaze caught on the brightness of a burning torch. A terrace ran outside the length of the ballroom, she realised, visible through a series of French doors. The torches burning at intervals along it indicated the hostess had had it lighted so that dancers might escape the heat of the ballroom and refresh themselves in the cool night air.

At the moment, it appeared deserted. Heedless of her lack of wrap or escort, Marcella strode through the nearest door and out on to the terrace.

With tears falling now, she sought out the dimmest corner. Wrapping her arms around herself, she gave in to silent sobs of misery and disappointment.

She'd really wanted to meet Dellamont again, wondering how he might react. Well, now she knew.

He might have looked and sounded like the

hero out of a storybook in Bristol, but in the brilliant candlelight of a London ballroom, she'd discovered what he truly was—just as high in the instep, dismissive and condescending as all the rest of them. It was probably best that her silly illusions about the sort of man he was had been shattered.

She should have known better. She knew better now.

After this, like she had with the girls at Miss Axminster's, she would be polite but distant. Play her part, ignore the provocations, smile, dance, endure the coldness and spite of the women, dismiss the entreaties of the supplicants. For a month. Then she'd hold her father to their bargain, go back where she belonged, and shake the dust of this world from her shoes for good.

'My, my, what have we here? Did all the adulation in the ballroom become too much for you?'

Marcella whirled around—to find herself confronted by her least favourite of all the unfavoured gentlemen. Though Lord Hoddleston was elegantly turned out, there was something about him beyond the mocking undertone of his voice that made her wary.

He was probably thought handsome, although in the brighter light of the candelabra last night she'd noted a bleariness in his eyes and lines on his face that hinted a life of excess was beginning to catch up to him. Not wanting Lady Arlsley to infer he interested her, she'd not enquired any further about his background or circumstances than the short summation her chaperon had given. But Marcella figured his finances must be truly desperate for him to be pursuing the likes of her, when she'd been told his title dated back almost four hundred years.

'I found the room...overwarm.'

'By contrast, it's rather chilly out here. And you without a wrap! Allow me to offer you...comfort.'

He stepped towards her. She sidestepped away. 'I'm doing quite well on my own. I just needed a little air. I'll return to ballroom presently. Please, go back in. I wouldn't want to keep you.'

'I might want to keep you,' he murmured, leaning closer. 'You're a pretty little thing, which is a bonus beyond the tidy sum you'll bring. You might as well take me, you know. You're not going to get a better offer. Certainly not from someone with a father as discriminating as Dellamont's.' He chuckled. 'Abandoning your partner and flouncing off the floor in the middle of a dance? After that charming little scene, even those in dire need of your blunt will think twice about pursuing you.'

So he'd been watching after all. As if the prospect of being abandoned by the other fortune hunters would make her look more favourably on this one! 'Kind of you to warn me, but unnecessary. And I must ask you to leave me in peace.'

'And if I don't want to?' he asked, stepping close enough to crowd her against the balustrade as he took her hand.

'It would create an even more shocking scene if I were to start screaming,' she retorted, trying to tug her arm free.

Hoddleston laughed. 'Scream if you like. I doubt anyone will hear you. Even if they should, by then, the damage will be done. Because I am going to kiss you.'

Panic beginning to well up, Marcella was calculating whether she should try gouging his leg with her sharp heel or kneeing him in his nether parts when a voice at her ear made her jump.

'I believe the lady asked you to leave, Hoddleston.'

Dellamont's voice. She was so relieved, for the moment, she forgave him for hurting and disappointing her.

'Lady?' Hoddleston echoed. 'I see no ladies here. Just a jumped-up cit's granddaughter who doesn't know her place. An opinion you demonstrated you share when you dragged her off the dance floor. Why don't you just take your leave, then—and leave her handsome dowry to me.'

Marcella gasped as Dellamont whipped out a hand to seize Hoddleston's lapel and jerk him backwards, away from her. 'Although I don't see any other gentlemen present here, save myself, I'd advise you to take *your* leave before I'm forced to resort to the crude sort of persuasion your behaviour merits. I know you'd be distressed to have that nose bleed all over your oh-so-pristine cravat.'

For a moment, the two men stared at each other, Hoddleston's face uncertain, as if calculating whether or not the Viscount would make good on his threat, Dellamont's stony with resolve.

The Baron must have believed him, for he took another step backwards. 'You threaten fisticuffs on the terrace outside a ball and still call yourself a gentleman? How...ill bred of you. I wouldn't stoop to that—not for the likes of *her*. But though your elevated sense of honour might prompt you to intervene now, I'm confident of reaching my goal. The high and mighty future Earl of Comeryn has no intention of aligning himself with a female like this one. In the end, I doubt any other men of breeding will either. I need merely bide my time.'

Glancing over at Marcella, he said, 'Because, in the end, you will have me.' Turning from her to the Viscount, with a look full of loathing, he growled, 'I won't forget this, Dellamont.'

'I assure you, neither will I. Are you in need of further encouragement to depart?'

'I believe I am sufficiently encouraged—about everything.' Making Marcella an elaborate bow, he said, 'Goodbye—for the moment, Miss Cranmore.'

Refusing to answer him, she turned her face away, listening for the sound of his footsteps fading.

She looked back up to see Dellamont watching Hoddleston, his alert vigilance not relaxing until the Baron disappeared back into ballroom. Then he turned to her.

'Are you all right, Miss Cranmore? He didn't harm you?'

She shook her head, shaken and close to tears again now that the unpleasant interlude was over. 'He threatened me with his attentions. Insulted me. Though in that regard, hardly more than most of the guests tonight.'

Since he'd been kind enough to get rid of Hoddleston, she didn't add *Like you did, too.*

To her surprise, he said it instead. 'As I did? Please, let me apologise. I had no right to be indignant with you for doing what every female must do—marry, and marry as well as she can. As you said in Bristol, a woman has little alternative. You'd already told me your mother had been pressing you to make a good match. It was just…'

'I'd assured you I didn't want to marry into

the aristocracy, and yet there I was? The *Factory Heiress*!' She spat out the term bitterly.

'I can hardly complain. I assured you I'd never marry for money either, yet here *I* am.'

'Did your family coerce you as well?'

Dellamont sighed. 'My father. Having heard about the arrival of a fabulously wealthy heiress and with the estate in need of cash, the Earl decided it was my duty to win and marry her. I have cash in hand if the estate needs it, but far be it for a d'Aubignon to accept money made in trade!'

'Although it is perfectly acceptable to marry it?'

'It makes no sense, I agree. The thing is, the Earl never allows my mother to spend the Season in London, and she does so love it. He would only allow her to stay if I agreed to go about in society, supposedly to court the Factory Heiress. Of course, I had no intention of actually doing that, but hoped agreeing would buy my mother some time to enjoy the city before Comeryn figured it out, delivered me a lecture, and dragged Mother back to Montwell Glen. I had no idea the "Factory Heiress" would be you.'

'When we met in Bristol, I had no idea it was going to be me, either,' she said wryly. 'I didn't discover until I returned to London that Sir Thomas, my mother's father, had made me his heir. Or that he'd accepted the baronetcy solely to help make my mother's fantasy of having me marry into the aristocracy come true. Grandda told me then that he'd arranged—manoeuvred is more accurate—to have a well-born lady introduce me. I hated the idea, but both Mama and Grandda begged me to go along. When even my father added his urging to theirs…

'Like you with your mother, I just couldn't refuse. But Father did agree that if I found the experience truly awful, he'd intervene to get me out of it. I'm going to try to make it for a month, but on nights like tonight—' she shuddered as she recalled the repellent confidence of Hoddleston, the cold contemptuous gazes of the people in the ballroom '—I'm not sure I can stand a whole month! I can't wait to get back to that engineering office!'

Dellamont laughed. 'I promised Mother I'd stick it out as long as I could, too. Or until my father realised he'd been hoodwinked and that I'd had no intention from the first of courting anyone. He lectures me frequently, but I suspect the rant I'll be subjected to on that occasion will be the most blistering ever. But it will be worth it, to let Mama enjoy town for a few weeks.'

Marcella sighed. 'The things we endure for family. But… I'm awfully glad to find I was mistaken about you tonight. That you really are the gentleman you appeared to be in Bristol.'

'As I am glad to confirm that you are truly the unusual lady I met in an engineer's office. But now, I'd better return you to the ballroom before you freeze.'

'Not that it will make much difference. As Hoddleston obligingly pointed out, after the "charming scene" I created by fleeing the dance floor, no one else is likely to want to stand up with me tonight. Maybe I can induce Lady Arlsley to let me go home.'

Marcella shook her head. 'I tried to tell her from the first that I was no more happy about the idea of going into society than she was at being saddled with presenting me. Of course, she didn't believe me. How could any female not be eager to join her precious exclusive little circle? But we made an uneasy truce. If she would not condescend to me or deliberately expose me to insult, I would endeavour not to embarrass her. I'm afraid my behaviour tonight didn't live up to that bargain.'

Dellamont had been walking her in, but at that, he halted. 'What if *we* were to make a bargain?'

'A bargain?' she repeated, angling a glance up at him. 'What do you mean?'

'Neither of us want to be here, wasting our

time idling around a society in which neither of us has any interest. What if we join forces? It would placate my father and allow my mother to enjoy the maximum amount of time in London if the Earl hears I'm spending time with the Heiress. While your chaperon will be pleased that a gentleman of good reputation and family is paying attention to you. I enjoy your company and would like to know you better—as a friend. At the least, I can keep reprobates like Hoddleston away from you.'

'Friends? To chat and dance together at the balls and routs I'm forced to attend? That would be wonderful!' she cried, energised by a vision of replacing the miserable evenings she was expecting with the delight of his company. With the one man in London who truly knew who she was and found her unique and interesting.

'Then, after a month or so, I can break off the relationship and go back where I belong. It will show Mama and Grandda that I made an effort— as you can show your father. We can then tell them we discovered we would not suit. It would be perfect!'

'It might be better if you let me break it off, rather than have you look like a jilt. I'll be thought a bounder, but no matter. I'm not interested in marrying soon anyway. I'm quite certain that once duty forces me to it, with the lure of a countess's coronet beckoning eligible females and their mamas will forgive me the lapse.'

Marcella shook her head. 'I'd not have you badly thought of. What do I care if society thinks me a jilt? Most already believe that, with my low birth, I possess no breeding. Once I make my escape, I devoutly hope never to encounter any of these people again, whereas they comprise the society you were born into, the one in which you will always move. Much better to let me break it off.'

'We can argue about that later. But for now… do we have a bargain?'

'For a month or so…we'll make what would otherwise be an ordeal much more pleasant for us both?'

'Exactly,' he confirmed.

'Then we have a bargain.' She held out a hand—and felt a little shiver go through her as he shook it.

'Back to the ballroom for you now. I'll tell Lady Arlsley that you became faint on the dance floor and needed some time alone to revive yourself on the terrace. That I waited to escort you back in.'

'But I told her I was going to the ladies' retiring room.'

'I'll tell her I intercepted you and recommended the terrace. It's cooler and more private, after all.'

'You think she'll believe that?'

Dellamont smiled. 'I can be quite persuasive. Especially if I request the honour of calling on you tomorrow.'

'She'll certainly be relieved to discover that I didn't give you a disgust of me after all,' Marcella said.

But not nearly as relieved as she was, Marcella thought as she put her hand on Dellamont's arm. She'd be able to continue seeing him—even if that might not be wise.

With him acting as that knight in shining armour in truth, it might be hard to keep her foolish feminine heart from fluttering.

Very well, she wouldn't deny that she was looking forward to enjoying his very attractive attentions—for a time. But he belonged to a society of which she wanted no part. Not that he would want her, either, for more than a temporary friendship. She was probably the least likely woman in England to make a proper countess.

No, this partnership would be as short-lived as she expected it would be pleasant. After which, she would return to her world—hopefully to exchange the escort of this knight in shining armour for that of her childhood hero Gilling—while he remained in his.

Two planets in different orbits, never to meet again.

Shaking off the sadness that thought evoked, she put a determined smile on her face and walked back into the ballroom on Dellamont's arm, looking forward with amusement to hearing the far-radiddle he would spin to placate Lady Arlsley for her absence.

Chapter Six

The following afternoon during calling hours, Marcella found herself seated in Lady Arlsley's parlour. The handful of gentlemen she'd danced with the evening before would make courtesy calls, making her attendance mandatory, her sponsor had informed her.

Although there was only one of last night's partners she really hoped to see. After having a night to think over the implications of their bargain, would Viscount Dellamont still want to follow through with it?

So far, she'd endured the attentions of two suitors, while several of Lady Arlsley's friends had called. After giving her a strictly proper greeting, two of those ladies were now settled on the sofa beside her sponsor, their heads together as they spoke in low tones. Their occasional glances in her direction told her that she—and last night's ball—were probably the topics of conversation.

The erstwhile suitors having departed after the obligatory fifteen minutes, Marcella wandered around the parlour, pausing to stare out the window on to the side garden. After Dellamont had left her last night, she'd been convinced he would honour his word, their bargain, and call today. But as she tossed and turned last night, anxiety keeping her from sleep, she'd begun to doubt that.

Having fulfilled his father's wishes by submitting to the required introductions, it would be much easier—and likely pleasanter—to continue the charade with the Earl by turning his attentions to some well-born girl of adequate dowry. There would be no need to single himself out and possibly invite criticism, branding himself as a fortune hunter by seeming to court her.

He'd disappointed her once. She told herself not to hope for too much, lest she be disappointed again.

The butler entered, bowing to introduce two newcomers, and her pulses leapt. Only to immediately settle as she recognised first Lord Charles, the foppish youngest son of a marquess. A few minutes of conversation last night been enough to demonstrate he possessed neither money nor sense. Following him was Lord Hoddleston.

Instinctive dislike had the hairs on the back of her neck rising. Giving her a knowing look, he walked over to pay his respects to Lady Arlsley and her friends on sofa. Then, while she steeled herself to endure him, with Lord Charles in tow, he walked in her direction.

'Miss Cranmore. How lovely you look this afternoon,' Lord Hoddleston said, bowing to her reluctant curtsy.

'Radiant as a daffodil in spring,' Lord Charles enthused.

'She'd need to be wearing a yellow gown to warrant that description,' Hoddleston said sardonically. 'In that pink confection, she's more like a vibrant tulip. Which inspires me to resume the conversation that was so rudely interrupted last night.'

'I didn't think anything more needed to be said,' Marcella replied, wishing she could be rude enough to ask him to leave.

'On the contrary, there's quite a bit. We were on the terrace, you'll remember. Alone.'

Was he trying to imply she'd agreed to meet him there—or hint she'd been compromised? she wondered, her irritation intensifying. 'Ah, yes, now I remember. I'd gone out for some fresh air and encountered you briefly on my way back in. Lord Charles,' she said, turning to the Marquess's son, 'you began telling me last night about the horse you'd been thinking of buying at Tattersall's?'

'Ah, the horse. Yes.' Looking uncomfortable under Lord Hoddleston's scornful gaze, which clearly said the Baron thought him of little account, he tugged at his neckcloth, but resisted the inclination to cut and run. 'A fine bay. Sixteen hands. Broad chest, fine withers. Looks to be a capital riding hack. Just have to convince m'father put out the blunt.'

Hoping to lure him into talking longer, she said, 'You will keep him for riding, or will he pull a carriage as well?'

Looking shocked, Lord Charles said, 'Oh, no, Miss Cranmore! One never puts a riding horse between the shafts! They're not bred nor trained for it. He'd be used solely for riding. Make quite a stir in the Park. He's a high-stepper, very showy.'

Hoddleston leaned in to murmur in her ear, 'You can take cover behind idiots like Lord Charles but you can't hide. After he bumbles off, I'll still be here—your inescapable destiny.'

Stepping back, she waved away his words, thinking if he were truly her destiny, she'd garrotte herself.

Before she could try to prod Lord Charles into further conversation, a stir at the doorway claimed their attention. 'Lord Dellamont,' the butler announced.

A wave of relief and delight ran through her. He'd called, just as he promised!

She had to suppress a smile as she watched the Viscount make full use of his entry to create a dramatic moment. After pausing on the threshold to survey the company, he proceeded slowly across the room, doubtless well aware of the ladies' admiring and the men's resentful gazes fixed on him, to make a courtly bow to the hostess and her friends.

'Ladies, a pleasure! I couldn't wait to see you again today, Lady Arlsley, and visit with your delightful charge. She promised to show me your garden, which I understand is superior. If I might claim her?'

Her gratified chaperon gave him her most gracious smile. 'Of course, Dellamont. As long as her maid accompanies you.'

'Thank you, my lady. I'm sure the garden will be as charming as the company.'

After giving her chaperon another bow, Dellamont turned to walk in her direction, the winning smile on his lips making her pulses pound with pleasure and anticipation. Ignoring both of the men beside her, he halted to say, 'I've come to hold you to your word, Miss Cranmore.'

'As you can see, Miss Cranmore is currently engaged with other guests,' Hoddleston said.

'She's already talked with you. It's my turn,'

Dellamont said, offering Marcella his arm. 'Shall you show me the garden as promised?'

'I'd never wish to default on a promise. Just let me go and find Mary. It's always so refreshing to take the air,' she added, with a deliberate look at Hoddleston.

'Why is she leaving with him?' she heard Lord Charles complain to the Baron as she walked out on Dellamont's arm.

'That was a fine bit of kidnapping,' she said after he closed the drawing room door behind them.

'Do you object?'

'Object to escaping that company? Not in the slightest! Do you really wish to see the garden?'

'Not especially. But I don't want to remain in the room with that young twit and the reprobate. Nor can we discuss the working of our bargain under the avid eyes of Lady Arlsley and her friends.'

So he meant to honour their bargain, too. The Season that had been forced on her might just become tolerable after all. 'Let me fetch Mary and get my pelisse, then.'

A few minutes later, Marcella hurried back, her maid trailing behind. After introductions, Mary bobbing a curtsy to Dellamont's nod, the three-some walked out the side door to the garden.

'You must come with us, but you needn't linger too close,' Marcella told the older woman as she held the door open for them.

'Never you mind, Miss Marcella,' the maid, who'd looked after her since she'd been a child, replied with a fond glance. 'You walk with your fine lord. I'll be near enough to call on if you should need me.'

'Don't worry, Mary,' Dellamont said. 'I won't attempt to ravish your charge on a garden bench— no matter how tempting she might be.'

'Just see you don't,' the maid replied tartly. 'I'd not be loath to give you a blow to the chops if you tried to take liberties, not even with you being a viscount and all.'

Dellamont laughed. 'I'll keep that in mind! You've a fine protector in Mary, Miss Cranmore. I'm relieved to know you will have someone nearby to keep your admirers in line.'

'Some need it more than others,' Marcella muttered, frowning as she thought of Lord Hoddleston. But she'd not waste this time with Dellamont fretting about the Baron.

'You've done your work well, my lord,' she said instead. 'By calling while Lady Arlsley's friends were visiting, the news will be all over London by suppertime that Viscount Dellamont is paying particular attention to Miss Cranmore.' She laughed. 'If I'm very lucky, knowing that an earl's son came calling will be discouraging enough to the competitors that I'll be spared further visits by Lord Hoddleston and Lord Charles.'

'Don't be too hard on them—at least, not on Lord Charles. He's the youngest son of a large family with no money of his own, so won't inherit either wealth or title. If he doesn't marry a well-dowered lady, he'll be reduced to spending his life as a hanger-on, dependent on the indulgence of his family. You are correct to lament the few options a female has beyond marriage, but opportunities for gentlemen to make their fortunes are limited as well.' He laughed. 'Poor Lord Charles doesn't strike me as having wit enough to succeed as a clergyman nor the boldness to prosper in the army.'

'Whereas you, my lord, have it all. Both the wit and boldness to invest in your own future, as well as land and title awaiting you. How I wish I had as many options!'

'Do you have any other options, save marriage?'

Marcella sighed. 'My family wouldn't hear of me working. I've been able thus far to assist Papa with his engineering work solely because he's indulged my interest. As a girl I'd actually hoped I might one day work in the business openly…but I realise now that could never happen. Too many men—and women—still believe that a female isn't capable of logical reasoning. I have considered becoming a teacher. But most schools that admit females have no interest in instructing their pupils in mathematics and the natural sciences. So I probably shall end up marrying, hopefully to someone who will allow me, if not to work outright, at least to remain around the world of engineering.'

'Someone like Mr Gilling?'

She felt herself flush. 'Was my interest so obvious?'

Dellamont smiled. 'You certainly gifted him with very engaging smiles. Would your engineer allow you to work with him, as your father does?'

'I'd hope to persuade him, but I don't really know. I'm guessing he thinks Papa allows me to do simple things around the office like record measurements because he enjoys having me near. I doubt Austin believes that I make any real contribution to figuring the calculations. But I'm not going to worry about that yet. Papa is still in his prime. I don't envision him handing over the business for years yet. I hope to delay marriage for as long as I can, in case my eventual husband frowns on my working with Papa and insists on restricting me to the usual female realm.'

'Do you have no interest in that at all? Children, running a household?'

'Not very much,' she admitted. 'I don't think I'd make a very good mother. I try to avoid the activities one is supposed to teach a daughter—

needlework, the minutiae of housekeeping and managing servants.'

'You'll need to entice your engineer, then.'

'It won't be easy,' she confessed. 'Gilling has worked for my father since I was a little girl and has always been so kind, thoughtful and support-ive, especially after my brother died. But I fear he stills sees me just as his employer's little girl. Not a woman grown.'

'He should open his eyes. They must be firmly shut, else I can't image how he could miss what a talented, engaging beauty that little girl has be-come.'

'Is…that how you see me?' she asked, not knowing him well enough to decide whether his words were sincere or gallantry.

He nodded. 'I'm not a flatterer, Miss Cran-more. Except to spare someone's feelings, I speak the truth as I see it.'

He truly thought her talented and beautiful? Absurdly gratified, she said, 'Then thank you kindly for the compliment.'

'Which is only returning the favour. How was it you described me? Possessed of "wit and bold-ness"? I should hope to merit that praise.'

'For someone of your background, who had no need to interest himself in anything outside his class and property, to take the time to investigate new technologies, then have the intelligence to evaluate and invest wisely in them, I think you merit both descriptions.'

He bowed. 'Then I must thank you kindly for the compliment.'

She'd like to talk with him for ever. It was so… liberating to be completely honest about what she felt and wanted, something she couldn't really do even with Papa. She loved her family dearly and knew they loved her, but they all wanted for her something she feared would never make her happy. While she yearned for something they would tell her could never be attained.

She might be doomed to unhappiness. But she wasn't yet ready to give up on her dreams.

'You an investor and me a mathematician—it seems we are both…out of the ordinary for our positions in society,' she said.

'Extraordinary, isn't it?' he murmured, looking down at her.

The intensity of his gaze held hers, making her catch her breath. Yes, he was extraordinary, compelling, mesmerising. Drawn by the power of his attraction, she felt herself drifting closer, lifting her face to his as he lowered his to her.

Then abruptly, he stepped away.

She'd been so entranced, she had to blink at that sudden return to reality. Shocked at how close she'd come to inviting his kiss, needing to compose herself, she said, 'I'd better walk you down all the pathways. I want to be able to honestly say I've shown you the garden. Besides, the spring bulbs truly are lovely.'

'Yes, I need to be able to comment on them to Lady Arlsley.'

'I do know quite a bit about plants—perhaps the one aspect of housewifery that does interest me. My father was so low after my brother's death, I worked with my mother to brew teas and tisanes to try to raise his spirits. I've discovered the herb garden here is exceptional.'

For the next few minutes, she walked him down that section of the border, pointing out the lemon balm, mint, and chamomile with its border of lavender.

After she'd finished giving her tour, Dellamont said, 'We've spent half an hour in the garden, which is about all the time your maid is going to allow us. Before I escort you back, we need to decide how we'll implement our plan.'

'I don't want to impose too much on your time. Perhaps I could send you word of one or two entertainments each week that we're to attend.'

Dellamont shook his head. 'Once or twice a week probably wouldn't be enough to satisfy my father. Better make it three or four events a week.'

'If it truly wouldn't be an imposition—that would be wonderful! My guess is that Lady Arlsley intends to drag me to every entertainment to which she can wangle us invitations, hoping to have me snag an offer as soon as possible and so as to rid herself of the burden of sponsoring me. Knowing that you will be at most of them will make getting through the month I've promised to endure much easier.'

'Balls, routs or musicales would be best,' Dellamont said. 'There will be dancing or performances to help pass the time before we can escape. Then there will be calls and rides in the park between the entertainments.'

'With only my maid looking on, instead of being the focus of the interested gazes of half the *ton*? That would be refreshing!'

'Precisely. You must send me notice once you know which invitations Lady Arlsley has accepted. I'll arrange to stop by most of them.'

'I'll talk to her tonight. We're dining with some of her friends, a previous engagement she wasn't able to put off. I'll try to let you know tomorrow what she has planned for the rest of the week.'

'Excellent. By banding together, we shall both run the social gauntlet and come out unscathed.'

Would she emerge unscathed? Marcella wondered. If Dellamont continued to be as attractive and interesting as he'd been thus far, it would be far too easy to fall more deeply under his spell.

But she need only remind herself what remaining in his world would entail—mingling with

Lady Arlsley and her condescending friends, the witless Lord Charles…and Lord Hoddleston. That prospect should be enough to discourage any ill-judged attachment.

Mary's 'harrumph' interrupted her thoughts. 'Best be getting back, Miss Marcella, before Her Fancy Ladyship sends out a search party.'

'She would hardly do that,' Marcella countered. 'If I were to stay out long enough to be considered compromised, she could insist on an engagement and be rid of me all the sooner. But I'd not do that to you, Dellamont, I promise.'

'I'd appreciate it,' he said drily. 'Though I am indebted to you already. The Earl sought me out at breakfast this morning. He must have had news of last night's ball from some of his cronies, for he actually congratulated me on making a promising start. I honestly can't remember him ever complimenting me before.'

Touched with sadness at that avowal, she countered, 'About time, then. Although his approval now is likely to make his anger when you don't claim my hand rather greater.'

Dellamont shrugged. 'I'll deal with that when it happens. But Mary is right; we should go in. I've already outstayed the requisite quarter-hour.'

'I only hope Lord Charles and Lord Hoddleston have already departed, too.'

'I doubt Lady Arlsley would encourage them

to linger. Not if it seems you have a future earl dangling after you.'

'Would that having you "dangle" might dissuade them from seeking me out at all future events!' Marcella said with some heat.

Once they'd reached the door back to the house, Dellamont paused. 'I will escort you to the drawing room, pay my respects to Lady Arlsley and take my leave.'

Marcella nodded. 'Here's to our bargain, then. Long may it continue.'

'Well, for a month or so, at any rate. You'll let me know about the next entertainment?'

'Yes. I'll try to send a note. Where should I address it?'

'Fortunately, I have my own quarters, so I'm not living under my father's thumb.' After giving her the address, he bowed. 'I think I'm going to enjoy this bargain. At least until the Earl discovers it and the retribution begins.'

'I hope the punishment won't be too severe,' Marcella said with a smile. 'Because I think I shall enjoy it, too.'

She just needed to be careful not to enjoy it too much.

Chapter Seven

Early the following morning, Crispin rode through the gates of Hyde Park, his younger sister, Lady Margaret, riding beside him. After calling on Miss Cranmore the day before, he'd paid a visit to his mother. As he was going out, he'd encountered his sibling, who confessed she'd been lying in wait for him so she might beg him to take her riding.

Though she loved being in London, she was finding it tiresome not being able to attend any events beyond afternoon calls and teas with their mother, she'd told him. Since their mother didn't ride and their groom frowned on any pace faster than a trot, she pleaded with him to offer her the treat of a real gallop.

Though Crispin had had little to do with his older sister, who in looks and temperament was too much like his father, Maggie had always been a merry, engaging child whose occasional company he enjoyed. She hadn't even balked at being ready at the unfashionably early hour he'd insisted was necessary if she wished to arrive before the park became too crowded for a proper gallop.

They rode along, Crispin required to do nothing more taxing than trot beside her, listening while she chattered to him about her impressions of London, the wonder of the shops and buildings, and the society ladies, the only common factor in her ramblings her frankness and complete lack of awe or deference for the leaders of fashionable world—or indeed, for her own father. Smiling as she made a particularly biting comment about the Earl, Crispin thought ruefully that it was as well for their mother's peace of mind that his little sister was seldom summoned into her sire's presence.

They'd just turned down the first pathway, approaching the long section suitable for galloping, when Crispin spotted a female on side-saddle cantering towards them. A female who looked very much like Miss Cranmore.

Within a few moments, she was near enough for Crispin to confirm that it was indeed Miss Cranmore, a groom trailing behind her. Though her eyes brightened and she smiled in recognition, she didn't bring her mount to a halt, merely gave him a slight nod, as one might to acknowledge stranger.

Allowing him, he realised, to ride by without greeting her, if he chose.

Knowing that though his father might wish him to marry an heiress, he'd object to having the daughter he had to marry off next year be seen to associate with the granddaughter of a coal miner, the wisest course would have been to do exactly that. But the fact that she'd been perceptive and courteous enough to allow him that option—with a smile that seemed to say she didn't even resent the ridiculousness of that double standard—made him decide not to take advantage of her discretion.

Bringing his mount to a halt, he called 'Miss Cranmore! How nice to see you.'

Her smile brightening, she reined in as well. 'And you, my lord. A lovely morning, isn't it? But don't let me delay or interrupt your ride with the lady.'

Was there a touch of jealousy in her tone? Secretly gratified by the thought, said, 'You may be easy, Miss Cranmore. This is no lady. May I present my sister, Lady Margaret d'Aubignon?'

'I am a lady—if only by title,' his sister objected. 'Delighted to meet you, Miss Cranmore.'

'And I you, Lady Margaret.'

Suddenly his sister's eyes widened. 'Miss *Cranmore*? I have heard a lot about you!'

Despite Crispin's embarrassed hiss at his sister to keep quiet, Miss Cranmore smiled. 'I suppose you have.'

'But you're lovely!'

Though Crispin groaned at the comment, the Heiress laughed outright. 'What were you expecting? A perfume of smoke hanging about me, a homespun gown and bits of cotton thread tangled in my hair? Or a costly, over-trimmed riding habit, my neck and arms festooned with jewels?'

'I don't know quite what I expected. I've never met a girl from the merchant class before.'

'Enough, Maggie,' Crispin said, feeling his face flush, and wishing he'd reminded himself before impulsively making the introductions just how frank his irrepressible sibling could be. 'You must excuse my sister, Miss Cranmore. She may be styled "Lady Margaret" but as you can see, her manners need substantial work.'

'I'm just being honest,' his sister protested. 'As you would surely have me be, wouldn't you, Miss Cranmore? Since it seems one can never be frank in society, and you must spend all your time there, I should think you would appreciate it.'

While Crispin silently berated himself for allowing the meeting, Miss Cranmore said, 'I do appreciate candour. And you are right, I am forced to spend much time in society, where honesty is in very short supply. Which is why I escape for a morning ride.'

'Well, I'm not "out" yet—not until next Season, but I'm enjoying a ride as well. I'm not allowed to go anywhere, you see, except to accompany Mama to teas and calls on horrid old dragons who assess me like some sort of merchandise at market. It's so annoying! All the while, I must keep my eyes modestly downcast and my opinions to myself, so that they will bestow their approval and promise to issue invitations to all the important parties next year. It's a wonder I've not burst from the strain.'

Her eyes dancing, Miss Cranmore gave Crispin a wink, to which he returned a weak smile, beyond relieved that she seemed amused rather than offended by his sister's unvarnished remarks. 'I understand perfectly. It *is* annoying to be assessed like goods in the marketplace. If it weren't for the promise I made my dear father, I would have abandoned society after the first event.'

His sister stared, her eyes widening in surprise. 'Your father is a *dear*? Truly?' She shook her head. 'I can't imagine. Mine is an ogre.'

'Maggie,' Crispin warned again.

'You know you think so too, Crispin, though you might be too polite to say it,' Lady Margaret retorted. 'My elder brother has more reason than any of us to think that. My older sister married as soon as possible and our younger brother escaped to India, but since Dellamont must one day take over from Papa, he receives the brunt of his abuse. Especially since he tries to intercede for Mama. And Heaven forbid he should express any ideas of his own! *I'm* going to escape when I wed next Season, but as the heir, he's trapped. I intend to marry a rich man and have a handsome allowance, so I may buy whatever I like. Papa is such a miser!'

'You might want to look for a gentleman who is kind, too. Marriage lasts a long time. Too long to wed someone who's disagreeable.'

'Well, if I beguile a rich older man, I might not have to tolerate him for too long. Then I can be a wealthy widow and do what I like.'

Crispin shook his head, resigned. 'My sister is incorrigible, as you see.'

'I am sorry to hear your family is so…contentious. I've been very lucky. There are only three of us now since my brother died and we get along so harmoniously. Mama and Papa have very different interests, but they have always had a great tenderness and care for each other. And my grandfather, too.'

Lady Margaret shook her head wonderingly. 'I can't imagine what that would be like. I've known only Papa shouting, Mama crying, everyone upset and servants scattering out of the way. Did your grandfather really work in a coal mine?'

'He did.'

'He was a clever lad, though,' Crispin said, 'who invented machinery that made moving coal easier. His talent got him promoted to foreman, then manager. He developed and patented other machinery, earning enough to become independent. He then applied the mechanical principles he'd perfected in mining to other industries, improving their efficiency and profitability. Making a fortune and getting himself knighted in the process.' At Miss Cranmore's look of surprise, he added, 'I knew of your father's reputation, but little about your grandfather. So I made some enquiries. He's quite an impressive individual. Beginning from nothing, he used his wit, ingenuity and drive to become a towering figure in his field.'

Looking gratified, she said, 'As you've become knowledgeable in your field of investments?'

'You mean railways?' Lady Margaret asked. 'Papa is always criticising his investments, but I think it's wonderful that he's found a way to become independent. At least, as independent as he can be, shackled to the estate as he is. At least he has an income that allows him to escape the house. Whereas I cannot get away until I marry. But I'll not allow myself to be bullied by my husband, like Papa bullies Mama. I shall stand up for myself!'

'I sincerely hope you marry a man who will treasure your uniqueness and seek to make you happy,' Miss Cranmore said with feeling.

'She's going to lead that hapless husband a merry dance, that's for sure,' Crispin said wryly.

Whipping her gaze back to Marcella, Lady Margaret said, 'Well I think you're perfect for Crispin.'

Once again, Crispin felt his face heat. 'Do you never tire of saying things you shouldn't, brat?'

'I like you, Miss Cranmore. The other young ladies I've met paying calls with Mama seem so spineless and simpering, trying to ingratiate themselves with the dragons no matter how unpleasantly they are treated by them. And the girls who are already out, especially the beauties, are so condescending. I'd much rather have Crispin marry someone who's kind and honest, like you, instead of a younger version of the dowagers who love to lord it over everyone. You know he can be quite nice once you get to know him.'

Miss Cranmore chuckled. 'We've only just become acquainted, so it's too early to tell. But I do hope we will be good friends.'

'Enough questioning, brat. Let's let Miss Cranmore continue her ride without further inquisition.'

'Very well, no more talk of marriage. Do you ride often, Miss Cranmore?'

'Every morning, unless the weather is bad.' She smiled. 'I have to gird myself to suffer the dragons, too. And I enjoy riding. My grandfather loves horses, and I often ride with my father when he goes to inspect works in progress.'

'Your father takes you riding with him?' Lady Margaret said. 'I can't imagine accompanying Papa anywhere, not that he'd ask for me. He thinks female children are an annoyance, a burden to be married off who take with them dowries that drain the assets of the estate. Sometimes I think if I walked by him on the street, he'd probably not even recognise me.'

'Surely not!' Miss Cranmore protested.

'I'm just as happy to keep my distance. I won't defer to him as Mama does, and he does hate to be crossed, so it's probably best that I seldom encounter him.'

'I'm sorry,' Miss Cranmore said softly, sadness in her eyes. 'Family should be a safe harbour from the world, where one is sheltered and protected. Not a place of contention.'

'Well, ours is the latter. If I see you again in

the park, can we ride together? I know I'm an inquisitive brat, but I do like you.'

'Only if your family approves. I… I wouldn't wish to make trouble for you. I'm not sure either your father or your mother would consider me an acceptable acquaintance for an earl's unmarried daughter.'

Lady Margaret gave a peal of laughter. 'How could they object, when Papa is pushing Dellamont to marry you?'

'Society's standards for gentlemen and ladies are quite different,' Miss Cranmore said drily.

'When I first heard what Papa intended, I thought Crispin ought to refuse to marry you just on principle. Now that I've met you, though, I think it would be a capital idea. Even though I'd hate for Papa to think he'd got his way.'

'I'm afraid I must be getting home. I want to have some time with my mother before I must go to Lady Arlsley's.'

'Are you not staying with Lady Arlsley?' Crispin asked in surprise.

'She did offer, but she was really no more eager to have me as her house guest than I was to become one. By staying home, at least I have mornings with Mama and can sometimes sneak away to Papa's office for a visit. I do sympathise about those society *beldames*, Lady Margaret. We are going to call on more of them today ourselves.' She shook her head. 'I can't wait for this to be over!'

'Do you mean—you didn't *want* a Season?' Lady Margaret asked.

'Not a bit! I don't want to marry yet, so it serves little purpose. I only agreed because my family was eager for me to give it a try. Mama thought it would be glamorous and exciting, attending glittering balls filled with fashionable, beautifully dressed people.' She sighed. 'I'd rather ride with Papa to inspect his projects.'

'But what will you do if you don't marry this Season?'

'Continue to work with my father. He builds bridges and railways. It's fascinating.'

Lady Margaret shook her head wonderingly. 'Bridges and railways? You really are unusual! I hope we can ride together again. Do say we can, Crispin!'

'After all your shockingly inquisitive questions, scamp, I should think Miss Cranmore would rather gallop in the opposite direction if she sees you coming.'

For once, his sister seemed abashed. Her face colouring, she said, 'I do apologise if I've been too vulgarly intrusive. But I think it's better to know more about the world than be ignorant. No one tells unmarried girls anything!'

'Too true. And contrary to what your brother

says, if we meet again, I'd be happy to ride together if it is deemed acceptable. But now I must go. It was good to see you, Lord Dellamont, and delightful to meet you, Lady Margaret.'

'Delightful to meet you, too!' his sister echoed.

With a nod, Miss Cranmore gave her horse the office to start, the groom resuming his place behind her as she trotted towards the gates of the park.

Crispin watched them ride off with a jumble of conflicting emotions, foremost among them annoyance at his sister. 'I ought to take my whip to you, brat.'

'I don't see why. You should know by now that I say what I think—when I can get away with it. Besides, I don't think Miss Cranmore minded.' Lady Margaret laughed. 'How differently one of those insufferable society misses would have acted, had *she* been the one you'd introduced me to! Probably would have ignored me completely while she made eyes at the future Earl.'

'Probably,' he admitted, his opinion of unmarried society girls mirroring his sister's.

'I do like Miss Cranmore. And I hope you convince her to marry you. She seems to really care that one is…happy, not just established.'

Married…and happy? He'd never considered the two could go together, at least not for very long.

'Well, as she said, we've only recently met.

Now, if you really want to gallop rather than just chat, we should do so immediately.' Pointing towards the saddle path, on which several riders appeared in the distance, he continued, 'The trail is already becoming more crowded.'

'Let's gallop. Race you to the far turn?'

'Off you go!'

As Crispin gave his horse its head and set off after his sister, he had to marvel at the exceptional conversation she had provoked.

He was relieved Lady Margaret hadn't offended Miss Cranmore. Had the positions been reversed, and a girl from the merchant class so freely expressed her opinions to anyone save a rebel like his sister, disapproval would have been instantaneous and severe. Miss Cranmore had borne his sister's sometimes embarrassing enquiries with good-humoured equanimity.

A recurring embarrassment heated his face when he recalled how his sister had baldly implied they should marry. And he'd felt a mix of surprise and scepticism at the view of family and marriage Miss Cranmore had expressed.

Home as a safe refuge from the world?

Urging his sister to consider marriage only to a man who would treasure her uniqueness and want to make her happy?

Was that what she expected for her own marriage, once she decided she could put it off no longer? Or had she only expressed that rosy view to encourage Maggie? Perhaps she hoped marrying her childhood hero engineer would guarantee her happiness. He only hoped she didn't end up being disappointed.

His sister's frankness reminded him of his unusually candid conversation with Miss Cranmore in Bristol. In fact, it reminded him of all their conversations. She hadn't always been that candid, but she was unfailingly honest. And she'd never attempted, as his sister agreed most unmarried females would, to cast out lures or ingratiate herself in his eyes.

Though she was highly alluring. Desire returned in a rush as he remembered halting beside her in Lady Arlsley's garden as she gazed up at him admiringly.

He'd been oh-so-tempted to kiss her. He'd been certain she would have welcomed his kiss. Would she have responded as well, urging him to tighten their embrace?

Feeling the wash of heat that prospect evoked, he warned himself that he would need to stay more on guard against the response she so easily aroused in him. Keep his distance and keep their interactions merely friendly. She might not be a lady born, but were he to let lust lead him into doing something compromising, his honour would demand he repair the lapse with the same remedy he would offer if she were in fact a Lady of Quality.

And though the view of marriage put forth by Marcella Cranmore might be more appealing than anything he'd ever envisaged, he had no desire to be forced into testing that unlikely vision for himself.

Chapter Eight

Towards the end of following evening, Crispin entered the ballroom where one of his mother's friends, Lady Richardson, was holding a rout. A note received earlier that day from Miss Cranmore had informed him that Lady Arlsley intended for them to attend this, the most prestigious society entertainment the evening had to offer.

He paused just inside the entrance, scanning the guests for the heiress. Then spied her at the far end of the dance floor, squired by Lord Charles.

Before she became aware of his presence, he allowed himself a moment to openly inspect her. A familiar heat built within as his gaze roved over the curvaceous body well displayed by the gown's bared shoulders, rounded bust, tight waist and voluminous skirts, admiring, as well, the graceful elegance with which she glided across the dance floor.

Though he'd need to keep tight hold over his physical response, he still looked forward to claiming his two dances. Being able to hold that tempting body as close as propriety permitted while he looked down into her animated face, his gaze claimed by those sparkling green eyes and beguiling lips. How fortuitous that neither of them was interested in marriage, for if he were in search of a countess, her unique loveliness might have him pursuing her in earnest.

Fortunately, neither of them had any desire to proceed in that direction. He'd simply enjoy the novelty of her conversation and unusual interests for the duration of their bargain, after which they would go their separate ways.

An unexpected wave of sadness chilled him.

They'd go their separate ways...unless he could figure out a means for them to remain friends after they both quit society. He wasn't sure how he'd manage it, 'friendship' between a young man and an unrelated single female from different social classes being virtually unheard of, but it was certainly a prospect worth exploring further. The reward for persistence and innovation would be the prospect of enjoying her company not just for a month, but for the foreseeable future.

His sadness dissipating at the possibility, he headed in her direction. It appeared she had successfully engaged Lord Charles in conversation, for the young man's eyes were bright and a smile of sheer enjoyment lit his face, making Crispin smile as well. Though Miss Cranmore had more wit half-asleep than her partner fully awake, she was evidently kind and forbearing enough not to let Lord Charles know that.

Just as she'd been kind and forbearing to his sister. Though it didn't particularly reveal excellence of character to be kind to someone with whom one intended to have few dealings, he knew how annoying it could be to spend time with a lackwit who did little to sustain the conversation. Having suffered through a number of conversations with Lord Charles, he wasn't sure he could be so tolerant.

She must possess patience as well.

As the last measures of the dance were played, he made his way over to the side of the ballroom where Lady Arlsley awaited her charge. 'Lord Dellamont,' the Baron's wife said, curtsying as she spotted him. 'How pleased I am to see you in attendance tonight.'

'Lady Richardson is one of my mother's oldest friends,' he replied as he bowed. 'She would be disappointed if I were not to make an appearance.'

'Miss Cranmore will be pleased as well,' she said as, the dance completed, the couples began leaving the floor.

'I was gratified to learn all about the bay colt,' he heard Miss Cranmore say as she and the Marquess's son approached. 'I do hope that you will be able to purchase him.'

Smiling at her, a slightly besotted look on his face, Lord Charles bowed—only to stop short, frowning, when he spied Crispin. 'Dellamont,' he said, his tone aggrieved. 'I suppose I might as well take my leave, Miss Cranmore.'

'Thank you again for the dance, my lord,' she said, giving the young man a curtsy. 'Lord Dellamont. What a delightful surprise to encounter you tonight.'

Crispin bit back a smile at the irony in her tone. 'A happy chance,' he agreed drily.

'It's also a happy chance that the dance about to begin is a waltz,' Lady Arlsley said. 'I'm sure you'll want to allow Dellamont the pleasure.'

'If he invites me,' she replied pointedly to her chaperon, giving Crispin an eye-roll that once again had him chuckling.

'It would be my honour, Miss Cranmore.'

'Then it will also be mine,' she replied, offering her hand.

As he led her out on to the dance floor, she sighed. 'Could Lady Arlsley be any more blatantly encouraging? If we hadn't already made our bargain, I'd be horribly embarrassed.'

'You can rest easy. I find her directness amusing.'

'What an interminable evening! Thank heaven you arrived at last! I'd about given up hope.'

'Sorry, I should have warned you that was my plan,' he told her as he moved her into the rhythm of the dance—forcing himself to concentrate on her conversation and ignore the warmth of the tempting body under his gloved fingers and the distracting scent of her rose perfume. 'Even if I seem to be dangling after you, we're only allowed to share two dances—any more, and society will expect us to be calling the banns. So I decided it would be better to arrive later in the evening, when I thought your patience with all this would be wearing thin.'

'It certainly is. Honestly, what do people see in events like this? Granted, despite my extravagant dowry, I'm an outsider and can't expect to be treated like one born into this select group. Still, I can't imagine spending four or five months in London every year enduring nights like this. Based on my admittedly limited observation, they consist of the same dances punctuated by the same conversations with the same inane topics—fashion, whose entertainments are the most superior and gossip about the latest scandal. How is everyone not bored to flinders?'

'There are other activities,' he countered, amused. 'Ladies make calls on one another and spend a great deal of time shopping for gowns,

shoes, pelisses, shawls, and other feminine fripperies. Gentlemen gather in clubs to gamble and
gossip and visit their tailors and go to Tattersall's to buy horses. All this frantic activity is
interspersed with attending the occasional opera
or theatre where one can show off the afore-
mentioned finery.'

'Opera or theatre performances where I'm betting they ignore the stage and continue gabbing
about fashion, entertainments, and the latest juicy
gossip.' She huffed in exasperation. 'I'd go mad
in a month. I *will* go mad in a month, so it's fortunate that I didn't promise myself to stick with
it longer than that.'

'What would you be doing if you were not
here?' he asked, genuinely curious about what
life was like in a stratum of society so different
from his own.

'Besides working with Father, I'd be attending
my mother. Assisting in parish visits to the poor,
the sick and those in need. Tending the herb garden, riding, visiting friends. Reading and studying. Papa often brings home to dinner associates
from work. And yes, from time to time, there
would be dinners and musical evenings with other
families.'

'Doesn't that amount to a social round very
similar to London society?'

She shook her head. 'Not really. There's nothing as formal as the London Season, more gatherings of friends and family punctuated by cotillions in town. But the subscription Season is short, and opportunities to attend private balls or the theatre is much more limited.'

'How do families fire off their daughters, then?'

'Through connections among families rather than formal presentations. Often the young couple has a good deal of choice in the matter, which from what I've overheard thus far, often does not happen in your world.'

He nodded. 'Very true. Marriages in the *ton* are generally made to enhance status, add wealth to the family coffers and to form links of blood to people with power. Surely families in *your* world want that for their children as well.'

'To some extent,' she admitted. 'First and foremost, they want daughters to wed men who can comfortably support a family, and sons to marry amiable girls trained to take care of that family. Beyond that, if business links can be solidified through marriage, that's all to the good. And I suppose there is gossip—people are people, whatever their rank—but it doesn't seem so malicious.'

'You seem to find the entire aristocracy rather repellent,' he observed, thinking it made it even more interesting that she'd agreed to this foray into society.

'I told you I spent a year at an exclusive ladies' finishing school. The most miserable year of my life! Almost all the girls were gentry born and they never let me forget I was not. Aside from me, the few students from wealthy merchant class families toadied to the others, tolerating the slights and condescension, always trying to ingratiate themselves and make connections they thought would help them marry into the gentry. A highly unlikely outcome, in my opinion. I tried to be cordial to everyone, but I had so little in common with any of them, I mostly stayed to myself. Even at that, I received all the condescension, insults and ostracising I needed for a lifetime. After the warmth and closeness of my family, I felt dreadfully alone.'

'Why did your parents insist you remain, if it was that awful?'

She sighed. 'I never told Mama how bad it was. She was so excited to send me there! She wanted the best for me, and thought exactly like those merchant class girls—that by attending the school, I would make social connections that could assist me in marrying well and perhaps help Father's business, too. My father knew the truth, but as he did in this current situation, for my mother's sake he asked me to endure it for as long as I could, after which he would support my desire to leave. So I managed to finish out the year. Neither of us wanted to disappoint Mama, and she would have felt terrible if she'd known how bad it truly was.'

'You made no friendships at all?' *Ton* females must be more shallow and snobbish even than he'd thought if they were able to overlook this intelligent, interesting person in their midst.

Or perhaps, recognising she added wit, beauty, and charm to her wealth, they were jealous of her advantages in the deadly serious competition for the most prized marriage prospects.

Miss Cranmore laughed. 'I've not yet encountered any of my former fellow students in London. If I should, I suspect the only reason they wouldn't give me the cut direct would be their shock at finding me sponsored by a baron's wife and elevated into their midst.'

'Sounds dreadful.'

'It was—mostly. There was one small group of girls who, like me, had little interest in beaux and balls and talk of advantageous marriages. But they were older, and though they were kind enough when I encountered them, they were gentry born as well, so I never tried to get to know them better. Although Miss Henley was very encouraging.'

'Henley?' Crispin echoed. 'Emma Henley?'

'Why, yes. Do you know her?'

'Not well. But Miss Henley—Lady Theo Collington now—is a dear friend of *my* good friend Gregory Lattimar's sister.'

'Lady Theo?' Miss Cranmore laughed. 'So much for her intentions to disdain marriage and work on reform causes.'

'You mustn't think she abandoned those efforts. She is still very much involved with the Ladies' Committee on Parliamentary Reform. And the man she married, Lord Theo, is becoming a well-known artist, so she didn't turn into some conventional society matron.'

'I'm pleased to hear it. But enough about my sad past. I visited Papa's office this afternoon, and his solicitor told me you'd invested in the Great Western. Bravo! I think you'll realise a handsome return.'

'I hope so. If only to further confound my father.'

'So you'll be looking for your next venture. Any idea what it might be?'

'There are a number of bills before Parliament now. The most promising will link London with areas to the north, south and west.'

'I told my grandfather that he would soon be able to journey from Newcastle to London by rail, much faster and in greater comfort that he does by riding! Which schemes are being proposed now?'

For the duration of the dance, she encouraged him to describe the bills that interested him, asking about potential routes, elevations and right of ways that would need to be acquired, which landowners would have to be persuaded or placated to have the routes pass through their land. A useful device, for talking about his greatest enthusiasm helped him block out the sensual appeal that might otherwise have his thoughts headed in other directions.

'When do you plan to ride out and inspect the next potential investment?' she asked after he'd concluded.

'Once we decide our bargain is over.' He laughed. 'I'll want to be well away from my father for some time after that anyway. A nice, long ramble around the English countryside should be just what's needed.'

'How exciting! I wish I could ride about exploring like that. I so enjoyed accompanying Papa along the way to Bristol. I, too, envision a network of rails that would run from one end of our island to the other, north to south, east to west. A way to move goods and people that won't be affected by bad weather, the availability of horses or oxen, or the stamina of animals.'

'And eventually, a more comfortable as well as more efficient means of transport,' he replied. 'At present, the wagons that transport people are rather basic. But I can envision entrepreneurs building carriages that are as opulent as the fanciest travelling vehicles designed for the wealthy. Larger ones, too, that could double as dining rooms or gentlemen's clubs.'

She laughed. 'Imagine, having a gentleman board the railway in the morning, have his breakfast, read his paper, play a hand of cards with friends, lunch, dine and disembark in the evening at his destination, halfway across the country!'

'Exactly,' Crispin said, pleased to find that she shared his vision. Though he knew he'd have to release his hold on her at the end of the dance, reluctant to lose her completely, as the last measures sounded, he said, 'Thank you for the dance. Can I escort you in for some refreshment?'

'Please! The longer you can protect me from the attentions of others, the better I will like it,' she said, putting her hand on his arm so he might lead her off the floor.

Guiltily aware of how much he relished that touch, he said, 'Alas, I can't monopolise you for the entire rest of the evening, but it will be permissible for us to share a glass of punch and have one more dance. Will I be aggravating too many other suitors?' he asked, interested to learn how her debut was progressing.

'Only a few have entered the lists,' she said with a smile. 'There's Mr Farnsworth, a widower of good family who is seeking a rich young wife to give him the male heir he lacks and to fund dowries for his five daughters. Lord Tolleridge, whom I understand lost a fortune on a banking scheme and needs a fat dowry to restore his finances. Both are polite, almost obsequiously flattering—but under it all, there's still that overtone that I ought to feel grateful that gentlemen of their breeding would condescend to court me.'

Though he knew such treatment was probably to be expected—his father's advice to marry the chit and then relegate her to the country echoed in his head—it still irritated him to hear that she'd been subjected to that indignity. 'Surely Lord Charles isn't so snobbish.'

'Oh, no. I probably like him best of the bunch. To be honest, I feel a little sorry for him. Of course, his real reason for pursuing me is his need of a fortune, but though he hardly has wit enough to follow a conversation from one end to the other, he has a kind heart. From some of the things he's mentioned, he's often been made the butt of jokes by cleverer men, which makes him more sympathetic to my position, I think. We share a love of horses, so I'm happy to encourage him to ramble on about his favourite mounts and the ones he aspires to purchase.'

She laughed as Crispin handed her the glass of punch. 'He declares I'm a "capital good fellow" to allow him to wax enthusiastic about them, since most females aren't the least bit interested.'

Crispin waved a finger at her. 'You'd better be careful. He had a rather besotted look on his face tonight. Give him much more encouragement, and he's liable to make you a declaration.'

'Oh, dear, that would never do!' she said with a look of alarm that reassured him. It was all well to insist she didn't wish to wed into the aristocracy, but when it came down to it, with her family pressing her on, he wasn't sure she'd truly be able to resist the temptation to claim the title and status. Even if it were only to become Lady Charles, wife of a marquess's younger son.

'I'll be careful to head off anything of that nature,' she replied after sipping her punch. 'I wouldn't wish to hurt his feelings by refusing him. Unlike Lord Hoddleston. I'd not regret wounding *his* sensibilities if it would discourage him from pursuing me!'

Recalling the anger on the Baron's face the night he'd routed him on the terrace, Crispin frowned. 'Is he still bothering you?'

'Not "bothering", exactly, but certainly not giving up, despite my marked lack of enthusiasm for his company. He actually told me he will be like the Grim Reaper—the final contender who'll claim me after all the rest had fallen away. An apt analogy, because being wed to him would be worse than death!'

So the man hadn't really taken to heart Crispin's warning that night on the balcony. 'I shall have to be more vigilant at protecting you from him,' Crispin said, silently vowing to do so.

'I'd love to give *him* the cut direct, but Lady Arlsley won't allow it.' She sighed. 'Like Hoddleston, her ladyship believes that you'll never come up to snuff, and therefore insists I must keep all my options open. And before you say her standards must be low indeed if she'd approve of me bestowing my hand on the Baron, I assure you they are.'

'I wish you'd been found a more protective protector,' he retorted.

'I can't fault her too much. She's been placed in a difficult situation, forced by her husband's indiscretion to lend her name and status to sponsor someone she doesn't consider worthy. Although I can't make myself like her, I do sometimes feel bad that I'm running this rig on her, accepting her patronage while having no real intention to marry. But then she says or does something condescending, and my sympathy evaporates. I tell myself that when this is over, she can congratulate herself on having done her duty to her husband while escaping the onus of foisting undeserving me on some well-born family.'

'She's a fool if she hasn't by now realised you are deserving of the highest place,' he said with some heat.

Looking up, she coloured. 'Thank you, Dellamont,' she said softly. 'How very…chivalrous.'

An odd warmth filled his chest as he realised he meant every word. 'It's not idle gallantry. I told you I only say what I mean. In wit, intelligence, ability you are superior to every female in this room. Despite that, I would have you return to the place you feel you belong, and end up in a marriage that lives up to your dreams. And I hope when you leave society, we can find a way to remain friends.'

'I would like that, too—very much,' she said, holding his gaze while that odd tightness in his chest intensified. The desire to kiss her washed through him again. Needing to resist it, he looked away and made himself take a gulp of punch.

Looking away as well, she set her own cup back on the tray. 'I suppose we must return to the ballroom.'

He'd rather find some quiet place to continue talking with her—but she was right, they needed to re-join the company before they exceed the time they could spend with their heads together without raising expectations of an imminent engagement. And he needed to be squiring her about on the dance floor, consciousness of the roomful of people observing them helping him overcome this nagging desire to kiss her.

Offering her his arm, he said, 'You'll let me

know if Hoddleston needs more…cogent persuasion to cease annoying you.'

'I will. He warned me that you are only amusing yourself by seeming to court me, and will drop me once the novelty of it fades. I told him if that were true, he ought to be relieved rather than annoyed about your attentions, since my supposed disappointment at your desertion would make me more amenable to marrying someone of lesser status.'

'I wouldn't provoke him too much,' Crispin said, a niggle of worry troubling him. 'I've never heard that he had a bad reputation with women, but I understand his financial situation is precarious. I'd not put it past him to try to compromise you into marriage, if gentler persuasion failed.'

'I've already had some indication of his readiness to proceed in that direction, so I stay on my guard. I never dance with him except in a ballroom full of people, never agree to go driving with him or to walk with him in Lady Arlsley's garden when he calls. And I keep Mary nearby. She doesn't like him, either, and has proclaimed she'd be happy to "cosh him on the noggin" if he gets out of line.'

'Bravo for Mary. Still, you'll let me know if his attentions become too pressing. I'll administer some additional "encouragement" for him to find redress for his financial problems elsewhere.'

She looked up at him, wide-eyed. 'You would do that for me?'

'We have a bargain to protect each other, don't we?' The intensity of his concern about Hoddleston made him realise he felt a good deal more protective towards her than he'd anticipated when he proposed this alliance.

He'd be just as protective of his sister or any other innocent female, he reassured himself, dismissing a stir of unease over the strength of his reaction.

'A bargain I believe I'll be getting the best of!' she was saying. 'Father has already promised to support me when I decide to abandon society. Whereas you will incur the wrath of your father.'

'But I'll have that long inspection trip in the countryside to look forward to. There hasn't been anyone else bothering you, has there?'

'I've just described the sum total of my four most assiduous suitors, save you, of course. So,' she continued as he led her back into the ballroom, 'to end the evening on the most pleasant note, I'll look for Lord Charles and entice him to dance with me again. Then you can claim your second waltz. After that, if I'm lucky, I can plead fatigue and persuade Lady Arlsley to let us leave.'

'Sounds like a good plan. Which entertainment will you be attending next?'

'There's a musicale at the Dellaneys' two evenings from now.'

'Are you musical?'

'I am, actually. It's my one feminine accomplishment. Not the harp, although the instructors at Miss Axminster's school recommended it as the best instrument for a girl to play in order to display the elegance of her figure. Which about sums up the quality of instruction at that school,' she added, wrinkling her nose with a distaste that set him chuckling. 'I prefer the pianoforte. Do you play?'

'Indifferently. But I'll arrange to get myself invited to the Dellaneys', so I may enjoy your performance.'

'Good. I'll count on seeing you there.'

By now, they'd reached Lady Arlsley's side. 'As I will you. Until I claim that next waltz?'

'I'll save it for you.'

'Excellent. In the interim, I'll go have a word with my mother. Miss Cranmore, Lady Arlsley.' Giving them a bow, Crispin walked off.

He found his mother in the card room, a smile on her face as she chatted with several friends. Love for his gentle mother welling up, Crispin told himself it would be worth whatever blistering scold he had to endure from his father when this was over to have been able to give her this treat.

Besides which, honesty forced him to admit, spending time with the enticing Miss Cranmore wasn't a hardship either. Good thing his dread of marriage was great enough to overcome even the temptation she provided.

Lady Comeryn turned her smile on her son when she spotted him walking over. 'Taking a break from the dancing, my dear? If so, will you escort me to get a glass of punch?'

She must want to talk, Crispin thought as he bent to kiss her cheek. So despite the fact that he'd just finished a glass, he replied, 'Of course, Mama. If these ladies will excuse you?'

'We'll deal you out of the next hand, Lady Comeryn,' her friend Lady Randolph said. 'Have a pleasant chat.'

Crispin smiled as his mother took his arm and he walked her out. 'They'll be waiting breathlessly, hoping to glean some news when you return.'

'Naturally. As I would be in their places. Have you any news for me to glean?'

'Only that I am pleased to see you enjoying yourself tonight, which hardly counts as "news".'

'I am indeed enjoying myself! And cannot thank you enough for giving me the opportunity to stay in London. I trust you haven't found society…too odious?'

'No. But I do limit my participation.'

By now they'd reached the refreshment room, and conversation halted while he obtained her a glass of punch. After she'd thanked him and taken a sip, she hesitated for a moment before saying, 'What do you think of the Heiress? I've heard that you stood up with her for a waltz tonight. And that you've called on her and gone riding with her—Maggie told me the last.'

'My, the London gossips are busy, aren't they?' Crispin said, a little irritated, though not surprised, that his movements were being tracked so closely.

'Your father stopped by my sitting room this morning to commend my help in introducing you to her. He was so pleased he even increased my clothing allowance! I'll be able to order some new gowns after all.'

Though this demonstration of the stranglehold his father kept over his mother angered him further—new gowns should not be parcelled out as reward for earning his approval—Crispin managed to keep his voice light. 'As you so richly deserve, and I know you will look charming in them. How did Father find out? I assume you hadn't discussed anything with him.'

'Oh, no, I hadn't spoken with him since he instructed me to find a way to introduce you. He heard about it at his club, I would imagine. I know you men accuse us ladies of being terrible gossips, but truly, men are much worse.'

Aside from dining on occasion, Crispin didn't spend much time at clubs, but he'd played enough hands of cards within their exclusive walls over the years not to dispute his mother's allegation.

'You are probably right.'

After a pause, his mother added, 'Apparently the wagers at the clubs favour you to win her hand.'

Crispin grimaced. He didn't regret his bargain with Miss Cranmore, but somehow having their relationship reduced to a crass wager offended him.

'I hope Father doesn't bet on me.'

'Do you...not like her?'

'I don't like any female enough to contemplate marriage,' he retorted. 'But that avowal is for your ears alone. I intend to continue calling on and dancing with her, eking out the time as long as possible so you can enjoy London.'

'I've already had nearly ten days of entertainments, which is far more than I am usually allowed. But if you are continuing your attentions to Miss Cranmore solely to buy time for me... you can begin backing away. As I've pointed out, your attentions have been particular enough to prompt wagers in the betting books. Not that Miss Cranmore has any relations of sufficient status to discover that, but it's still not kind to raise expectations you know won't be fulfilled. Your eventual abandonment will expose her to malicious gossip, even if it doesn't break her heart.'

'Because though she isn't of "sufficient status", she still has feelings?' he asked with asperity.

'Of course she does. And if she has any sensibility at all, how could she not fall in love with my handsome son, if he gave her any encouragement? I'd not have her wounded just so I can enjoy London.'

His irritation that his mother seemed to share the condescension of her class softened. His mother knew more than most about being wounded.

'You needn't worry. We understand each other. Her father is a railway engineer, by the way. It gives us something to talk about.'

'So you do like her, then?'

At the hopeful note in her voice, Crispin immediately regretted saying anything. 'Don't be weaving plans, Mama.'

'You know I wouldn't!' she protested. 'I'd just like to see you wed eventually to someone whose company you could enjoy. My marriage to your father…hasn't provided the best example of matrimony. There are couples who do much better. Who deal congenially with each other, even seek to make their spouse happy. I would wish that sort of match for you.'

Pretty much any marriage would be an improvement on his parents'. But he didn't mean to wound his mother by agreeing. So he said instead, 'I'm not interested in exploring those unknown waters yet. Nor is there any need. Father is going strong, and I'm sure will be fully capable of overseeing Montwell Glen for the foreseeable future.'

After sipping her punch, his mother gave him a little smile. 'I wouldn't mind having some grandchildren sooner, though.

'My older sister has already fulfilled that requirement.'

'Yes, but those aren't *your* children.'

'I expect to have some eventually—it's my duty as the heir, after all. But I intend to ensure my present happiness continues by delaying that blessed event until the last possible moment. Now, having offered you refreshment and as much news as can be had, I'll escort you back to your friends.'

'Very well, no more marital advice from one hardly qualified to offer it. Just remember that your happiness matters to me more than anything else. Don't continue the social round solely for my sake. And please don't continue it long enough to engage the feelings of an innocent girl just to gratify me.'

'I shall be very careful to do neither.'

'Then I shall be content.'

After depositing his mother back in the card room, Crispin made his way back to the ballroom, where he observed Miss Cranmore once again dancing with Lord Charles.

Would they both be able to continue this charade for as long as a month? And might Marcella Cranmore actually be in danger of falling for him?

After considering that gratifying possibility for a moment, he dismissed it. His mother was naturally prejudiced about the strength of his appeal to women, and Miss Cranmore seemed quite set on enticing her engineer. Nor would he wish to have her develop feelings for him warmer than the friendship he felt for her.

Friendship underpinned by a layer of desire that was a good bit warmer, he admitted. A sensual attraction that she felt as well. Since he was older, well aware of how insidiously passion could overcome prudence, it was his responsibility to avoid letting the physical pull simmering between them result in a lapse that would catapult them into a marriage neither wanted.

A duty he needed to keep uppermost in mind when in her tantalising proximity.

Chapter Nine

Two evenings later, Marcella scanned the room at the Dellaneys' musicale from her seat next to Lady Arlsley. Several young ladies had already performed on the pianoforte, and another was presently doing a fair job singing a ballad, accompanied on the piano by one of her beaux.

Lord Hoddleston had arrived earlier, spotted her at once and come over to offer his compliments. Under Lady Arlsley's insistent gaze, she was forced to respond cordially and acknowledge that she would soon be performing herself. But since she'd taken the precaution of steering her sponsor to seats in a section that was already fully occupied, Hoddleston was not able to ruin her enjoyment of the ensuing musical selections by taking a chair nearby.

He seemed to have sensed she'd deliberately arranged that situation. As he took his leave before the next number began, he leaned closer to murmur, 'You can't escape me, you know. I will catch up with you later.'

She gave him no answer, which only deepened his smile and her annoyance. Honestly, she thought as she recalled his sardonic expression, she wasn't the only well-dowered maiden on the Marriage Mart this Season. She would have thought, with his ancient lineage and her pointed lack of enthusiasm, he would by now have turned his efforts to a more promising object. What sort of man persisted in paying his attentions to a woman who clearly didn't want them?

Someone who wanted to subdue and dominate, probably, she thought, pressing her lips together. That observation made her even more determined to avoid his company. If he gave any sign of trying to coerce her, she would cut him dead whether her sponsor agreed or not.

The singer concluded her selection to a smattering of applause. As this performance was the last before an intermission, newcomers were then admitted. With a stir of delight, Marcella recognised Dellamont among them.

What a fine figure he always cut! she thought, watching admiringly as he walked in. With that handsome face and commanding presence even more striking in his black evening wear, she wasn't surprised that the gazes of all the unmarried ladies—and quite a few of the married ones—followed him as he walked across room.

She had to admit, her own pulse beat a little faster as he approached. Trying to calm the flutter, she told herself to remember she was the focus of his flattering attentions only because of their bargain. Otherwise, he'd have already quit society, or be appeasing his father by dangling after some female of his own class.

A reminder she would do well to heed. As he halted beside her chair and she felt the energising force of his presence in every nerve, it could otherwise be too easy to get carried away, risking both her heart and her virtue.

Surely she was too level-headed for that. Forcing the flutter in her stomach to still, she rose with Lady Arlsley to greet him.

'Good evening, ladies!' he said, bowing to their curtsies. 'Have you been enjoying the music?'

'Very much,' Lady Arlsley replied. 'It has been quite superior. Which is impressive, considering all the performers have been young ladies just out.'

'All superior, and they so young? Amazing,' he said. Though Lady Arlsley seemed not to notice the irony in his tone, Marcella had to choke back a laugh. 'I understand this set has just concluded. Might I escort you ladies for some refreshment?'

'A friend has just arrived with whom I must

speak before the next set begins,' Lady Arlsley replied. 'But I'm sure Miss Cranmore would enjoy partaking of the repast Lady Dellaney set out.'

Marcella shook her head at Dellamont as she took his arm, trying to ignore the little shiver that went through her at his touch. 'My charming sponsor. As lacking in subtlety as ever.'

'Now, now. She probably does have a friend just arrived with whom she wishes to speak.'

'Doubtless on a matter of such urgency, it could not wait for a glass of punch. But she'd probably go speak with the potted fern in the corner if it meant she could send me off with you. And you shouldn't disparage tonight's performances. They have been so surprisingly good, I'm quite impressed. Obviously some aristocratic maidens practise much harder than the students at Miss Axminster's did.'

'Or more likely, only those who have achieved a reasonable level of skill are permitted by their mamas to perform in society. So, are you going to favour the company with a selection?'

'In the next set,' Marcella replied with a nod.

'We'd better make sure you are well refreshed, then.' They stopped by the table in the dining room, which was set with a variety of dishes. 'Would you like a glass of wine? A plateful of the assorted offerings?'

'Nothing to eat, thank you. We dined before we came. But a glass of wine would be welcome.'

'I see Hoddleston is here tonight,' Dellamont said as he handed her a glass. 'He hasn't been bothering you, has he?'

'No—not yet, at any rate. He stopped by to greet us after he arrived, but as I'd made sure there were no vacant seats near us, I was spared making further conversation.'

Marcella debated relating Hoddleston's parting remark, but decided against it. Though she appreciated Dellamont's offer to watch over her, she needed to be able to take care of herself. He was unlikely to be present every time the Baron found an opportunity to approach her. And it was her challenge to master anyway.

'No Lord Charles?'

Marcella laughed. 'He called this afternoon and enquired which event we'd be attending tonight. Upon learning it would be a musicale, he positively blanched. Then apologised for not being able to bear attending, years of being forced to listen to the "screeching sopranos and out-of-tune melodies of his sisters" having given him a permanent distaste of musical evenings. He promised to meet me at the next ball we attend.'

'With your common love of riding, I'm surprised he hasn't asked to accompany you to the park.'

She hesitated, but she might as well tell him.

'He has, actually. But mindful of your warning, I turned him down. If he is becoming enamoured, it wouldn't do to indulge in an activity that would likely feed his infatuation.' She chuckled. 'I told him that I am promised to ride with a lady friend each morning, which is our only time to put our heads together for a good gossip, and I was sure he wouldn't want to listen in. The prospect made him almost as pale as the idea of listening to a screeching soprano.'

Dellamont chuckled as well. 'I suppose you can be pardoned your little white lie in a good cause.'

'It wasn't exactly a lie. I have met your sister each morning, not by design. But not entirely by chance, either, I don't think. I believe she's been lying in wait for me, eager to pepper me with questions about the events I attend, what the ladies and gentlemen are wearing, what they talk about, whether I find the entertainments interesting. Knowing I will tell her the unvarnished truth, as she suspects her acquaintances do not. But I do enjoy her company. One never knows what she will say!'

'She's outrageous, for certain,' Dellamont said with a sigh. 'I pity her eventual husband.'

'I only hope she is able to marry a man who will appreciate her. I shall enjoy her company while I can. She seems so enthusiastic about the prospect of our marrying, I *will* have to jilt you, else she will be furious with you. Although she will then be furious with me for slighting her beloved brother.'

'Don't worry about her sending her maid to poison your soup. I'll placate her by telling her about our bargain—once it's over. Since one can never know what she will say, I wouldn't trust her not to natter on to someone about what a great joke we are playing on society if I were to tell her about it now.'

'I hope she will be amused. I wouldn't want her to think I didn't like and highly esteem you.'

As she delivered that assessment, Marcella glanced up at Dellamont. His compelling dark eyes seem to draw her in, as if she'd moved physically closer. Planting her feet to resist that impulse, she felt a tingling awareness shiver over her skin.

How easy it would be to be drawn in! So easy, if this conversation were taking place in a secluded nook, rather than in the middle of a refreshment room full of people, to take that step closer. So hard to resist raising her lips for the kiss his molten gaze seemed to promise.

If they were to find themselves in that dark nook some time in future, dare she invite that kiss? In defiance of prudence and caution, she was becoming less and less sure she could end their bargain without having tasted the kiss she found herself craving more and more.

But if she wanted to salvage a friendship once their bargain was over, she couldn't allow herself to stumble down that path.

Seeming as captivated as she was, for a long moment Dellamont simply gazed at her. Then he abruptly stepped away, turning towards the table and seizing a plate. 'I'm pleased to know you esteem me, as I do you,' he said, his tone light. 'I shall sample a bit of this while you finish your wine. Which you should do rather quickly. The guests are beginning to move back into the music room. Your time to shine approaches.'

She was glad that he'd defused the moment—before she let her unruly senses lead her any farther astray. Silently scolding herself for forgetting this was only a temporary bargain, she said tartly, 'If I shine, it will be whispered that I perform like a hired musician—evidence of my inferior birth. If I stumble, heads will shake knowingly and observe how my inferior skill reflects my lack of breeding.'

Dellamont shook his head. 'You truly are a cynic! So what's it to be? Shine or stumble?'

'Shine, for certain. I wouldn't give them the satisfaction of performing badly.' She chuckled. 'Although those whose only interest is my dowry wouldn't care if I lost the rhythm and played every note wrong.'

Putting down his plate and taking her empty glass, Dellamont said, 'Then go show up the maidens of Miss Axminster's.'

Half an hour later, after the guests had settled back in their chairs and one other young lady had performed a halting rendition of a Mozart concerto, Lady Arlsley rose to introduce Marcella as she walked to the pianoforte. She was arranging her music, running over the melody in her head, when a shadow fell over the keyboard.

'That Beethoven is quite a complicated selection, Miss Cranmore,' Lord Hoddleston said. 'You must allow me to turn the pages for you.'

Instinctive dislike making it difficult for her to keep her tone cordial, she replied, 'Kind of you to offer, but I'm quite accustomed to turning pages on my own. I would find it distracting to have someone hovering nearby.'

'If I can distract you, all the better,' he murmured, stepping close enough that his pant leg brushed her full sleeve.

Finding his proximity as distasteful as she'd anticipated, she repeated, 'I really prefer to turn the pages myself. If you would move away, please, my lord?'

'And if it doesn't please me? If I prefer to see you…disturbed by my nearness?'

Marcella hesitated, not sure how to proceed. Aggravated as she was by his persistence, unless she gritted her teeth and allowed Hoddleston to remain, she'd end up causing a scene, either by jumping up and abandoning the instrument, or by demanding that he retreat.

Before she could decide, she felt a touch on her other shoulder—and looked up to see Dellamont, smiling down at her. 'Sorry I'm tardy, Miss Cranmore. A chatty acquaintance in the refreshment room detained me. But I'm very much looking forward to performing our duet.'

'Duet?' Hoddleston echoed, frowning. 'Since when do you play, Dellamont?'

'I'm a great lover of music—as all my *friends* know,' he replied coolly. 'If you would take a seat, Hoddleston, we need to prepare. The guests are waiting.'

For a moment, the Baron hesitated, as if ready to dispute further. Then, probably realising that doing so under the interested gaze of dozens of eyes would only make him look ridiculous, he gave Marcella a stiff bow. 'You may have escaped for the moment, my dear,' he said in her ear. 'But I'll be waiting.'

'I shall never be his "dear",' she muttered as she slid over to make room for Dellamont on the piano bench. Not realising, until her anger faded, how difficult it was going to be to not become *pleasurably* distracted with the Viscount seated so close beside her on the small, narrow bench.

Heavens, she might well play all the notes wrong!

Trying to quell her nervousness, she murmured, 'Thank you for the rescue. It was a rescue, wasn't it?'

Dellamont nodded. 'I saw Hoddleston approach and kept watch. Since it appeared you were trying to persuade him to depart without success, I decided to intervene.' He smiled wryly. 'I only hope you have something less complicated to play than the Beethoven, or I shall embarrass myself completely.'

She felt the hairs on her bare neck and shoulder quiver in the slight draught created as he took his seat and suppressed a sigh. He wasn't the only one who needed to play a simple piece that demanded less skill and concentration.

Savouring the usually forbidden closeness, she said, 'Do you sing?'

'Sometimes.'

'Then how about "Robin Adair"? I have the music for that.'

Dellamont blew out a breath of relief. 'Yes, I could manage that.'

Marcella pulled the music from the portfolio

she'd brought and gave it to the Viscount, who arranged it on the holder. 'Would you prefer to play the bass or treble clef?' she asked.

'It would be more manly to do the bass,' he teased. 'Then we'd not have to change places.'

She suppressed the naughty thought that if they did change sides, she might be able to slide even closer to him. Chiding herself to behave, she said, 'Let's play through one verse before we start singing. Tell me when you're ready.'

He lifted his hands into position. 'Any time now.'

After counting off two measures' worth of beats, she nodded and they began.

It took them a few minutes to fully coordinate their fingering, but after that, they continued playing in perfect sync. Dellamont had a pleasant singing voice, a deep, rich baritone that matched well with her bright soprano. By the time they finished the song, Marcella was thoroughly enjoying herself.

'Thank you!' she said as they lifted their fingers from the keys to enthusiastic applause. 'I don't often get to play duets. That was delightful.'

Nodding towards the assembly, he said, 'The audience seems to want an encore. If you have another selection you think I could play.'

'I would love to! I've collected music for a great many airs, ballads and glees. My grandfather prefers them to the more complex works of the major composers.' Spying one particular piece, she seized it with a grin. 'In honour of our bargain, "No One Shall Govern Me" would be perfect, if we repeat only the first verse. Perhaps Hoddleston—and the assembled company—will take the hint.'

After scanning the lyrics, Dellamont laughed. 'You're right, it *is* perfect for us. I don't know the tune, but the music looks simple enough. Hum it through for me once and I think I can manage.'

She sang through a verse softly, then said, 'That's the tempo. Let's play through a verse first, like last time, and then sing the first verse three times.'

'You don't wish to sing all the verses?'

'And reach the dreary conclusion that Laura becomes a sad old maid who wishes she'd allowed herself to be governed after all? Definitely not!'

He grinned. 'I thought not. Very well, Miss Independent. Let's confound the assembly.' After assuming a playing position, he nodded.

They played through the music once, then began to sing.

When young and thoughtless
Laura said,
'No one shall win my heart';
But little dreamt the simple maid

Of love's delusive art.
At ball or play
She'd flirt away
But always said
'I'll never wed,
No one shall govern me.
No, no, no, no, no, no,
No one shall govern me.'

By the time they'd sung the verse the third time, Dellamont was chuckling. Looking over at the audience, who after they finished wore faintly puzzled expressions as they clapped politely, Marcella had to choke down laughter of her own.

'I only like the first verse,' she told the assembly. 'Thank you for your kindness. Now we must cede our place to another performer.'

They rose from the bench, Dellamont offering his arm as they walked away. 'Having gone above and beyond your duty, you can return me to Lady Arlsley. Thank you again for the rescue—and a very enjoyable duet!'

'You are very welcome. I enjoyed playing with you, too.'

Marcella was resigning herself to losing the pleasure of his conversation—and the delicious frisson of awareness of his nearness—but just before they reached where Lady Arlsley was sitting, he halted. 'Hoddleston is still watching. Perhaps I should sit with you for a while to make sure you don't need any further reinforcements.'

Marcella made a wry grimace. 'From the thundering look he gave you when you forced him to walk away, you might be the one needing help.'

Dellamont laughed shortly. 'Hoddleston is no match for me with fists or swords and he knows it. He'll stay out of my way. I can assure you. But I'll stay long enough to make sure he doesn't try to take out his displeasure at being outmanoeuvred on you.'

'Are you sure society won't think I've enjoyed…too much of your company for one evening? I'd not have you being pressured by public opinion.'

'You should know by now I'm never pressured by public opinion. If my father's rants are unable to make me conform, the expectations of mere acquaintances are hardly likely to affect me.'

'Very well. As long as you think it's…safe.'

Whether it was safe for *her* might be a more pertinent question. It was all well and good to spend time with Prince Charming as long as one remembered one was living a fairy tale. Something that could become increasingly hard to keep in mind, if she spent too much time with him.

Soon she'd be returning to her own world—the world she preferred. Hopefully to entice a man she'd admired for half her life to make her his wife and sweep her into a future more rich and rewarding than anything the *ton* could ever offer.

Somehow, she was no longer quite so excited about the prospect.

'How kind of you to play with Miss Cranmore, Lord Dellamont,' Lady Arlsley said approvingly as they took seats adjacent to her. 'And how well you play.'

'You are too kind. But Miss Cranmore is a superior musician. Her talent made up for my lack.'

'What a perfect couple you made, performing together! Ah—there's my dear friend, Lady Collingwood, beckoning to me. I'll just be a minute.'

'If she is any more syrupy-sweet, I think I shall be ill,' Marcella muttered as her sponsor walked across the room.

'She does rather empty the butter boat.'

'After pouring it over the sugar cone.'

Smiling, Dellamont said, 'My compliment about your playing wasn't empty praise. Even though the pieces we performed were simple, your technique is admirable. And just the fact that you would attempt the Beethoven leaves me in awe.'

'I've had plenty of practice. Father always found music soothing. When he was devastated after my brother's death, I began playing for him every night. Mama encouraged me, too, after she saw how much it seemed to help him relax.'

'So you were a congenial family group, entertaining each other in the evening.'

She nodded. 'Very. We still spend the evenings together, me playing while Father reads and Mother does her needlework. If Father brings home an associate who enjoys music, I'll play for them, too. Did—does your family not gather together after dinner to play cards or read aloud?'

He laughed shortly. 'When I was growing up, we children dined in the nursery. When I returned after being away at school and was considered old enough to have a place at the dinner table, a meal conducted mostly in silence was followed by my mother retreating to her rooms while I was either dismissed, or beckoned to Father's study, if he wished to harangue me about some lapse while he drank his brandy.'

No wonder he had so little taste for family life, Marcella thought, grieved by all he had missed. 'I'm sorry,' she said softly. 'It...it shouldn't be like that.'

'From what the other boys said about their lives when we were at school, such an arrangement wasn't that unusual. Except most of their families had more guests to dine with them. Montwell Glen is isolated enough that Papa generally goes to London when he wishes to consult friends or needs to attend the Lords. There are no families who live nearby of sufficient rank for him to consider them worthy of an invitation to an earl's table.'

'When you do eventually marry, you must choose someone who will make your domestic life much more enjoyable.'

He shook his head. 'I've had little enough evidence that such households exist, but I won't dispute your memories of your own experience. Is... is that the sort of home you expect to establish with your engineer?'

'I certainly hope to. Austin became indispensable to us all after my brother's death. He carried the load at the office while Papa was too grief-stricken to work, watched out for Mama, and was so incredibly kind and attentive to the lost little girl I'd become. Having him nearby is like...like being in a wrapped in a warm shawl before a cosy fire on a bitter winter day. One feels safe, comfortable and cared for. Of course, he does still treat me like Papa's little girl. I... I hope he will allow me to continue working in the office if we marry, but of course, since he hasn't as yet indicated he *wishes* to marry me, I've had no opportunity to enquire about that. If he should not want me there, I suppose I shall have to accept it, and be content.'

He angled a probing glance at her. 'Can you be content? With comfort and kindness, instead of the stimulating intellectual partnership you're looking for?'

A question she often asked herself—and had such difficulty answering, she usually pushed away thinking about it. 'I suppose I shall have to be.'

'Content with comfort, rather than…passion?'

She looked up sharply, a zing of awareness jolting through her. It was well and good to dream about kisses…about closeness and more. Giddy, tempting—and far too dangerous.

When she looked away without answering, he said, 'I might not know much about domestic harmony, but I do know one should not live without passion. Especially not someone with your intelligence and fire.'

'That's easy enough for a man to say!' she flung back. 'You can behave as you wish, without facing consequences. It's very different for a female.'

'Not so different,' he argued. 'A gentleman, too, has to marry in the end.'

'Ah, but before he does, he can have the pleasure of riding about England where and when he chooses, answering to no one. No doubt catching the eye of any number of appreciative females.'

He grinned. 'You think I catch the eye of appreciative females?'

'I think, unless they are of invincible virtue, they would be quite vulnerable.'

'How invincible is your virtue?'

'Until now, I'd thought it infallible.' Breaking free of his intent gaze to stare down at his hand beside hers, so very conscious of his beguiling nearness, she said frankly, 'Now I'm not so sure. So you mustn't tempt me.'

He tipped her chin back up to face him, smiling faintly. 'Sadly, you are right. I mustn't tempt you—or myself. Not if we want to salvage friendship once your Season ends. I do look forward to meeting you again, perhaps chatting in your father's office when I come to enquire about the progress on the Great Western.'

'I would love to see you! I could make you tea. Go over engineering drawings with you.'

'We must make it happen. But I see Lady Arlsley returning, so I should take myself off before I truly outstay the acceptable interval. I'll linger in the refreshment room, watching, until you depart, just in case. Signal if you should need me.'

'That's very kind.' Much as she wanted to press him to stay, she knew it was time for him to quit her company. There were already far too many eyes avidly watching them—probably with mental timepieces ticking in their ears to calculate just how long he remained chatting with her. 'I shall probably have to suffer through a few minutes of conversation with Hoddleston, but with

Lady Arlsley so delighted by the continuing attentions of a far greater prize, she'll not want to risk discouraging your pursuit by seeming too ardent about encouraging his.'

As he stood, she said, 'Thank you again for playing duets with me. Perhaps we can play again some time.'

'I can't imagine where, but I'd enjoy it. We must look for an opportunity.'

'We should. Good evening, my lord.'

'You'll ride again tomorrow? Maybe I can accompany Lady Margaret. Restrain her from saying anything too outrageous.'

Marcella laughed. 'I wish you luck with that.'

He smiled back. 'Thank you—for an evening that was much more enjoyable than I expected.'

'My pleasure.' After pressing her fingers briefly, he bowed and walked away.

Marcella cradled her tingling hand. Dellamont wasn't hers and wasn't going to be. She needed to school herself to let him go without feeling this pointless sense of regret.

Nor did she dare *want* him to be hers…since in the unlikely event he wanted *her*, any fairy-tale dreams of happiness would surely be doomed by all the obstacles such an ill-matched couple would face. A fact she needed to emphasise to her sometimes heedless heart.

Better to focus her attention instead on thinking about venues and opportunities at which she might meet him in future as a *friend*, at her father's office or elsewhere.

Such meetings being the only prudent way to maintain any contact with him once their bargain ended.

Chapter Ten

In the morning two days later, Marcella rode to the park, her groom trailing her. She was looking forward to seeing Dellamont, who had been unable to accompany her and Lady Margaret yesterday, but had promised his sister to attend her this morning.

As they trotted along, she mulled over the brief conversation she'd had with Austin Gilling when she stopped by the office to have tea with her father the previous afternoon.

Gilling had declined to join them, but as she was leaving, he rose from his desk to walk her out, asking how she was enjoying her debut. When she replied drily that she was enduring it, he said, 'So you don't intend to marry an aristocrat?'

Had she detected an interest deeper than politeness in that enquiry? 'That was my mother's dream, not mine,' she replied. 'I entered society to please her and Grandfather. My hope since I started assisting Papa at the office has been to wed someone from my own world…the world of engineering. Someone I esteem and trust.'

She could have hardly made her intention clearer without actually proposing to him. Hoping she hadn't gone too far, she held her breath until he finally replied, 'Sometimes it's difficult to realise the sweet little girl who sobbed on my shoulder after her brother's death has grown up. It was a…shock to learn you'd embarked on a debut.'

'A shock to me, too. But even Papa agrees I must wed some time.'

Pausing by the door, his fair face colouring, he said, 'I think it quite likely that your hopes for a husband from the engineering world will be realised.'

Then, bowing, as she left.

Had he been hinting he himself would help her realise it? Had she detected a change in the way he treated her—something deeper, more personal than the avuncular affection he'd always shown her since childhood? Or was that only her wishful imagining at work?

At the least, he'd seemed to say he had been shocked into recognising she was now a woman grown. Perhaps if he'd not decided what he wanted to do about that fact by the time she left society, the calls she hoped Dellamont would make to her father's office would prompt him into further action.

Turning her cherished vision of wedding her childhood hero into reality. It was what she'd wanted for years now, wasn't it?

If a certain virile, dark-haired, dark-eyed gentleman was currently distracting her from that vision, it was hardly alarming—he was, after all, handsome and charming. But like the Season she'd embarked upon, he was a temporary detour from the path of her life. The sugar icing on a delicious dessert, something to be enjoyed for the moment, but not the nourishing stuff that sustained one over the long years.

As she rode through the park gates, a rider on side-saddle in the distance waved at her. Recognising Lady Margaret, she waved back, her pulse kicking up a notch when she saw Dellamont on his black gelding beside his sister.

Might as well savour every bit of sweetness while the dessert lasted, she told herself, signalling her horse to a trot as she rode to meet them.

'Lady Margaret, Lord Dellamont, so good to see you,' she said as she reined in beside them.

'Delighted to see you again,' Dellamont replied, giving her a smile that set off an annoying little flutter in her belly.

Trying to quell the feeling, she turned her attention to his sister. 'How was the call on the Almack's patronesses, Lady Margaret? As gruelling as you had expected?'

'Lady Cowper was frosty, Lady Jersey condescending, but Mama is so sweet and earnest and unassuming, they both gradually thawed. Towards her, of course, not towards me. I'm only a chit of no account who's not even out yet.'

'Mama's just trying to establish the contacts you'll need during next year's presentation,' Dellamont reminded his sister. 'Something she will surely accomplish, as long as you're not countering her efforts by being sulky or impertinent to the matrons whose approval will make or break your success.'

'I was, as required, meek and monosyllabic.'

Dellamont laughed. 'I wish I'd been a fly on the wall to observe it. I have a hard time imagining you maintaining a bashful demeanour for more than a few minutes without exploding from the strain.'

'Fortunately, a proper call only lasts half an hour,' Lady Margaret said. 'I'm able to contain myself that long. How did you spend your afternoon, Miss Cranmore?'

'I called on my father at his office. I haven't had much time with him since all this began, and I have missed our afternoon teas.'

Lady Margaret shook her head wonderingly. 'I

still find it remarkable that you and your father have tea together and chat.'

'I am very fortunate in his affection,' Marcella said simply.

'I wouldn't know about that,' Lady Margaret retorted. 'Well, shall we have a good gallop before the park becomes too crowded?'

'Absolutely,' Marcella replied, eager to indulge in one of the few favourite pursuits the time-consuming constraints of the Season had left her.

'Let's be off, then,' Dellamont said. 'Race you to the bend, Maggie.'

'As long as *you* don't sulk when I beat you!' his sister retorted, spurring her mount.

Laughing, Marcella set her mare to follow them, enjoying the gallop but not trying to best them, content to observe the brother and sister's friendly competition. Though the unhappiness of the childhood Dellamont had described saddened her, she was cheered to know that he at least maintained a warm relationship with his mother and sister.

She truly hoped his eventual wife would make up for those grim, unhappy years. Surely he could find a society beauty with the wit and liveliness of his sister who would also have as much appreciation for Dellamont's fine qualities as for the status she would enjoy as a countess.

She chuckled as the siblings reached the finish

point neck and neck. Lady Margaret turned her mount towards Marcella when she reached them a moment later, calling out 'I won, didn't I!'

'Well, I don't know. It was a very close thing.'

'You'd better tell her she's the victor, else she will sulk,' Dellamont said, his eyes merry as he teased his sister.

'I will not sulk. Besides, I don't have to. You know I beat you, even if it salves your masculine pride to pretend you did. It's only fair that you get beaten upon occasion, for gentlemen hold all the advantages, don't they, Miss Cranmore? My mare is still fast, but Fancy Lady is getting older. I thought being in London would offer a good opportunity to choose another mare to replace her, but Crispin informs me that females are not allowed in Tattersall's. I very much resent that I don't get to choose my own horse, when silly fops with more money than horse sense can inspect the offerings at their leisure.'

'You know your groom would do the evaluating, even if you were permitted to attend,' Dellamont countered. 'The prohibition on females at Tattersall's is intended to protect them from the coarse language they would overhear from the grooms, trainers and stable hands assembled to tend the horses.'

'And from the gentlemen looking to purchase those horses?' his sister added tartly.

'Them, too,' Dellamont admitted with a laugh.

'Are you allowed a say in the purchase of your mount, Miss Cranmore?' Lady Margaret asked. 'Your mare is very fine.'

'Yes, she's a delight. And yes, I was present when she was purchased. There are often horse fairs on market days in the country. All the local people, men, women and children, are free to attend.'

'How lucky you are! As for the language at Tattersall's, it's not as if anyone who rides isn't around the stables often enough to overhear salty language—inadvertently, of course,' Lady Margaret added after a speaking glance from her brother. 'It's hardly likely that my "innocent ears" would be sullied.'

'Perhaps you should listen less intently when you're in the stables,' her brother suggested.

Making a face at him, she said, 'How I wish I could see all the horses on offer for myself.' Her gaze turning mischievous, she continued, 'Maybe I should visit your rooms and borrow a gentleman's rig, so I might sneak into Tattersall's unobserved.'

Dellamont cast his eyes skywards. 'Heaven forfend! Promise me you won't do anything of the sort, brat. Should anyone catch you out dressed as a boy, your reputation would be ruined before you'd even been presented.'

Lady Margaret sighed. 'It's all so ridiculous, what a female must do to preserve her reputation. If I weren't so anxious to make an advantageous match next year so I can escape Montwell Glen, I'd be tempted to chance it. Though I will be sorry to abandon Mama after I'm wed. With me gone and you avoiding the place, she'll have no one to protect her.'

Marcella's heart ached not just for a girl so eager to leave her childhood home, she seemed willing to marry almost anyone with suitable wealth, but also for the mother both siblings evidently loved dearly. 'Once you are married, as mistress of a household of your own, you shall be able to invite your mother for long visits.'

Brightening, Lady Margaret said, 'Yes, I will, won't I? I must marry someone with a town house in London, so I can have Mama stay with me for the Season every year. She would love that, wouldn't she, Crispin? It would serve Papa right to rusticate in the country by himself. He'd have to find another object for his tantrums—hopefully not you!'

Pained again at this further indication of family discord, Marcella could think of nothing to say. Looking embarrassed by his sister's frank disclosures, Dellamont said, 'Enough about Montwell Glen. Shall we make a slow circuit of the park and cool down the horses?'

'Please do, but I'll need to leave you,' Marcella said. 'I want to stop at Hatchard's this morning, and if I am to present myself on time for Lady Arlsley's at-home this afternoon, I shall have to go there now.'

'What are you seeking at Hatchard's?' Dellamont asked. 'The latest novel?'

'I do so love the Minerva Press novels,' Lady Margaret said. 'Such evil villains and dashing heroes! Do you have favourites, Miss Cranmore?'

'At the risk of sounding very dull, I've never read any,' Marcella admitted. 'I stop by Hatchard's periodically to check if there are new scientific reprints available. They generally carry them, when smaller bookshops don't.' Laughing at the expression of distaste crossing Lady Margaret's face, she continued, 'I'm afraid I prefer tomes about mathematics and botany by female authors to scandalous novels.'

Lady Margaret's eyes widened in surprise. '*Females* have written about such things?'

'Not many,' Marcella replied. 'Women are rarely allowed to receive enough education to qualify them to write scholarly reports. Which is why the few who have are my heroines. Imagine, being able to pursue a vocation other than marriage! Few manage it now, but some day I hope that women will be able to follow their interests wherever they lead.'

'A woman offered a choice other than marriage or penury? What an appealing notion!' Lady Margaret said. 'Though I'm not sure I'd want to delve into mathematics to secure the opportunity.'

Marcella laughed. 'Continue to enjoy your novels and leave the mathematics to odd ducks like me.'

'Maggie, will your groom's escort home be sufficient? If Miss Cranmore doesn't mind, I'd like to accompany her to Hatchard's. I'd be curious to learn more about the authors she is seeking.'

'I'm sure I could find my way back to Portman Square even without Jamison's help,' Lady Margaret said. Giving her brother and Marcella a coy glance, she said, 'By all means, accompany Miss Cranmore to Hatchard's—and discover what an educated female can achieve.'

Dellamont smiled. 'So I shall, brat.'

'Can you ride tomorrow, Crispin?' his sister asked.

'Probably not. There are some meetings about a proposed Parliamentary offering I want to attend.'

'Very well. But I suspect it's more to avoid being beaten by me again than a desire for information that prevents you,' she said saucily. 'I hope to see you, though, Miss Cranmore.'

'Unless the weather is bad, I shall probably ride,' Marcella confirmed.

'Shall we head to Hatchard's, Miss Cranmore?' Dellamont asked.

'With pleasure,' she replied.

With Marcella's groom riding behind them as chaperon, they parted with Lady Margaret and her escort and proceeded out of the park towards Piccadilly. 'Did you see your engineer when you had tea with your father yesterday?' Dellamont asked.

'Yes. Though Mr Gilling didn't join us, we shared a few words before I left.'

'And?' He raised his eyebrows in enquiry.

She blew out a sigh. 'He admitted he'd been surprised to learn I was making my debut— meaning that he was shocked to suddenly realise I am old enough to wed.' Recalling the conversation, she flushed. 'I was actually brazen enough to tell him when I did marry, I hoped my husband would be an engineer...someone I knew well and valued.'

'Bold indeed! What did he say to that?'

'Well, he didn't run in the other direction. I *think* he'll finally consider the possibility, once he full accepts the fact that I've grown up. We've been dear friends for ever, after all. But I don't know. He did say he was confident that my hopes to marry the sort of man I wanted would be realised. But I couldn't tell if he meant that remark in a general way, or was referring to possibly making me an offer himself.'

'If he's at least thinking in that direction, then enduring the Season will have been worth it, don't you think? Bravo!'

'Don't be celebrating my nuptials yet! Having you call at Papa's office once I leave society might help continue to move his thoughts in that direction, if he's not progressed there on his own.'

'Delighted to offer my assistance. But I'd not wish to move his thoughts along *too* quickly. After all, he may prefer to have his wife remain at home and stay out of the office, even while your father is still working. Which would make it difficult, if not impossible, for us to maintain a friendship.'

Once she married, remaining friends with a man who was neither a relation nor a member of her own society would probably prove impossible in any event, she thought with a trace of sadness. But then, she wasn't married yet and didn't intend to be for some time.

Which gave Austin time to realise she'd grown up enough to become his wife, and herself a chance to continue her friendship with Dellamont.

She'd not think about how bereft she might feel when she had to bid the Viscount a final goodbye.

'Well, I shall not yet consider the dispiriting

possibility that my spouse might bar me from working with Papa. Which is why, while I'm eager to get Mr Gilling thinking of me as a woman grown, I don't really want him to make me a declaration any time soon.'

Dellamont shook his head. 'You might not be able to have it both ways, you know. Once your engineer realises he wants the woman you've become, he may not want to delay wedding you.'

'I'll worry about that later. For now, I need to gird myself to suffer through a bit more of the Season.'

'How much longer do you intend to keep at it?'

'Lady Arlsley has already accepted invitations for entertainments for the next two weeks, so that long at least. Perhaps not much longer than that. Would that be long enough for your purposes?'

'My mother has already assured me I can abandon society whenever I want. Not that she isn't thoroughly enjoying this rare chance to stay in London, but she doesn't want me to hang on just for her.' He looked over at her. 'She also doesn't want me to continue my attentions to you long enough for your reputation—or your heart—to be damaged when they cease. I didn't tell her about our bargain, of course, but I did tell her we understood each other well enough that there was no possibility of that happening. We...do have that understanding, don't we?'

If Dellamont had developed any warmer feelings for her, he would have confessed them just now, Marcella thought. Illogically unsure whether to be relieved or disappointed that he hadn't, she said stoutly, 'Of course. We entered this bargain both knowing what we wanted, and an attachment beyond friendship was never part of that. Nothing has happened to change that agreement—except, perhaps, my gratitude for your protection from Lord Hoddleston. And my growing appreciation for your talent as a musician and a horseman.'

He smiled—in relief at knowing she wasn't developing a *tendre* for him? 'As my appreciation for your talents increases. So, when do we meet next?'

'We should probably allow a few days to pass before you seek me out at another ball or rout, where all of society can watch and speculate about your attentions.'

He nodded. 'Maintain that "discreet interval".'

'Yes. That said, if you wish to call tomorrow afternoon and walk in the garden, I think that would be good strategy. Lady Arlsley is already pushing for an attachment, so it will not cause any more speculation on her part, and there will be at most a handful of her friends present. Enough to spread gossip that will encourage your father, but not enough to lead to widespread expectations that you are close to a declaration.'

'You are getting a rather deft feel for all this,' he said wryly.

'It's like a well-choreographed dance,' Marcella said. 'Advance, retreat, attract notice, discreetly withdraw, so as to slowly progress only as far and as fast as one wishes.'

By now, they'd arrived at the bookstore in Piccadilly. 'Thank you for escorting me,' Marcella said. 'It was helpful to be able to plan strategy, something we can't do when surrounded by a bevy of interested listeners.'

'Yes. So we continue. For another two weeks, at least.'

She nodded. 'Two weeks more. Then we'll see where we are. Shall we go in?'

After Dellamont helped her dismount, she turned to the groom with a smile. 'You'll walk the horses, won't you, Thompson? He's very patient,' she told Dellamont, 'having accompanied me on this errand several times before.'

'Of course, miss. I can manage three horses, no problems.'

'There will be an extra coin for a tankard of ale tonight,' she promised. 'Very well, my lord. Are you ready to be instructed?'

He offered his arm, and she took it. 'Miss Cranmore, I'm ready to have you instruct me... in whatever you most enjoy,' he murmured as he walked her through the door.

A shiver rippling over her skin at the double entendre, Marcella swallowed hard. She could just imagine some of the pleasures in which he could instruct her... Jerking her thoughts back from imagining his kiss, she said, 'We'll confine your education today to learning more about female savants.'

Smiling, he said, 'Lead on.'

Chapter Eleven

Still smiling faintly, Crispin followed Miss Cranmore into the bookstore. So they were to search out tomes on mathematics and astronomy written by females. He'd been as surprised as his sister to learn such women existed, and genuinely curious to know more about them.

If the son of land-owning aristocracy could involve himself in new, radically different pursuits from most of his class, why shouldn't females have more options?

With Miss Cranmore's enthusiasm for engineering design, he could appreciate how such learned women would be her heroines. Not one whose aspirations were limited to catching a suitable husband and raising a family, his Miss Cranmore.

Many men disdained women of intelligence. Society disparaged them as 'bluestockings'. But from the first, he'd found that Marcella Cranmore's lively intellect and mathematical abilities made her more, rather than less attractive to him. That the lithe, curvaceous body with its speaking eyes and tempting lips also housed a keen mind piqued both his interest and his desire.

He was delighted at the opportunity to accompany her to the bookstore—to extend his time in her enchanting presence and learn more about what fascinated her.

He assumed she would make enquiries of the store clerk who greeted them, but telling the man she knew where the material she sought would be shelved, she waved him away and set off down the aisle, not halting until they reached an obscure corner.

'Priding themselves on stocking most everything that can be obtained in print, Hatchard's does carry these ladies' writings. But believing interest in them to be minimal, the shop doesn't display them in a prominent place,' she explained as she gestured towards the out-of-the-way shelf.

'They can't expect to sell any to casual browsers if they place them here,' he observed.

'As long as they are at least available, I'm content. The majority of the writers are botanists, which is understandable. Females may be barred from studying at university, but no one can keep a curious girl from examining, classifying and drawing the plants that grow in the fields and gardens around her. Maria Jacson published several works, from *Botanical Lectures by a Lady* to several volumes about Linnaean botany and plant physiology to this *Florist's Manual*,' she said, tapping the spine of the book.

'And several volumes of it, I see,' Crispin noted.

'Elizabeth Andrew Warren works with the Royal Horticultural Society of Cornwall,' she continued, 'organising their yearly plant collections and along the way, discovering a number of new, rare specimens. Anna Worsley studies plants in the Bristol area and has contributed her lists to H. C. Watson's *New Botanist's Guide*, which the staff here tell me will be available next year. Sarah Drake does the illustrations for this horticultural magazine, *Edwards's Botanical Register*,' she said, handing him a copy.

Dellamont took the magazine and flipped through. 'I'm no botanist, but these are beautiful.'

'And of much more value to the world than painting violets on china plates,' Miss Cranmore said with a disgust that made him laugh.

'Were you ever tasked with painting flowers on china plates?' he asked. 'No—let me guess. It was the subject of an entire course at Miss Axminster's School.'

'So it was. Embroidering flowers on chair

covers was also much studied,' she replied drily. 'Whereas I preferred studying the work of Caroline Herschel, who actually earned a *salary* for assisting her brother, the royal astronomer at Windsor, and won a Gold Medal from the Royal Astronomical Society in 1828 for her discovery of comets and nebulae. But my true heroine is this lady,' she said, reverently drawing out a slim volume.

'*The Mechanism of the Heavens* by Mary Somerville,' Crispin read. 'What is this about?'

'It's an explanation in algebraic terms of the workings of the solar system, a clear, understandable rendition of celestial mechanics so excellently written it made Mrs Somerville famous when it was published in 1831. She'd already had reports about her experiments on the relationship of light and magnetism printed in the journals of the Royal Society. She never studied at university, of course, but she acquired the best books available and taught herself algebra, geometry and Euclidian principals. Later she was able to work in laboratories to expand her knowledge to chemistry, electricity and magnetism. John Murray is to publish her second book, *On the Connection of the Physical Sciences*, some time soon. Indeed, I was hoping Hatchard's might have it today, but I see it isn't in stock yet. I can't wait to read it!'

She couldn't wait to read a volume about chemistry and mathematics, he thought, marvelling. A book that someone with his limited grasp of advanced scientific principles would probably find incomprehensible. He already appreciated how intelligent she was, but the depth of her intellectual curiosity struck him anew.

She was like one of those comets her heroines studied—blazing with life and enthusiasm, a bright star. How he was drawn to that fierce light!

And how important he remember the risk of being drawn in too closely, he thought, deliberately reining back his admiration.

Focusing instead on the writings, he said, 'I expect the content of the next volume will be about as far as one can get from the histrionic villains and fainting heroines that so delight my sister.'

She chuckled. 'Probably.'

'I've always thought of myself as rather liberal when it came to my estimation of a woman's abilities. But I had no idea they might be capable of something like this.'

She smiled wryly. 'Mrs Somerville said that from her youngest days, she resented that the privileges of education so lavishly bestowed on men were denied to women. Even her first husband—who fortunately passed away before he could curtail her intellectual growth—doubted a female was capable of profiting from academic study.'

Crispin looked down at the book in his hand. 'She certainly proved him wrong.'

'If you are truly a forward-looking gentleman, you might want to read Maria Jacson's *Botanical Lectures*. Besides the erudite description and lovely illustrations, she expresses quite eloquently her frustration that, and I paraphrase, a female must refrain from "obtruding" her knowledge on a world that condemns a woman to working with her hands, rather than her head.'

'Perhaps men have always been drawn to admire the beauty of those heads, rather than the intellect within them.'

'Drawn to outward beauty—which poses no challenge to their sense of superiority?' she retorted.

He laughed. 'There is that.' He pulled out the Jacson book and stacked it on the Somerville volume. 'I have to admit—I'm impressed. You've given me a lot to think—and read—about.'

Her eyes widening, she said, 'You mean—you actually intend to read these?'

He shook a reproving finger. 'Haven't you learned by now that I never say things I don't mean?'

Her surprise turned to a smile of such engaging delight, he had to once again suppress the urge to kiss her. 'Then I, too, am impressed.'

'It's a mutual admiration society we have,' he murmured.

Her gaze locked on his, the desire that always simmered between them intensifying. 'I suppose it is.'

He had to look away from those tempting lips before his yearning to taste her, here and now in this shadowy nook of the bookstore, overcame prudence. Dangerous, how the more intelligent and unique he found her, the stronger his passion grew.

'Will you purchase anything?' he asked after he'd got himself back under control.

'I don't own the latest copy of the *Botanical Register*, so I'll take that. But then I really must get home. Mary will think I've been kidnapped and scold that she doesn't have sufficient time to turn me out looking like a proper young lady before I must appear at Lady Arlsley's.'

'We should get you home, then.' Much as he regretted the necessity. Much as he'd prefer to further extend their time together by asking her to take tea at Gunter's, or make another circuit around the park.

He walked with her to the sales counter, amused when she not only refused to allow him to pay for her book, but tried to talk him into letting her pay for his selections.

'Which would only have been fair, since I induced you to get them,' she said, still arguing the point as they walked out to reclaim their horses.

'I may be willing to concede I have much to learn about the female intellect, but as a gentleman, I have some standards—which include forbidding a lady to pay for my purchases.'

'Well, if you enjoy the books, I shall be content.'

'I will certainly find them interesting. Until tomorrow afternoon, then. Enjoy your evening.'

'And you yours.'

He retrieved his reins from her groom, who then turned to help her remount. Once her attendant vaulted back in the saddle, with a little wave to Crispin, she rode off.

He watched her go, thoughtful as he remounted his gelding.

He wasn't sure whether to be glad or regretful that their bargain would likely end in two weeks. She intrigued, stimulated and amused him, and he looked forward with anticipation to spending time with her.

Though being near her less often would be a boon to a conscience that was having increasing trouble restraining his physical desire, having their future interactions after they left society limited to occasional meetings in her father's office was a most unappealing prospect.

He'd have to give more thought to finding other places he might see her—more often.

He'd made the acquaintance of a number of beauties since his university days, but he'd never met a woman who ignited such a strong and immediate physical response. And compared to her blazing intellect and unconventional interests, the other women he'd known seemed commonplace and forgettable.

How fortunate he didn't intend to wed any time soon, he thought as he turned his mount towards Jasmin Street. Though Marcella Cranmore seemed adamant about refusing to marry into his class, he might otherwise be tempted to try to change her mind.

The afternoon of the following day, Crispin presented himself at Lady Arlsley's town house in Upper Brook Street. After having read several chapters in the books he'd bought at Hatchard's, he looked forward to discussing them with Miss Cranmore…even as he warned himself not to be distracted by the romantic possibilities offered by a stroll down pathways whose trees were now coming into leaf, accompanied by a maid who might trail just far enough behind to afford them some privacy.

If those circumstances developed, would he be able to resist temptation?

As before, he walked into the parlour to greet his hostess and subject himself to the speculative looks of the two friends currently visiting her. He returned a bland smile to her enthusiastic acquiescence when he asked permission to escort Miss Cranmore on a walk through the garden.

Giving him an amused look at her sponsor's blatant encouragement, the lady in question walked out with him, pausing in the hallway to await the maid who was approaching with her bonnet and pelisse.

To his surprise, when Mary halted beside them, she directed her scowl not towards the unworthy male offering his arm to her charge—but to her mistress. 'I put that parcel with your things, miss,' she said as she helped her Miss Cranmore into her pelisse. 'But I hope you come to your senses and decide not to use it.'

After giving him a quick glance, Miss Cranmore frowned at the maid. 'We'll talk about that later.'

'I've not kept watch over you since you were a wee babe to see you ruin yourself now and spoil all the opportunities given to you—or something worse!' the maid grumbled as she followed them out—ostensibly to herself, but loud enough that he was able to catch her words.

'That's quite enough, Mary,' Miss Cranmore said sharply.

Amused by the maid's scolding, his curiosity piqued by what he'd overheard, Crispin was about to interrupt Miss Cranmore's determined monologue about the early-blooming tulips and enquire what had prompted her maid's distress when the woman's next muttering made his levity evaporate. He cast a startled look back at Mary, who replied to his questioning glance with a disapproving nod.

Gripping the hand Miss Cranmore had laid on his arm, he picked up the pace, walking her away from Mary, who for once seemed content to have her mistress spirited away.

'You had Mary purchase gentleman's clothing?' he asked incredulously. 'Is that true?'

Not meeting his eyes, she said in an exasperated tone, 'Mary shouldn't comment about what is none of her business.'

'Keeping you from harm *is* her business. You're not… *Please* assure me you're going to try to sneak my sister into Tattersall's!' Recalling Lady Margaret's chatter yesterday about the unfairness of men having exclusive clubs into which they could retreat, he added, 'Or worse still, try to gain admittance to a gentlemen's club!'

'Of course not!' she replied, her surprise too genuine for him to doubt. 'I'd never do anything to put your sister in harm's way.'

Relieved, he retorted, 'It's more likely she

would try to persuade you into doing something that would put *you* at risk. Or threaten to do something so outrageous that you felt it necessary to go along to protect her. I know you like her.'

'I do like her. So I would never let her manoeuvre me into letting her do something rash.'

'Thank Heaven. Then what do you intend to do with boy's garb?'

'What makes you think I shall do anything with it?'

'So you don't deny you had her procure some?'

She gave a huff of frustration, knowing he'd just caught her out. 'It wasn't good of you to try to trick me. But I assure you, my intentions are perfectly respectable.'

Crispin gave her a disbelieving look. 'Having you wear male attire anywhere but hidden away in the country—and probably not even there—could never be respectable. Besides, Mary must be quite worried if she let me overhear her scolding. She'd never have betrayed you otherwise. She must hope I might be able to talk you out of whatever it is you are planning. So—what *are* you planning?'

Still silent, she looked at him resentfully, but he just shook his head. 'I'm not going to leave until you tell me, so you might as well do it straight away. If I sit on the doorstep for too long, Lady Arlsley will be making enquiries as well.'

'Oh, very well. But you must promise not to tell anyone.'

'I can't in good conscience promise that until I know what it is. But I do promise to hear you out—and not betray you unless I think what you're planning will truly put you in danger.'

Probably realising that was the best bargain he would offer—and that he would indeed refuse to leave until she confessed to him—she said, 'I so sympathised with your sister when she complained that men have all the freedom, while women are restricted from going so many places, including venues that are useful and quite harmless, like Tattersall's. Then…an opportunity arose that was so enticing, I just couldn't bring myself to overlook it.'

'If it were an opportunity you could safely take, you wouldn't need to disguise yourself in men's garments,' he shot back.

'But it would be safe. Entirely safe! There's a lecture to be held tomorrow at the Institution of Civil Engineers. Unfortunately, as with the Royal Society meetings, only gentlemen are admitted. Papa told me at tea yesterday that George Stephenson himself will be speaking.'

She sighed, her eyes alight. '*George Stephenson!* Imagine, being able to listen to the man who invented the first workable railway carriages and constructed the first commercially successful railway! Who pioneered the design of iron and masonry bridges, developed standards for the correct degree of slope and turn for railway tracks. Who designed the multi-arched skew bridge at Rainhill! Papa had been given admission tickets, but has a consultation with a potential investor and won't be able to use them. So, when Mr Gilling called him away to answer a question I... I slipped them out of the drawer and put them in my reticule. And had Mary procure me a suit of clothes.'

Crispin shook his head. 'You can't be seriously contemplating trying to get into the meeting dressed as a boy!'

'Why not? I only need to kit myself out properly, present my admission ticket, find a seat at the back of the room and remain unobtrusive. Even you must admit it will be a perfectly respectable gathering.'

She was so aglow with enthusiasm, he hated to discourage her, but he could see nothing resulting from such a rash stunt but catastrophe and embarrassment. Trying to let her down gently, he said, 'You will have to speak to the doorman who admits you, to the person who takes your ticket, and probably extend polite greetings to other members who happen to be nearby when you come in. Don't you think someone will ask you where you are from, with whom you work? Any one of those could recognise your voice as feminine. Now, walk ahead of me.'

Looking puzzled, she angled her head. 'Walk ahead?'

'Just walk,' he ordered.

With an exasperated expression, she turned and proceeded away from him.

He shook his head. The idea was madness. Heat flashed through his body at the mental image of seeing the swaying hips now sending her skirts fluttering outlined by a tight-fitting coat. He dared not let himself think what her trim derrière and shapely legs would look like in a figure-revealing pair of trousers.

'You can stop now.' As she turned back to him he said, 'You'd never get away with it.'

'Why not?' she demanded.

'You walk like a woman, for one,' he said shortly. He took a step accompanied by an ex-aggerated swing of his hips and watched as her face coloured.

'Oh. I see.'

'It's not just your walk. Only consider. You appearing there, a person unknown to any of the members, a stranger who doesn't attempt to speak with anyone, would immediately draw attention and excite speculation. Being scientific gentle-men, the members would almost certainly wish to satisfy their natural curiosity, forcing you into conversation, with every word you utter and every half-truth you invent about your background bringing you closer to discovery and disaster. Think of the embarrassment—for your family, if not for you. The humiliation to your father.'

She stopped beside him, her eager expression fading as his arguments sank in. 'I suppose you're right,' she said dully after a moment. 'Ah, but how much I'd like to go! It would be an experience I would remember for ever, the highlight of my life. It's only a lecture, a few hours of time. But for one who will never be allowed to study at university, never permitted to practise as an engineer herself, could I not have at least those few hours to treasure?'

As tears formed in the corners of her eyes, Crispin felt terrible. He wouldn't change her into a man even if he could—what a waste of beauty that would be—but he did wish with all his heart that it wasn't imperative to prevent her from committing this folly. That there was a way to allow her the treat she longed for.

Knowing there was nothing he could offer to make up for its loss, he was struggling to think of a sympathetic reply while she impatiently swiped the tears from face. 'I suppose that's it, then. Unless…'

She rounded to face him, her eyes once again bright with excitement. 'You are probably right.

If I were to go by myself, I'd be forced to have a minimum of conversation. I couldn't just slip in and remain unnoticed. But if I were to trail along behind someone else... Someone with a well-known interest in railways, someone of importance who would become the focus of everyone's attention, the obscure young clerk attending with him would be ignored.'

'No,' he said flatly.

'At least consider it!'

'I wouldn't bring a mere clerk, who could have little interest in the lecture.'

'I could be...your young cousin from the country, who's become interested in railways because of your investments. Your bashful country cousin who has little to say for himself.'

'No.'

'Please! I'll practise in front of a mirror so I can stay straight as stick as I walk. I'll keep my head down and mumble and slip into the background. The other engineers will be curious to meet you, talk with you. They'd have no interest in a bumbling young cousin who has neither expertise nor money to invest. And...and if the ruse were discovered, you could say you'd done it on a lark. Or a wager! Everyone knows society gentlemen agree to do all sorts of outrageous things on a bet. Even then, no one would discover who I really am. And none of the engineers travel in your social circles, where they might comment on the escapade to someone who knows you. They might shake their heads over you showing such a lack of respect for their organisation, but no one would be offended enough to refuse accepting your investment in their next venture. It could work!'

'Even if I agreed, how do you think you'd manage to don your "costume"? You could hardly dress in gentlemen's attire in your own bedchamber—assuming Mary would let you out the door—and then waltz down the stairway and out into the street without some gawking servant noticing you.'

'I intend to bring the garments to Father's office. Walk out with him when he leaves for his consultation, circle around to the back entrance and change in the storeroom, then exit the same way. The room contains just surveying equipment and measuring rods, so unless there is an active survey going on, no one goes into it. Please say you'll do this! Whatever happens, even if I should be discovered, no harm will come to you, and there's only a very small chance that my true identity would be discovered to embarrass my family. I've never wanted anything as badly as I want this, perhaps my one chance to attend a scientific lecture. Please?'

Her pleading face was hard to resist. What he'd

read of Miss Jacson's book and her eloquent comments about the discrimination against education for women made it impossible for him not to sympathise with the restrictions that restrained her. It would be such a small thing—one lecture stolen from the whole realm of study denied her.

He was an idiot to even consider it.

While he dithered, trying to get his tongue to produce the refusal his common sense told him was imperative, her expression altered again, from eager to guarded. 'Never mind, Dellamont. I shouldn't have asked. Please forget that I did.'

Her swift change from entreaty to capitulation set alarm bells clanging in his head. 'Promise me you're not going to attempt this on your own.' When she said nothing, merely gazed into the distance, he repeated, 'Promise me!'

'I can't,' she burst out. 'It's bad enough that my options are reduced to marrying someone in order to remain close to the work I love, that I'm barred from practising the trade even though I know I would do an excellent job, as good as Austin or any of Father's engineers. It's one small chance to seize something for my own. Besides, I don't see how it could be that disastrous. Even if I were discovered and word of it reached my sponsor—though I can't imagine how it could, since no one from the *ton* would be attending the lecture anyway—if my Season were to be abruptly ended, that would be fine with me. If I were caught out, I'd probably just be escorted out with heavy disapproval. No one there knows me and I doubt I'd be forced to reveal my name, so my family wouldn't be shamed. But instead of being passive, responding only to what others do, for once I could take the initiative and do what I wanted. I might even succeed.'

'You're going to do it anyway.'

She nodded. 'I think I will. I think I must.'

Should he participate in this folly, if he couldn't dissuade her? If he were present, he could at least protect her from abuse if she were discovered. He had to admit, he too would be interested in hearing Stephenson speak. He could do as she suggested, grandly announce his presence, make a short introduction of his 'cousin' and then monopolise attention, letting her recede into the background.

He was still an idiot to consider it.

But in the end, he was too worried about what might happen to her if she went on her own. While prudence screamed in protest and every instinct for self-preservation argued against it, he said, 'Very well. I'll attend and do my best to deflect any attention from you.'

She'd started walking back towards the house,

but at that, she stopped short and turned to face him, her eyes going wide. 'You will? Truly?'

'Haven't I told you several times—?'

'That you never say anything you don't mean?' she interrupted. Running back to him, such a look of joy on her face that for a moment he forgot the enormity of the folly he'd just committed himself to, she cried, 'Oh, Dellamont, thank you! I'll never forget this!'

'I should be clapped up in Bedlam. But if we're going to do this thing, we'd better figure out how.'

Placing her hand back on his arm, she said, 'Let's walk, then.'

For the next half-hour, they considered and discarded plans of action, finally coming up with one he thought had a reasonable chance of not ending in disaster. As they finished the final circuit, she turned to him, smiling. 'I'll see you outside the back entrance to Father's office tomorrow afternoon at three.'

'I'll wait until four. If you haven't appeared by then, I'll know something came up to prevent you.'

'Yes. Any later, and we would miss the beginning of the lecture.' She shook her head wonderingly. 'I can hardly believe it. I shall actually be able to attend a meeting of the Institution and listen to George Stephenson speak. It's a dream come true. I cannot thank you enough!'

Throwing her arms around Crispin, she went up on tiptoe and kissed him.

What she lacked in expertise, she made up for in enthusiasm. Response roaring through him, he pulled her closer, deepening the kiss, captivated by the honeyed taste of her, the rapture of pulling that luscious body close to his.

From a distant somewhere, a voice pitched with outrage seemed to be hailing them. As if suddenly awakening to what she'd done, Miss Cranmore stepped back abruptly, requiring him to release her.

'Now, Mary,' he heard her say, his wits still foggy with passion, 'you mustn't rail at Lord Dellamont. It was my fault.'

'Sure and it was,' the maid scolded, watching them from the turn in the pathway. 'What will his lordship be thinking of you? If you wasn't a lady grown, I'd take a switch to you. You come in now and let me fix your hair before it comes altogether unpinned.'

The glare Mary gave Crispin told him that Miss Cranmore's accepting blame for the kiss hadn't exonerated him completely. Standing with hands on hips, the maid waited for her charge to accompany her.

'I'd better soothe Mary's ruffled feelings, or

she'll not let me out of the house tomorrow,' she told him softly, a thrill in her voice. 'What an adventure it will be!'

'I only hope it won't end with me clapped up in Newgate,' Crispin muttered. 'Very well, I'll bid you good day, Miss Cranmore,' he said more loudly. Nodding to the maid, he walked towards the house.

As he passed Mary, she murmured, 'You will protect her, won't you?'

Surprised, he checked his step long enough to murmur back, 'You can count on it.'

Giving her head a satisfied shake, the maid walked over to collect her mistress.

Still somewhat astounded by what Miss Cranmore had induced him to agree to, a few minutes later Crispin found himself back outside on the street. Their careful planning having ensured as much as possible that disaster would be avoided, he would worry no more about it.

And despite the risk of all the things that could go wrong, he felt himself catching Miss Cranmore's enthusiasm, his thoughts turning instead to what a grand adventure it could be if all turned out right.

As long as he was able to steel his response to seeing her lovely body revealed in breeches. Fortunately, travelling to and from the meeting in his phaeton with his tiger up behind and sitting in the midst of a group listening to a lecture on bridge construction—with his 'cousin' dressed in male attire—ought to hold in check his desire to kiss her again.

Chapter Twelve

Precisely at three the following afternoon, Crispin pulled up his phaeton on the narrow alleyway behind Richard Cranmore's engineering office. Telling his tiger to walk the horses back towards the street, he hopped down from the carriage and walked to the door to the servants' entrance.

He trusted his tiger, but he'd rather the boy not know precisely where his passenger had come from—and have as little chance as possible to observe her walking.

A few minutes later, a slim figure emerged through the doorway. He halted, watching her as she walked towards him.

Even her brilliant smile couldn't distract him from the effect of seeing her in male garb. Saints preserve him, she looked every bit as fetching as he'd feared.

The fashionable coat nipped in snugly at her

waist, and though the tails belled out in the back to end below her thighs, masking her derrière, it was open in front to reveal trousers that hugged her belly and showed tantalising glimpses of her legs—her long, lovely, shapely legs. His mouth drying, his gaze traced them down to where the trouser legs topped polished shoes.

While he tried to unstick his tongue from the roof of his suddenly dry mouth, he noticed how stilted she was as she advanced towards him, obviously trying to remove the natural sway from her gait.

'What do you think?' she asked, beaming as she halted beside him.

'I think I just made the most colossal mistake of my life.'

Obviously too excited to be abashed by his comment, she only laughed. 'Now you're just being pettish. I thought I looked quite well—the style not so exaggerated as to draw the eye, but the suit well enough put together not to invite comment.'

Well put together. More like *excellently* put together. So excellently, he was seized by the desire to march her back into the storeroom and remove all those garments. Slowly, one by one, his hands cherishing her calves, thighs, belly…

Sweat broke out on his brow.

Dragging his thoughts from the physical, as he

forced himself to make a more objective inspection, he realised she was right. Her ensemble was stylish enough, but not too stylish, the garments neat and well made, but not extravagant enough to draw unusual notice. She'd got the tone just right, appearing to be exactly what she sought to be: a young, well-to-do but not flashy *ton* gentleman.

'I suppose you'll do,' he admitted at last. 'As long as none of the engineers looks at you too closely.'

As long as no gentleman's eye lingered on the unusually rounded swell beneath the neatly tied cravat or the extravagant curve of hips under her jacket.

'You'll be there to deflect attention and make sure no one gives me a second glance,' she replied. 'I'd worried over how to camouflage my excessive amount of hair, but I've managed to sweep it up underneath and pin the top down over the fullness, most of it hidden under the wide neck of the cravat, so if I remove my hat carefully, I think I can get by. I can't thank you enough for this! But shouldn't we be going? It would be better not to be the focus of too many glances by arriving late.'

Nodding, Crispin paced to the end of the alley and waved to his tiger, who turned the horses and brought the equipage to them. About to offer her a hand up, he remembered just in time and watched instead as she grabbed the strap and jumped up herself.

'Wonderful,' she murmured to him after he'd climbed up and set the team in motion. 'So much easier than if I'd been wearing skirts!'

He gave her a warning look, jerking his chin towards the tiger perched behind them and hoping the clatter of wheels on the cobblestones had muffled her words. 'Better start being bashful and monosyllabic now.'

Nodding, she slid a finger across her mouth in a 'my lips are sealed' gesture—which, alas, only recalled his attention to that tempting mouth.

Clearly unaware of the havoc her apparel was causing him, as merry as a child given a bag of sweetmeats, she grinned at him, her eyes dancing and her whole body almost vibrating with excitement.

While his vibrated with tension of a different sort.

Or rather, two sorts—the sensual response he must hold in check, and dread over how this episode would end.

All too soon, they arrived at the institution's headquarters, a fine Georgian building in Westminster. *The game begins*, he told himself as he watched her hop down, then climbed down himself. After sending his tiger off to a nearby posting inn with enough coins to buy himself some ale and a meat pie, Crispin turned towards Miss Cranmore.

She'd been practising keeping silent during their drive, but now he could feel her anticipation as they stood facing the entry stairs. 'Ready?'

'Beyond ready,' she answered.

Reminding himself not to offer her his arm, he walked up the steps beside her, having to check a grin when, halting before the entry door, he heard her long, awed sigh. 'Don't you dare swoon on me,' he murmured.

She turned to him with a chuckle. 'That wouldn't be very politic, with me in trousers. No, I shall be serious, respectful, and defer completely to you.'

'If only you had deferred to my request not to go ahead with this enterprise,' he retorted.

'Don't be a spoilsport. Shall we enter?'

He anticipated that two of the greatest hurdles would be getting past the attendant who took their hats and canes and then the member taking their tickets. To his relief, both events occurred without incident, Miss Cranmore's hair remaining securely hidden as she doffed her hat, and neither man sparing her a glance.

They proceeded into the vestibule in front of the assembly room where the lecture would take place, Crispin halting at the edge of the room so that Miss Cranmore would be able to stand behind him by the wall, partially shielded from view. The few engineers already present, who stood around chatting, nodded to acknowledge their arrival.

Then, as he'd feared and anticipated, one man detached himself from the group and came over to them.

'Lord Dellamont, isn't it?' he asked. When Crispin nodded, he continued, 'I thought I recognised you. I sat in the gallery near you during Parliament's debate about the Great Western. Did you decide to invest in it?'

'I did.'

'A chancy endeavour. But Isambard Brunel and Richard Cranmore are excellent engineers. I'd give good odds for it being successfully built, although it remains to be seen if construction costs can be kept low enough to make it profitable. But here, I'm forgetting my manners. I'm Forsythe, Reginald Forsythe, a member of the Institution's Board of Directors. How pleased I am to welcome such a forward-thinking investor to our lecture today—and your companion, of course,' he added, gesturing to Miss Cranmore.

'John Mathews, my young cousin from the country. He's still at school, but has become infected by my enthusiasm for railways.'

The three exchanged bows, Crispin checking a smile over how correct Miss Cranmore's was, just the right angle and degree of bend. She must indeed have been practising in front of her mirror.

Several other gentlemen come over to join them, Forsythe performing the introductions, before talk turned into a general discussion about the tunnels, bridges and viaducts the assorted engineers were building or in the process of designing.

Crispin asked a question here, made a comment there, ensuring the conversation flowed briskly. As he'd hoped, the fully engaged gentlemen completely ignored the shy young man standing behind him.

He didn't dare look at her himself. She was probably bursting to take part in the conversation. He didn't want to do anything that might encourage her to abandon her prudent silence.

Once he'd decided they'd chatted long enough, he said, 'The lecture will begin soon. We'd better take our seats, don't you think?'

With a murmur of agreement, the group set off. Ever conscious of the potential for discovery, Crispin chose chairs at the side of room furthest from the entry door, where they would not be immediately seen by everyone who came in or went out, in a shadowy corner furthest removed from the pale afternoon light filtering in through two large windows.

A few minutes later, the chairman of the lecture series rose to welcome them and introduce their speaker. A stir went through the room—Crispin heard Miss Cranmore's sharp intake of breath—as the guest lecturer walked in.

A tall, genial, grey-haired man, George Stephenson greeted the group, nodding to several he recognised in the audience. Speaking in his north country accent with the assurance of vast expertise, he launched into a discussion of the factors to be considered in the design of bridge spans, noting the advantages and disadvantages of construction wholly with stone versus a combination of stone and iron.

It was definitely a lecture for a professional practitioner, including terms and calculations with which, despite Crispin's investigations into railway building, he was not entirely familiar. But when he stole a glance at Miss Cranmore, she was gazing raptly at the speaker, occasionally nodding at something he said, evidently comprehending every word.

Crispin's already elevated opinion of her intellectual gifts rose even higher.

After a while, the ever-present worry of discovery abating as the lecture continued, Crispin relaxed enough to be able to focus on the speech himself. Though he hadn't sufficient training to appreciate all the mathematical details involved in the construction of arches and spans, he found them as fascinating at Miss Cranmore. Who, when he once again glanced her way, looked as if she were trying to memorise the lecturer's words so she might rush home and transfer his comments to notes on paper.

At length, Stephenson concluded his talk to enthusiastic applause. When the committee chairman stood and announced their speaker would entertain questions from the audience, Crispin leaned over to murmur, 'We would be wise to take our leave now, before everyone files out.'

Miss Cranmore gave a little sigh, but nodded. 'I'd love to stay until the last possible minute, but you're correct. It would be better to get away while our luck still holds.'

Several other members had also stood and begun moving around, so they attracted no notice as they walked around the back edge of the room and out the entry door. In the deserted vestibule, they collected their hats and canes from the attendant.

Crispin was about to walk out when Miss Cranmore halted, requiring him to pause beside her. 'It's the Menai Bridge,' she said, pointing at a framed print on the wall. 'Papa told me about it. Quite a feat of engineering!'

'Looks impressive,' he agreed.

'Thomas Telford designed it to link the island

of Anglesey to the mainland. The island's principal source of income was the sale of cattle, and before the bridge, with the current so swift ferry crossing was difficult, they often tried to have the poor beasts swim across the strait—losing many of their valuable animals. So the bridge was a boon not just to the cattlemen, but to their herds. It was one of the first bridges to incorporate both stone supports and iron suspension elements.' She sighed. 'Isn't it beautiful?'

She spoke of the bridge with the awed admiration other women might express when viewing a beautiful gown or a necklace of sparkling gems. How truly singular she was!

Approaching voices spurring him from his contemplation of her, he said, 'We'd better keep going. The members are starting to emerge, so we need to make our escape.'

Nodding, she quickly walked out beside him, then slowed her pace as they strolled to the nearby hostelry where he retrieved his phaeton. Flipping his tiger another coin and then taking the reins, Crispin said, 'You can have the rest of the day to yourself, Tim. Take a hackney back when you're ready. I'll drive the team home.'

'Don't you need me to walk the team for you when you stop...somewhere?' the boy asked with a glance at Miss Cranmore.

'No. I'll be bringing them straight back to the stables after I drop my, um, cousin off at his lodgings.'

The boy grinned. After tipping his hat to them, he said, 'Good day to you then, my lord—and to you, miss.'

While Miss Cranmore's eyes widened in shock, Crispin groaned as the lad strolled off, whistling. 'Tim is a former street rat who doesn't miss much,' he told her, not altogether surprised the tiger's sharp eyes had penetrated her disguise. 'Fortunately, he's in my employ, so he won't say anything. Even so, I didn't want him to make note of the building to which I bring you back.'

Miss Cranmore gave a dismissive wave, apparently already recovered from that momentary worry. 'I'm sure he will cause no trouble. In any event, the risk was all worth it. Wasn't Stephenson's lecture glorious? I could have listened to him for ever! I only wish he'd brought a slate so he could have worked out for us some of the problems of slope and turn radius he was describing.'

'I actually understood more of it than I'd expected. I suppose you comprehended everything?'

She shook her head excitedly, confirming his appraisal of her abilities. 'Oh, yes. How I wish I could attend all the Institution's lectures! But I must not be greedy. I'm already for ever in your debt for allowing me this one glorious, marvellous afternoon of freedom. In fact,' she added, turning to him, 'you needn't drive me home. I should like to walk. Maybe I'll even stop at a tavern and order some ale. Because I can! It's such a delight to stroll about in trousers. I never realised just how cumbersome and confining it is, being restricted by yards of skirts and petticoats. To say nothing of the even greater restrictions on where a female can go and what she can do. I feel so...free!'

Laughing, she wiggled her legs, then leapt in the air and spun in a circle. 'I must figure out a way to wear trousers more often.'

'Heaven forbid,' he objected with a shudder, trying to keep his gaze focused on her face and not on those beguiling legs. He was certainly *not* going to tell her that his irrepressible sister often wore breeches when riding at Montwell Glen.

'I'll be sending up prayers of thanks for the rest of my days that we got though that episode unscathed. And if females started wearing trousers, the effect would be disastrous. Men all over London would be walking into lampposts, too distracted to pay attention to where they were going while they stared at all those nether limbs.'

She stopped short and looked over at him. 'Have you been staring at my nether limbs?'

'Blatantly. I was so overcome, I hardly heard a word of the lecture.'

That was skirting dangerously close to the truth, but given his teasing tone, she didn't believe him—thankfully. 'Liar. How can I ever thank you enough for providing what will remain one of the highlights of my life! I'm even prepared to admit I probably couldn't have carried it off—at least, not as successfully—without your help. Now, I intend to find that tavern and enjoy an ale, so with my final thanks, I'll set off.'

She truly meant to stroll off on her own. As she passed him, he caught her shoulder with his free hand. 'Here now, you can't go wandering around by yourself! Tim's not the only one with a critical eye. You've been lucky enough to pass unnoticed so far, when you weren't subjected to much attention, but you can't count on that luck holding if you jaunt all over London. What if someone suspected, or someone jostled you and your hair tumbled down?'

'The cat would be in with the pigeons then,' she admitted with a sigh. 'Please, can I have just one ale? I cannot bear the prospect of returning just yet. Besides, I need to delay long enough to make sure Papa has finished his meeting, dropped his papers off at the office and returned home. I don't want to risk going back in to change if there's a chance of encountering him.'

'Won't he make sure the office is locked up before he leaves? How will you get in?'

She grinned and patted her waistcoat pocket. 'I brought a key. An engineer needs to think out every detail of a project. So you see, I can't go back just yet.'

'Very well, but you'll have to suffer my escort. I'm not setting you loose in London on your own. Hop in, Miss Cranmore.'

'That sounds very formal. After all we've succeeded in doing today, don't you think you should call me "Marcella"? At least when there's no one about to overhear.'

'Not while you are wearing men's garments,' he retorted.

After she climbed up, laughing, he gathered the reins and hopped into the vehicle, searching his brain for a tavern that was respectable, but not too fashionable or close to anywhere he might run into someone he knew. Any *ton* acquaintance he chanced to encounter would look far more closely at his 'cousin's' attire than the preoccupied engineers had. And most of them knew his family tree well enough to be suspicious of some unknown relation from the country. He'd rather not have to invent some elaborate fiction that might come back to bite him.

He finally decided on a small tavern not far from Parliament that was frequented by travellers, drovers and common folk who served the members of Parliament, rather than by the legislators themselves. It also boasted a small back terrace set off from the busy road by a stand of evergreens. If his luck held, they could bring their tankards to that sheltered spot and converse with no one nearby to watch or overhear.

He drove to the location, handed the phaeton over to a stable boy in the attached livery, then walked in with her beside him to order their ale. He felt a prickling all over his skin, so sensitive was he to possible observation, but as at the lecture, the two labourers at the bar and the few gathered at a scattering of tables paid them no attention.

Still, he breathed a heartfelt sigh of relief when, mugs in hand, he was able to lead Marcella to the deserted side terrace.

'It's lovely here,' she said, looking about. 'You know the inn well, I take it?'

'The tap man's wife makes an excellent stew. It's fortunate we arrived before workmen break for the day to take their supper, for it can get quite crowded. I often stop here for a bowl and a mug of ale after a Parliamentary debate, if I want to mull over what's been presented alone, without a chattering multitude around me. The others attending the debate generally take their refreshment at more fashionable establishments.'

She was silent for a long time, her expression pensive. 'I should have been born a boy. I did what I could to comfort Papa after my brother's death, but nothing would have helped him recover like knowing he had another heir. Someone he could send to Edinburgh to study as he had, someone to train up and eventually turn over his business to. Oh, I've been terribly fortunate that he was willing to share as much of his career with me as he has. But even so, I was never...adequate. Never enough.'

Never adequate. Never enough. The words resonated through Crispin. Hadn't he so often felt that way with a father he could never please? A mother whose unhappiness he'd tried to ease but ultimately couldn't prevent?

She paused to take a sip of her ale. 'After this taste of freedom, it will be even harder for me to reconcile myself to playing that lesser role.'

Disturbed by her melancholy, Crispin didn't know what to say to console her. It *was* regrettable that her brilliance and drive were destined to be wasted on domestic tasks that didn't interest her. 'You'll just have to marry that man who will make you happy to be his wife.'

'I suppose so.' But she didn't sound as enthused about her engineer as she had when discussing him previously. After taking a last sip of her ale, she set down her mug. 'I must steel myself to return. Back to propriety. Back to performing my *proper* role,' she concluded, a bitter note in her voice.

While he watched, unhappy at her distress, she walked over to the screen of tall evergreens. 'Sometimes I wish I could stay hidden away, like this garden.'

'I wouldn't have brought you to the lecture if I'd known it would make you sad.'

'No, be glad you did. Despite having to go back, I'm still so grateful that I got to attend. You've given me the only taste of what life might have been I shall likely ever have. I shall be fiercely grateful for that for ever. More grateful than you can imagine.'

He walked over to her, trying to think of something consoling to say, when abruptly she turned to face him. 'This grateful.' Lifting her chin, she reached up, pulled his head down and kissed him.

The desire he'd been containing all day strained his control to the breaking point. While he fought to keep it from disintegrating completely, he couldn't help responding to the kiss he'd wanted too much for too long.

Just a bit deeper, just a bit longer, his senses urged. She didn't help his unravelling restraint by meeting his lips with fervent eagerness, pressing her body against his.

He wrapped his arms around her, his tongue tracing her lips. When she opened for him, he couldn't keep himself from plunging inside, seeking her tongue and tangling it with his while he taught her the sweet dance of advance and retreat.

A loud screech of carriage brakes and the shouting of two carters whose vehicles had almost collided on the road beyond finally recalled him from madness. Breathing hard, he broke away.

Madness it was. Not just kissing her, which was madness enough. But kissing her when anyone from the tavern who happened to walk on to the terrace would think he'd just been passionately embracing another man.

She stood staring at him, eyes foggy with desire, her breathing rapid as his own.

'Good thing this place is so secluded,' he said when he could catch his breath. 'Not that I have any personal objections myself, but had anyone seen us, I might have got myself arrested.'

Initial puzzlement was followed by comprehension, then her face blushed. 'Better arrested than married,' she retorted, 'which is what could have happened if I were in female garb. One is only temporary, the other permanent. In any event, I suppose it's time to leave. Papa should be on his way home by now.'

Still unsettled, he gathered the mugs and let her walk with him back into the tavern to deposit them.

Though he didn't want to let her go. He wanted

to take her back to her father's office and follow her into that storeroom, kiss her again and caress the full length of those lovely legs whose presence titillated him with every step she took.

A lady's ball gown might get the prize for best displaying bare shoulders, the tempting upper curve of breasts. But a gown couldn't compare to the breath-stealing impact of imagining how a pair of snug knit riding breeches would outline that trim bottom, rounded hips and slim legs. It was a wonder his overheated brain didn't melt at the image.

Still fighting to beat back his unslaked desire, he walked with her to the stables, retrieved his phaeton, then unashamedly took his last chance to frankly stare at her trouser-clad form as she pulled herself up into the vehicle.

Turning to him after he'd set the vehicle in motion, she said with a brave smile, 'We had a splendid adventure, didn't we?'

'Once I get you safely back into your father's office, see you emerge dressed in your normal attire and sent home in a hackney, then I'll agree it has been.'

'An adventure that will remain our secret.'

He liked the idea of having a secret she shared only with him. A rare, unprecedented experience, just as unique and exceptional as she was.

A woman who made him burn with a desire as fierce as his admiration for her talent and intellect.

He'd better be glad she was soon to return to her own world—before she tempted him beyond all prudence.

'I don't know,' he replied, keeping his voice light, wanting to prevent a return of her melancholy, now that that adventure was almost over. 'I'm not sure how I'm going to be able to see you in skirts again without remembering how you look in trousers.'

She laughed, as he'd hoped she would. 'Perhaps you'll see me like that again some day.'

Unlikely, much as he would love it. He'd love to see much more of her—without the gown or the trousers. He could envision having an animated discussion of bridges and railway viaducts over dinner…then carrying her up to his chamber and making love to her all through the night.

Every night.

Shocked at the direction his thoughts had taken, he quickly reminded himself that such a scenario would require the one sacrifice he wasn't willing to make for her, or anyone. Marriage.

While he wrestled with his thoughts, Miss Cranmore remained silent on the drive back, in marked contrast to her excitement on the way to the lecture.

'Are you still regretting that glimpse into a life

you cannot have?' he asked quietly as he pulled up the team in the alleyway behind the office.

'No. Not really. Well, maybe a little. But I would never have had even this taste—except for you.' She put a hand up, caressing his cheek. Unable to prevent himself, he put his hand on hers to hold it against him.

'What a marvel you are,' she said softly. 'I can't imagine anyone else who would have done that for me. Not Papa, certainly not Mr Gilling. I'll never forget it. If ever I can do you such a signal service, you have only to ask.'

It was on the tip of his tongue to ask her— what? *Stay with me? Let me make love to you?*

Desire really had addled his brain, he thought, allowing the ugly memories of his unhappy youth to overwhelm the enticing vision of her wrapped in his arms. If he were to risk marrying her, it was highly unlikely their initial harmony would last. How much more bitter would it be to begin on such a note of joy, only to have that harmony disintegrate over years of life's disappointments and inevitable disagreements into a mutual indifference, even active dislike?

No, it wasn't worth the risk. When he married, he would choose someone who'd fulfil his minimum expectations. A woman who'd wed him to become a countess, who would run his household with efficiency, produce heirs—and leave him to experience the highs and lows of life on his own. He'd not be responsible for ensuring her happiness, or she his.

A lifetime of failing to protect his mother's had taught him what an impossible task that would be.

Still, he hated to end what had been a magical interlude. 'Are you sure you can get home safely? I'd feel better if drove you.'

'That wouldn't be prudent. I took a hackney to the office. Papa thinks I was going afterwards to Lady Arlsley's, while Lady Arlsley believes I was to return home after tea with Papa. How could I explain turning up under your escort? No, better that I return in a hackney, as I always do after visiting Upper Brook Street.'

'I'll linger here, then, and keep watch until you are in that hackney on your way home.'

'Watch out for me, like you did at the musicale?'

'We protect each other, don't we? That's our bargain, isn't it—Marcella.'

She smiled. 'So it is, Dellamont.'

'My family calls me "Crispin".'

'Then I would be honoured… Crispin.'

She slipped down from the vehicle and hurried over to unlock the door to the servants' entrance.

Crispin hopped down as well and went to his horses' heads, rubbing their noses and speaking softly. He idled there until, a short time later,

Marcella emerged, once again properly attired in skirts. He led the team beside her until they reached the nearby hackney stand, then waited until she climbed into a vehicle and waved good-bye to him through the window.

Watching her drive off, he was able finally to completely relax.

It *had* been an extraordinary adventure. Even now, he marvelled that he'd had the audacity and foolhardiness to go through with it. Although once he learned she was adamant about attending the lecture, he didn't see what else he could have done. He had to protect her and make sure she didn't come to grief.

A warm feeling expanded in his chest at knowing he had given her a memory she would treasure.

Now that the threat of disaster was over, he was beginning to think he would treasure it, too. He must set his to mind to figuring out how to guarantee he'd have the enjoyment and stimulation of meeting with her at her father's office after their society bargain concluded.

Because he didn't dare allow himself to contemplate sharing anything more.

Chapter Thirteen

Two afternoons later, Marcella rode in the carriage with Lady Arlsley out of London towards Norwalk House in Highgate Village. Lady Norwalk's annual garden party to display the beauty of her extensive grounds was one of the highlights of the early Season, her sponsor told her, the plantings magnificent and the view over the city to the south and the forests to the north incomparable.

A country girl at heart, Marcella was looking forward to some fresh air and perhaps a longer walk than was possible in Lady Arlsley's small city garden.

A long walk with Lord Dellamont, who'd assured her he planned to attend.

It would be a relief to be able to converse freely with him, something she'd not been able to do at the crowded rout last night. She had little more than a week left of the month she'd promised herself to endure the Season. Though she was tempted to extend that deadline in order to enjoy more of Dellamont's company, it would be wiser to hold to it…lest she grow fonder of him than she was willing to admit, to him or herself.

There was also the problem of her apparent inability to resist kissing him whenever an opportunity arose.

Yes, she'd been beyond thankful for the gift he'd given her by agreeing to accompany her to the Stephenson lecture. But she was too honest to attribute her impulsive kiss in Lady Arlsley's garden—or the longer, more lingering, more passionate one on the tavern terrace—simply to a need to thank him.

The bald truth was she desired him, and had practically from the moment she first saw him. An attraction that had only deepened over time, while her consciousness of his presence when he was near grew ever more acute.

She'd wanted his kisses, and thrilled at the response she evoked in him. She'd never felt anything more wonderful than soft pressure of his tongue caressing hers, setting off explosions of sensation all over her body and a heated ache at her very centre.

Though she'd never experienced such feelings before, she was well aware of the dangers of indulging them. Were she and Dellamont interested in a relationship closer than friendship, she might be willing to risk ever more intimate moments. Like the feel of his hands all over her body that she dreamed about as she tossed and turned at night.

But with him uninterested in marriage and her unwilling to consider wedding into the *ton*, even if he changed his mind about wedlock, continually subjecting herself to a temptation she'd already demonstrated she was ill equipped to resist could end in disaster.

Disaster to her reputation...and her heart, which found him ever more appealing.

She couldn't in good conscience try to entice Austin Gilling into marrying her if she'd already given herself—or her affections—to someone else. She'd be a fool to risk losing the possibility of securing Gilling's love and commitment to savour a passion she found incomparable—and that an experienced gentleman like Dellamont, if he thought about his reaction at all, probably considered only the normal physical response of a healthy male for an attractive female. Pleasant, but nothing out of the ordinary.

It was time to return to her rightful place, to limited goals that were capable of being realised. Return this Cinderella to the ash-strewn hearth of domestic reality and leave the fairy-tale prince alone in his glittering world.

Despite how incredibly sweet and stirring it was to have his lips on hers, his arms wrapped around her, she must prevent it from happening again.

Besides, much as she desired him, she admired and cared for him even more. If she were sensible enough to resist his physical appeal, she would protect the possibility of maintaining her friendship with an exceptional man who appreciated the things she loved. Who accepted and even admired her unconventional talents.

Since, much as her heart sometimes imagined otherwise, she knew nothing more than friendship was feasible.

So she must concentrate on doing whatever was necessary to ensure she could continue meeting her dear friend after she abandoned society. At her father's office, at least, and perhaps also riding in the park, properly chaperoned by her groom.

It was simply unthinkable now that she could give Crispin up completely.

Despite knowing that trading his almost daily escort for more occasional meetings was the smart, the prudent, the *only* course, the prospect still made her melancholy.

At least she had the event today, a few more balls and a handful of morning rides to look forward to before she was forced to reduce their interactions.

After the carriage halted, Marcella followed her sponsor out and through the gate into the walled Norwalk House gardens, curtsying to the hostess who'd set up a reception line just inside the door. After being directed to refreshment tables placed out on the lawn and given a map of the various paths and allées leading to a rose garden not yet in bloom, garden rooms of spring bulbs in a variety of hues, and several evergreen walks that led to a small maze, she accompanied her sponsor over to a group of Lady Arlsley's friends.

She stood at Lady Arlsley's elbow after greetings had been exchanged, smiling politely, hoping Crispin would arrive soon and that Lord Hoddleston would not arrive at all.

She'd encountered the Baron at each of the last two evening entertainments they'd attended, a ball and last night's rout. Though she couldn't avoid dancing with him, she'd been careful to make sure she was promised to someone else—last night, to Crispin—for the waltzes. But though the country dances kept him at a safe distance, he still walked too close to her as he escorted her on or off the floor and retained her hands too long after the movements of the dance dictated he release them. She made little attempt at conversation, leaving it to him when she was forced to endure his presence.

He could have no doubt about her lack of enthusiasm for his company, but still he persisted. And when she wasn't dancing or talking with him, she felt his gaze fixed on her from across the room—the greedy eyes of a cat waiting to pounce on a mouse.

It was fortunate that she would quit society soon, before she felt forced to cut him, regardless of what Lady Arlsley might say. There seemed no other way to avoid him, since he persisted in asking her to dance and stopping by to converse, despite her several times baldly asserting that she had no intention of marrying him.

To which he inevitably replied that he'd wait to see what her answer was after Dellamont dropped her—an event he predicted to be imminent every time he spoke with her.

An event, sadly, that *was* imminent, if not in the way Hoddleston meant.

To her relief, she spotted the Viscount's tall form striding in through the entrance gate. Ready to be rescued, she turned to greet him as he walked over to join her.

Smiling, he bowed and paid his compliments to Lady Arlsley and her friends before turning to Marcella. 'A lovely day, isn't it? Lady Arlsley, might I be permitted to take your charge for a turn around the garden?' He held up his guide. 'I have my map, so I promise I won't get us lost.'

'As long as you keep to the main pathways where other couples are strolling. Do avoid the temptation of exploring one of the deserted side-allées,' Lady Arlsley said with a knowing look. 'Enjoy your walk.'

Putting her hand on his arm as they set off, Marcella murmured, 'Not exactly overwhelmed with concern for my reputation, was she, sending us off alone with thinly veiled hints encouraging impropriety? I thought, with Mary not present, she'd insist on accompanying us. Apparently she'd rather us take advantage of her permission to do something compromising.'

'With hopes that another strolling couple would see and report it.'

'The sooner to have me affianced or disgraced and off her hands.' Marcella sighed. 'I shall have to be on my best behaviour, then—something I've signally failed to be thus far.'

'A delightful failure I wish I could encourage,' Crispin said wryly. 'But that wouldn't be a wise move—for either of us.'

'How unfortunate that wisdom must be so—*unfulfilling.*'

'Whereas rashness promises so much delight?' He sighed, too, and pressed her hand. 'We must both be on our best behaviour—no matter how difficult that is.'

It was probably unmaidenly to ask such a brazen question, but she couldn't help it. 'You also find it...difficult?'

He halted, looking down at her, the intensity of his gaze unmistakable. 'I've found resisting you difficult from the moment we met.'

Both surprised and gratified by his response, she could think of nothing to reply but a brainless, 'Oh.'

'Exactly,' he said, making her chuckle. 'So, it *is* a lovely day, the sun bright with the hint of summer to come and that azure sky dotted with lazy white clouds. And Lady Arlsley, however ignoble her motives, has allowed us the chance to talk freely. Let us enjoy that gift and not mourn... what we dare not have.'

The sun seemed brighter, the day warmer in his company, she thought, that now-familiar ripple of response going through her as she placed her hand on his arm. Walking side by side through the garden, virtually alone, was an intimacy that *could* easily lead to her wanting more. Another reason to limit herself in future to intellectual discussions in her father's office or forays on horseback, both of them mounted on their respective steeds, a safe distance apart.

'Are you enjoying this event?' he asked, startling her out of her reflections.

'I like being in London, but I've missed the country. Though we spend a good deal of time in the city, accompanying Papa when he's working in the office here, I grew up riding the trails and rambling along the paths of my grandfather's country house outside Tynemouth. Mother and I always return there when Papa is off on his frequent travels.'

'Indeed? I thought you lived all the year in London.'

'Oh, no! My father has another office in Newcastle, and we almost always spend the summers at Faircastle House. Papa says the city isn't salubrious in the hot summer months.'

'Fleeing the city in the heat? See, you do share something with the *ton*, who also retreat to their country estates after Parliament adjourns. Do you enjoy garden parties like this one at your grandfather's house?'

She shook her head. 'No, it's my first time to attend a *petit déjeuner champêtre*—such a pretentious name, by the way! Although I find it ridiculous to refer to an event held in the afternoon as a "breakfast".'

Crispin chuckled. 'Ah, but for *ton* fashionables who attend balls until the wee hours or gamble until dawn, this probably is when they normally breakfast.'

'If so, another reason to dislike the group. I admit, the setting is lovely, but when I look at all the chairs that have been placed around the grounds, the tables brought out and loaded with refreshments that servants must scurry back and forth from the kitchens to replenish, all I can think about is how much trouble it must have been for the staff to set up and serve this event. I'm sure the maids and footmen with sore feet and aching arms wish the affair could have been held inside in one of the salons or ballrooms already furnished with chairs and tables that wouldn't have to be moved. Where the kitchens in which the refreshments are prepared are much closer to the places where they are being served.'

'Like the French, are you, ready to abolish the monarchy and create a republic?' he teased.

'No, just someone who appreciates the hard work of my staff and doesn't wish to make it unnecessarily more difficult. But then,' she added, 'Lady Arlsley told me Lady Norwalk takes great pride in the excellence, grand scale and uniqueness of her affair. She—and aristocrats like her—probably never spare a thought for the extra work she creates for her servants. Yet another reason to be glad I—and my egalitarian beliefs—shall soon be exiting aristocratic society.'

'Ah, but if Lady Norwalk had greater sensibility, we'd not be walking here with this backdrop of glorious spring flowers. The ladies do look like brilliant blooms or colourful butterflies beside the allées of greenery, don't they?'

'I grant you it makes a pretty picture. But the ladies could stroll just as prettily if the tables and refreshments remained inside.'

'Point taken. Have you seen more of Lord Charles? I didn't notice him hovering near you at the rout last night.'

Marcella sighed. 'It appears you were right; he *was* about to make me a declaration. I tried to refuse him as gently as I could, telling him how honoured I was by his esteem, but that I couldn't consider anything warmer than friendship. I hope I didn't wound his sensibilities too much.'

'I can understand his disappointment. He's unlikely ever to find another treasure like you, with the sense to appreciate his good character and the kindness to overlook his lack of wit.'

His assessment sent a shock of surprise through her. Did Crispin think her a 'treasure'? She was about to ask him, then remembered he'd already told her several times he never said anything he didn't mean.

She felt immensely pleased to know she figured so highly in his esteem. Of course, she esteemed him pretty highly too. If only…

She jerked her imaginings to a halt before they could venture down that futile path. Not only was Dellamont neither an engineer nor someone from her world, he'd already assured her several times he did not wish to marry. What he wanted to treasure from her was *friendship*.

If she were lucky, Austin would end up deciding to make her an offer. She'd be able to wrap herself in his cherished, long-familiar affection. An affection whose warmth would insulate her from the chill of losing her close association with Dellamont.

She gave herself a mental shake, telling herself not to waste the time she did have being melancholy about the changes that must happen in the future. It was a beautiful day, she was walking through a lovely country garden accompanied by an enticingly handsome escort she liked and admired. How foolish of her to be anything but joyful!

While she ordered her emotions, Crispin had paused to consult the map. 'We're very near where the path leads off to the maze. What do you think, my engineering marvel? Do you believe you could figure out the pathways and beat me to the centre?'

'I've never been in a maze before, but I'm ready to give it a try,' she said, glad to be distracted by his light-hearted challenge.

He swept out a hand. 'Ladies first. Choose your pathway, I'll take the other. After we find the centre and make our way back, you'll have had enough exertion that even you will be ready to snag an outdoor glass of punch from those poor overworked servants.'

'Perhaps,' she admitted. 'Shall we be off?'

'After you. I'll be waiting for you at the centre.'

'No,' she said, waving a finger at him. '*I'll* be waiting there for *you*.'

Marcella proceeded quickly to the first corner, then once out of view of Crispin, halted and went up on tiptoe, trying to see if she could get a sense of the way the pathways were laid out and what might prove the shortest route to the centre.

But the hedges were too tall and grew too thickly together. She would have to proceed by guess.

Ten minutes later, after being confounded by several dead ends and having to reverse course, her excitement grew as she realised she had to be approaching the centre. She turned one of the ever-tightening corners—and almost collided with Lord Hoddleston.

Stopping short, she stiffened with dislike. Standing before her was the very last person she wanted to meet along the twisting pathways.

'Lord Hoddleston,' she said coldly, giving him a curtsy. 'You must have already found the centre and be making your way out. Don't let me detain you.'

'I have, but it's you I wanted to find. I spied

you enter the maze with Dellamont, a number of others following in your wake. Which means I'm sure someone will come upon us shortly.'

As he stepped closer, she stepped away. But he continued until he'd backed her into the corner of one of the pathway's sharp curves. Truly annoyed now, she said, 'You may have found the centre, but I have not yet. It's not sporting of you to restrain me.'

'Oh, the game's not been sporting for some time. I admit, Dellamont has carried on his charade of courtship longer than I expected. Which makes me impatient. It's time to take matters out of his hands—into mine. Since that requires taking *you* into my hands, I'm quite willing to proceed.'

While he stood there, towering over her, heat in his eyes and a self-satisfied smile on his face, she said angrily, 'Don't you understand that you only make yourself ridiculous by persisting? I've already assured you I would not entertain your suit under any circumstances. So act as the gentleman you were born and release me.'

'But where you are concerned, I can no longer afford to be a gentleman. My creditors are becoming a bit too pressing, you see. But I'm not at all averse to speeding up the process. You'll be a prize I intend to savour, in addition to all that lovely dowry.'

He leaned down and grabbed her shoulders,

trying to force her into his arms. While she struggled to prevent it, he said, 'Fight if you want, but I'm too strong for you. The next couple that comes around the corner is going to see you in my arms and realise they've interrupted a scandalous tryst. Dellamont will bow out, and you will have to marry me.'

He was stronger than she'd expected, his arms longer than the ones she was using to try to push him away. She continued to resist, though, trying to manoeuvre into a position where she might stomp a heel on his instep, since he'd already moved too close for her to get a knee up to slam into his breeches.

He pushed harder, pressing her back until the trimmed ends of the clipped shrubs bit into her back, trying to kiss her as she jerked her face from side to side to avoid his mouth. She was considering how she might succeed in biting him if he managed to get his lips on hers when suddenly, his weight was lifted off her.

'Dellamont!' she cried, relief flooding her. Had anyone else come to her aid, news of the episode would quickly have become the subject of gossip—just as Hoddleston had planned.

By the thundercloud expression on Dellamont's face, it might become the subject of murder. After pulling the Baron away from her, he shoved the man in the opposite direction. Then, facing him, he said, 'I thought I'd warned you to cease troubling Miss Cranmore.'

'What Miss Cranmore and I do is none of your concern.'

'It becomes mine when you persist in paying her attentions she has told you repeatedly she does not want. And punishment becomes my concern when you trespass far beyond the line anyone who calls himself a gentleman should proceed with a lady.'

Before Hoddleston could reply—probably with another snide remark that Marcella was no lady—Crispin slammed a sharp left jab into the Baron's jaw, followed by a right hook that sent him tumbling to the ground.

'Need any further persuasion?' Crispin snarled. 'This time, hear me well. You are never to approach Miss Cranmore again or by heaven, our next encounter will be much more painful. If you see her walking down the street, you'd better cross to the other side. I'd advise you to concentrate instead on finding the gold you need from some other money pot.'

The Baron pulled himself up from the dust, glaring. Taking a handkerchief from his pocket, he wiped the trickle of blood from the corner of his mouth. 'You're going to be sorry you did this, Dellamont.'

'I'm only sorry I didn't do it sooner. Might I

suggest you quickly repair to your residence before anyone sees you and asks how you acquired that cut lip and swollen jaw?'

'You may think you've won. But this is not over.' Hoddleston transferred his gaze to Marcella, his expression furious. 'You'll pay for it, too.'

She shrank back from the venom in his eyes, doubly glad now that she would soon be back in her own world and safely out of his.

After brushing off his coat, Hoddleston set his hat back on his head and stalked off.

After the Baron had disappeared, Crispin blew out a breath. 'You are unharmed, I trust?'

'Y-yes,' she replied, surprised to find her voice shaky.

Then, to her shock and delight, the Viscount pulled her into his arms. 'I'm so sorry! I shouldn't have left you alone. I wouldn't have, if I'd known Hoddleston was on the grounds.'

Marcella snuggled against his chest, relishing the feeling of being safe and protected even as his nearness set off the usual swooping sensation in her stomach and tingling in her nerves. Determined to enjoy this forbidden embrace to the fullest before she had to bring it to an end, she allowed herself another few precious seconds before she pushed away.

'Truly, I am fine. You arrived before he succeeded in kissing me, which, if I didn't manage to bite him to prevent it, probably would have ended the situation anyway. If he'd placed his mouth on mine, I would almost certainly have cast up my accounts all over him.'

Shaking his head at her, Crispin laughed. 'No screaming or swooning?'

'I had thought to scream when he first seized me, but that might have attracted the witnesses he needed to be able to successfully compromise me in the eyes of the *ton*. Not that the idea of scandal bothers me, since I intend to quit their august company soon anyway, and good riddance. But I am grateful you found us first. I wouldn't have wanted to soil my gown with his blood.'

Crispin studied her for a moment. 'You truly are remarkable. But I'm confident you won't need rescuing again. I meant what I told him. If he comes anywhere near, you have only to tell me and I will deal with him. The outcome for him, I promise you, will be even less pretty. Now, are you certain you are recovered? I could take you back to Lady Arlsley with you claiming to feel faint from the sun and ask that she take you home.'

'I'd only have felt ill if Lord Hoddleston had succeeded in kissing me. I've lost my enthusiasm for the maze, though, so I'd like you to escort me back to the terrace, where we can remain well in sight of the other guests.' After hesitating a minute, she continued, 'Just in case someone might have seen or overheard something, I don't wish to make any mention of the…episode.'

'Understood. I'll take you back, fix you a plate and fetch some wine. We can sit in one of the tables beside the arbour where the orchestra is playing.'

She nodded agreement, and he walked her back, from time to time pressing her hand, as if wanting to make sure she had truly recovered. After he'd obtained the refreshments he promised, he took a seat beside her, his serious expression telling her he was still concerned, despite her assurances that she was fine.

'Truly, I'm not upset, so you may cease worrying. My remaining time in society will be short, and even if Lord Hoddleston should decide obtaining my dowry is worth risking your wrath, I don't think he'd actually attempt to despoil me. As I said, I care nothing for being "compromised", since the *ton*'s opinion of me carries no weight in my world. I would prefer that Mr Gilling not learn of Hoddleston's boorish behaviour. He, like you, might feel compelled to do something about it. The Baron might be no match for you, but I'm not sure how handy Mr Gilling is with his fists.'

'So you are determined to leave society…in little over a week?'

She nodded, unwilling to put her feelings into words.

How could she explain that she needed to leave before she started longing for more of his embraces? Before her control slipped, and she kissed him again? Before losing the near daily camaraderie they'd been sharing hurt too much?

Before she truly lost her heart to the unattainable Prince Charming?

She couldn't, of course.

'I shall have to inform Lady Arlsley soon,' she said instead. 'Her ladyship is going to be incredulous that anyone would voluntarily reject the privilege of mingling among the *ton*'s elite. Incredulous, and perhaps resentful that she was forced to tarnish her good name by having to sponsor my unworthiness.'

'I thought you said she'd be relieved not to be blamed for finding you an aristocratic husband.'

'That too.'

He hesitated and she held her breath, wondering what he might say. Express his own sorrow that their glorious bargain would soon end?

But when he did speak, he said only, 'Make sure I know which final events you will attend. I'll warn my mother and make plans to leave London immediately after. Perhaps I'll escort Mama back to Montwell Glen, so as to better shield her from my father's...disappointment. Shall we ride again tomorrow? If your time in the *ton* is about to end, we need to start making plans about how and when we can meet at your father's office.'

She was foolish to think what they'd shared had shaken his world as much as it had hers. All he treasures is your *friendship*, she reminded herself.

Despite the hollow feeling in her chest, she nodded. 'Yes, I'd like that.'

'Let me bring you another fortifying glass of wine before you depart, then.'

He walked away, Marcella watching as he sought out one of the servants carrying trays of glasses.

Sadness filled the hollow in her chest, even though she knew leaving society was the right choice. The prudent choice. The necessary choice.

She would simply have to savour these last few times he would escort her, partner her for a dance, bring her refreshments while they were both part of the same world, his company a delight it had been all too easy to become accustomed to.

She would become accustomed to its lack, she told herself. She'd turn her focus instead into exploring whether the long-time affection she'd shared with Austin could transform from her girl-hood worship and his fondness for a charming child into the mature love necessary between a man and a wife. As his wife, she could at least remain near her family, near her father's office, once she had to let go the work she loved and take up the domestic duties she'd never wanted.

The excitement of Crispin's attention, like the course of a shooting star, had been like a brilliant streak of light through the night sky of her life, swift and as swiftly vanishing. Austin was the north star, perhaps not as exciting, but a reliable, guiding presence. Solid and dependable as the rock base of a bridge support designed to carry heavy loads for a lifetime.

Even if the prospect of wedding him no longer thrilled her as much as it once had.

Chapter Fourteen

The following morning, Marcella rode with her groom through the gates into Hyde Park. With only a handful of days left in her Season, she intended to enjoy every possible activity with Crispin, even riding, though she hoped this one shared venture might be salvaged for…after.

A smile of irony curved her lips. When had she mentally begun dividing up her life into before she left society—and his frequent company—and after?

If they could continue to ride together, it wouldn't happen again soon. After their bargain ended, he would have to leave London, escorting his mother into the country before taking himself off on that extended trip around England to avoid the wrath of his father.

She'd be riding in the park alone, attended only by her groom, for the foreseeable future.

The sound of hoof beats drew her attention to the entry gates. Her upsurge of delight at seeing him was doubtless magnified by knowing how soon their days together would end. Never, she thought with a sigh, had she imagined when they struck this bargain how dear his presence would become.

Now she was lapsing into melancholy again, something she'd promised herself she would not do.

Putting a determined smile on her face, she wheeled her mount and rode over to greet him. 'A lovely morning, is it not, my lord? Lady Margaret is not accompanying you today?'

Some emotion passed swiftly over his face, instantly concerning her. 'What is it? Nothing has happened to her, has it? She's not ill or injured?'

He gave her a wry smile. 'Knowing how impulsive and careless she can be, you might well wonder. But no, she is in perfect health.'

'It's unusual for her not to ride, especially when she could secure your escort. Your lady mother has her engaged on more important business? Fittings for gowns, or calls to charm society dragons?'

Crispin blew out sigh. 'I could prevaricate, but I probably should just tell you straight out. Especially since Maggie is so incensed, I wouldn't put it past her to try to sneak out and contact you on her own.'

With a chill of foreboding, Marcella braced herself for what she feared was coming. 'Go on,' she said, her initial excitement at this ride in the park evaporating.

'Not that we tried to keep our rides together a secret, but we've not gone out of our way to advertise them either. I don't recall noticing anyone in particular the last time we were in the park, but someone did make note of us. Some gentleman, who apparently joked to my father at his club that he must be pretty sure of my capturing your dowry if he was allowing his unmarried daughter to risk her reputation being seen with you.'

'The Earl was not pleased,' Marcella said drily.

'No. He came home in a tearing rage, delivered my mother a thunderous scold that saw her take to her bed, and restricted my sister to her rooms, telling her if she had so little discernment—' Breaking off, his face colouring, he continued, 'I expect you can imagine the rest of what he said.'

She'd acknowledged from the first that his family might be happy to get her wealth, but wouldn't want her ill-bred presence to contaminate their innocent daughter. 'He railed that if you should somehow fail to secure my hand, and marriage didn't elevate my position, her association with me could harm your sister's chances of a successful presentation next year.'

He nodded. 'That was the gist of it, yes.'

It shouldn't hurt so much, but it did. She'd come to enjoy the uninhibited, plain-speaking Lady Margaret, to laugh at her verbal excesses, to try to gently recommend that she not pursue some of her more outlandish ideas. To feel that they were…friends.

What an insulting and bitter reminder that however much her money might be sought, his family and his peers would never consider her worthy of associating with them.

Suddenly she was furious—with the Earl, the whole condescending, superior, pampered lot of the *ton*, and with the man who'd beguiled himself into her affections when his family looked on her with contempt.

How could she have been such a fool?

'I'm sorry, Marcella. I know you've experienced this sort of ill treatment before, but I feel terrible that you are suffering it now at the hands of my own family.'

'Please, think nothing of it,' she said icily. 'It's only what I expected, after all.'

'Surely you know I don't share the Earl's views! I may have grown up blindly accepting them, I grant you, but I've had years of riding the country, meeting and talking in depth with engineers, builders, and craftsmen, most of whom possess more skill than I ever will and many of them more intelligence. No one class has a monopoly on talent, ability or inherent worth.'

'How enlightened you've become. But I must let you go. I don't believe I will ride in the park after all.'

She wasn't sure where she meant to go, only that she was too angry, disturbed, and yes, wounded, to tolerate riding where she might encounter any other obnoxious, supremely self-satisfied members of the *ton*. Nor, until she got her emotions under control, did she wish to go home, where Mary was certain to push and pry, trying to discover what had upset her.

A destination suddenly occurred. 'We'll head out the gate at Hyde Park Corner, Thompson,' she told her groom. Turning to nod at the Viscount, she said, 'Goodbye, Lord Dellamont.'

She rode off without a backward look—but soon heard the hoof beats of his mount following her. 'So I'm Dellamont again?' he said as he caught up to her. 'I know you're angry, and I don't blame you. But please don't lay this insult at my door.'

She ignored him, stemming back the tears that threatened by running a map of London through her head, trying to determine the best route to reach her chosen destination.

'Where are you going?' the Viscount asked after they rode out of the park and turned south, evidently not heading back to her family's home north of Oxford Street.

'Nowhere that would be of interest to a society gentleman. A place where engineers and common people of low birth work. A location that would be beneath the dignity of a viscount to visit.'

'If you think I'll allow you to ride off around London with a single groom to attend you just because you're in tearing rage, you're mistaken,' Dellamont countered.

'Suit yourself,' she said, determined to ignore him lest her turbulent emotions get the better of her and the threatening tears leak out.

Not sure of the fastest way to proceed, she led the groom from Hyde Park through Green Park and St James's Park, then threaded her way down to Westminster Bridge.

'Where exactly are you going?' Dellamont, who'd silently trailed her thus far, rode up to ask.

'If you must know, I want to look at the foundations being built for the London & Greenwich Railway,' she said, her anger beginning to dissipate, although the hurt was still there and she refused to look at him.

'Ah, yes. I understand the bill for that passed Parliament last year. Quite a project it will be, since the legislators insisted that the entire span must be elevated.'

'Papa says the viaduct will be more than three

miles long when it's completed, with more than eight hundred brick arches. Mr McIntosh, the engineer in charge, told Papa last winter that he planned to begin construction in February. I want to see how it's progressing.'

'Should be interesting. I'll come with you.'

Marcella shrugged. 'As you wish.'

It took them the better part of an hour to weave their way through the busy streets, transiting through Mayfair to Westminster, across the bridge and then through the less crowded roads south of the river to London Bridge. Finally arriving near the building site, Marcella found the area swarming with activity, some workmen unloading bricks from barges, some mixing mortar in large tubs, and others laying the bricks. Forgetting her anger, she pointed towards several immense brick arches that were rising on top of the excavated foundations.

'I've seen prints of bridges like the Menai, but never a bridge like this up close,' she said, awed. 'Those arches are *massive*. How magnificent the viaduct is going to be!'

'Have you never ridden on a railway?'

'Yes, but just some of the smaller ones constructed for the collieries around Newcastle.'

'You should travel on the Liverpool & Manchester. There aren't as many bridges and viaducts, but the ones that were constructed are very fine. It's thrilling, racing through the countryside faster than a horse can gallop.'

'I'm sure it is. Papa has promised to take Mama and me for the whole journey from London to Bristol once the Great Western is complete.'

'With the bridge crossing the River Avon and the Box Hill tunnel, that will be a fascinating ride. I can't wait to travel the line either.'

'And see your investment prosper?'

'That, too.'

She fell silent, studying the half-completed arches, estimating what the radius would be and mentally calculating the angles of stress.

'Working out the geometry of the support system?' Dellamont asked, bringing his mount closer until his booted leg nearly touched hers.

Despite her unsettled emotions, she felt that familiar shiver of awareness as he drew near. Finally, she looked over at him. 'How did you guess?'

'Because you are an engineer through and through.'

'Certainly not a proper *ton* maiden,' she said ruefully. 'And I should apologise. Your father's reaction is only what I expected to receive from members of the gentry. It was silly of me to become angry, and I certainly shouldn't have directed that anger at you.'

'No apologies necessary. How could you not have felt insulted when the Earl has been pushing me to court you?' Dellamont said quietly. 'And then insinuating that you are somehow unworthy to associate with my sister? When in truth, you are a far superior companion for Maggie than that impulsive scapegrace is for you.'

'I liked her, too,' Marcella admitted. 'But I should have known better than begin to imagine us friends. I won't make that mistake again.'

She should let go of her anger, but it would be wise to hold on to the hurt. Store it away so she could remember and relive it any time she indulged in the foolish daydream that somehow, somewhere, she and Viscount Dellamont, heir to the Earl of Comeryn, could meet as equals and friends.

How wise she'd been to reject from the outset any temptation to marry into the *ton*. To imagine they might be more than friends.

It would also be wise to let this experience begin to wean her from her unrealistic desire to remain in close contact with him once she returned to her proper place. Any attempt to meet him outside her own world would invite more condescending disapproval from any of his friends or family who chanced to learn of it.

He'd fallen silent, but at length, he said, 'Maggie considers you her friend, too. I wouldn't be at all surprised if she tried to see you, or at least write to you. Though you have every right to be, I hope you won't be too…dismissive with her if she does contact you. None of this was her fault.'

'No, it wasn't. But I can hardly maintain a friendship with your sister, given your father's serious objections.' Recalling Lady Margaret's frequently expressed dislike of her sire, Marcella laughed. 'Even if Lady Margaret would probably relish doing something he'd forbidden.'

Dellamont laughed, too. 'She probably would. But…have you forgiven *me*? I value your friendship and esteem. I'd be loath to discover something my imperious father had done caused me to lose it.'

She would be so much wiser to give him a polite reply and steel her heart and mind against him. And yet…this was the man who'd delighted in discussing mathematics with her. Who'd gone out of his way to protect her from bounders like Lord Hoddleston. And who, against his better judgement, had allowed her to experience the most stimulating afternoon of her life.

How could she turn away from him?

'There's nothing to forgive,' she said at last. Despite knowing she should armour herself against him, somehow, she couldn't.

He blew out a sigh of relief. 'Thank you. I was beginning to fear not even the credit the Stephenson lecture had earned me was going to be enough to salvage my standing in your eyes.'

'The Stephenson lecture will cover a great many faults,' she admitted.

'Good. So I may redeem myself further, will you let me buy you tea and ices at Gunter's? We can take it out under the plane trees in the square, all perfectly respectable. After a long ride, you must be ready for refreshment.'

She should refuse. She needed to begin preparing herself to see less of him, which would be easier if she curtailed rather than extended her time in his presence. But the voice of prudence was countered by an irresponsible longing to eke out as much as time with him as she could while she could.

In the end, irresponsible won out.

'I could do with a cup of tea,' she admitted. 'Then I must get back. Mama ordered me a new gown for the Thaxford ball that is to be delivered this morning. Mary wants me to model it so she has time to make corrections if she's not satisfied with the fit, after which I shall have to attend Lady Arlsley. Thank goodness I am able to dine with Papa and Mama tonight!'

'We'd better go quickly, then.'

Relief foremost among his tangle of emotions, Crispin escorted Marcella towards the refreshment establishment in Berkeley Square. He must have redeemed himself somewhat, since she allowed him to ride beside her, rather than ignoring him while he trailed behind her like a glorified groom as she had on the way to the Tower Bridge construction site.

He was as angry as she was about his father's illogical double standard. Guilty and appalled at the pain he'd seen in her eyes when he'd first revealed the reason his sister had not accompanied him, before anger overtook her hurt and surprise.

She deserved to be angry. Once again, he found himself much more in sympathy with her than with the views held by most of his own class. As he'd told her, after several years of exploring plans for building the new railway technology, he'd developed a high regard for the industry and expertise of the 'lower class' men who made it possible.

How could he not consider them at least equal, if not superior, to so many of his peers? Some, like his friend Gregory Lattimar, worked hard at managing and improving their estates, but many he knew from Oxford or in London felt their privileged status belonged to them by right. As Marcella asserted, they never spared a thought to the needs of their servants or the burdens their demands placed upon the people who worked for them, taking service as their due.

Privileges, for most part, won in antiquity by

ancestors who'd served as soldiers in battles supporting the throne. Privileges the current holders had done nothing to earn.

He'd have to summon every bit of charm he possessed while he beguiled her with tea and ices. He hadn't realised until she'd suddenly withdrawn from him just how much he'd come to count on her sunny companionship, her straightforward friendship untainted by the usual feminine wiles. Her approval of the man he really was.

It was more important than he could have imagined that he win back that approval and make sure he never placed it in jeopardy again.

With the streets busy, they didn't attempt any further conversation until they arrived at their destination. Not wanting to press his luck, Crispin allowed her groom to assist her to dismount.

'Thompson, isn't it?' he asked as the man guided her to her feet. After the groom nodded, Crispin continued, 'Can we impose on you to walk the horses one more time? I realise this additional delay must be keeping you from completing your other duties. For which you deserve additional thanks.' He pressed a coin into the groom's hand as he passed over his reins.

After the groom left to walk their mounts, Marcella turned to him. 'I'm quite capable of compensating my staff for extra services performed,' she said stiffly.

'Are we going to brangle over payment again?' he asked, hoping to disarm her by teasing, and relieved when her frown lifted.

'No. Because I will take care of my servant.'

'Very well. I will take care of tea. Have you tried Gunter's ices before?' he asked, waving her to a table under one of the trees.

'The ices have been featured at several *ton* entertainments.'

'Pineapple is the most exotic. I prefer strawberry myself.'

'I enjoy all the fruit ices. Their turtle soup is quite good, too.'

After he gave their order to the waiter who trotted over, Crispin turned back to her.

Recalling her plans for the evening, he said, 'What sort of suppers does your family prefer when you dine together? Truly, I'd like to know,' he asserted when she gave him a suspicious look. 'Our family dinners were always stiff, uncomfortable affairs. You describe yours as being so different. Knowing so little about what a happy family life is like, I hoped you might describe them further.'

And he did. He longed to discover more about the environment that had moulded her, not just into an accomplished mathematician, but also into the compassionate person who was concerned about a servant's aching arms, the kind person careful to spare the feelings of an earnest but un-intelligent suitor. A woman who increasingly intrigued and excited him.

At the mention of his own experience, her wariness dissipated. She even gave him a sympathetic look he found vastly encouraging. It appeared this topic would not only satisfy his curiosity, but would further reconcile her to him.

'Papa doesn't like a fuss. No enormous dinners with five courses and ten removes for us, even if Mama would love to try some from time to time. We have simple hearty fare. Papa enjoys fine ale and a brandy after dinner, but he takes it in the parlour with us. After dinner, I often read aloud to them, or play the pianoforte, especially if we are with Grandfather at Faircastle House. Or we'll sometimes play a few hands of cards, if Papa is not too tired.'

'Do you play cards or music when friends come to dine?'

'Yes. Though we more often host Papa's business associates or staff, like Mr Gilling, than friends.'

'Mr Gilling dines with you often?'

'Quite frequently. He did so much for all of us during the awful time after my brother died, Papa often treats him as the second son he never had.'

'Does that...pain you?'

'No. Well, a little. It's hard, sometimes, to see an outsider receive his full confidence and encouragement, but I'm so fond of Gilling myself, I can't really resent Papa's partiality for him.'

'If he's already virtually part of the family, your current circumstances will only be formalised if you wed him.'

'Yes. In a way, it will just be an extension of how we have gone on these past ten years.'

Conversation halted for a moment as the waiter brought over their tea and ices. As they sipped their tea and sampled the ice, Crispin reflected that wedding her engineer had been Marcella's sole aim since the Season began, prompting Gilling to declare himself the reason she'd agreed to their bargain. But he found he no longer viewed her marriage to the man with quite the disinterested equanimity he had at first.

'You truly think Gilling is worthy of you?' he asked a moment later, his tone sharper than he'd intended.

'He's certainly proved himself worthy over the years.'

'But?' he prompted, hearing an uncertain note in her voice.

'But...nothing. It will be best for me to proceed with my original plan, and see if he can envision me as his wife. Especially if I can persuade him to let me continue my work in the office.'

'Will he?'

She shook her head. 'As I told you before, I really don't know.'

'If he doesn't? Would you look for someone else? Though I can't imagine he wouldn't want to wed you if you gave him the slightest encouragement.'

'A flattering assessment I hope will prove correct. Since he has observed how Papa and I work together, there's a better chance of him allowing our continued association than there would be with someone unfamiliar with our arrangement. And I know Austin so well. We're comfortable with each other. The transition from friends to partners could happen with minimal... awkwardness.'

Crispin found he didn't really want to further discuss or envision her wedding Gilling—or anyone else. 'But you did say you prefer to delay marriage as long as possible.'

'Yes, I still hope to do that. Even if Mr Gilling will allow me to work in the office, in the natural way of things, there will eventually be children to supervise and the house to run. My time will no longer be entirely my own.'

Crispin found he liked envisioning what would be necessary to create those children even less. In fact, his whole being revolted at the idea of some other man kissing those lips, holding that body close, caressing the slender legs he'd so admired when she'd worn her trousers.

Which was ridiculous, when he had no claim on her, nor any intention of making one beyond friendship—a bond that would not extend to the privilege of making love to her.

Despite logic, his instinctive revulsion at the idea of someone else touching her didn't dissipate.

'The pineapple was delicious,' she said, finishing the ice in her bowl as he struggled to order his reaction. 'Thank you for that, and for tea. But I really must be getting home. I'll see you at the ball tomorrow night?'

'Definitely. I shall claim all your waltzes.'

Though he would be seeing her again the next evening, Crispin found himself reluctant to let her go. Perhaps because he was beginning to realise how very few additional occasions he would have to dance with her, squire her for ices or escort her to view railway viaduct construction sites.

Something deep within protested at that conclusion.

He recalled again the warmth and tenderness that had swelled his chest when she'd looked in awe at the railway viaduct construction at London Bridge and called it 'magnificent'.

While, watching her, he was thinking the most magnificent thing within view—was her.

His shock at her withdrawal today made him

realise he didn't want their close association to grow more distant. How could he prevent that when their interactions became limited to only occasional visits to her father's office and rides in park?

There had to be something else, something more, he could do, he thought as he signalled her groom to bring over their mounts. This time, he dared to give her a hand up into saddle, resisting the urge to stroke that booted ankle.

Somehow, he was going to figure out a better way forward.

Chapter Fifteen

~~~~~~~~~~~~~~~~~

Setting aside for the moment his need to figure out what to do about Marcella, the following afternoon, Crispin rode to the family town house on Portman Square. He'd been concerned about whether his tender-hearted mother had yet recovered from her husband's blistering reproof, and was relieved to find her out of her chamber, working on some needlework before the hearth in her sitting room.

'Crispin, what a delightful surprise!' she said as he walked in.

'No, don't get up and disturb your work,' he said as he came over to give her a kiss. 'I'm pleased to see you up and about.'

Sighing, she patted his hand. 'After all these years, one would think I would have developed a tougher skin. But the Earl still seems to so easily overcome me. What a poor honey I am! But I had a comfortable coze this morning with Lady Richardson, getting all the latest gossip, so I'm feeling better now.'

'You are a darling, and don't let anyone ever convince you otherwise.'

'And you are a darling to say so,' she said warmly. 'Can you stay for tea?'

'I'd be happy to. So what is new? Any juicy titbits for me?'

She hesitated, a troubled look passing over her face before her expression cleared and she smiled again. 'One thing you will truly find amazing, if you don't know about it yet.'

'And what would that be?' he asked, taking a seat on the sofa beside her after she rang for tea.

'You may have heard that the Duke of Faris-deen's heir, Lord Penlowe, passed away unexpect-edly a month or so ago.'

'Yes. Considering he was often the bane of Alex Cheverton's existence, I didn't feel much regret, although it is always sad for anyone to die so young. Is the gossip about the new heir? Some distant cousin, I would expect.'

'A very distant cousin. Also someone you know quite well.' As he raised his eyebrows in enquiry, she continued, 'The new heir is… Alex Cheverton.'

'Alex?' he exclaimed. 'How is that possible?'

For a moment, his mother traced the vagaries of a family tree that had seen his friend become the Duke's nearest male descendant. 'So you hadn't heard?'

'No! Nor have I heard a word from that rascal. Lattimar's back in Northumberland, but I would have thought Alex would have written us both.'

'It was all very sudden. Alex is actually in London now, and has been for several weeks. The Duke is running him to a frazzle, trying to educate him about assuming a title he wasn't bred to inherit, Lady Richardson said, so I expect that's why you've not heard from him.'

'He probably doesn't know I'm in London either,' Crispin said. 'When we all met last February, I was setting off on my exploratory trip for the Great Western, with no clear idea of when I might be back in the city.'

'He has been out in society a bit,' his mother said. 'But with the family in mourning, they've attended only a few select events. And since Farisdeen and your father loathe one another, it would be highly unlikely for anyone in our family to be bid to an entertainment at which the Duke or his new heir were to appear.'

'Alex—a duke. What a fine joke that will be on him! He was always so smug about how, as simply the master of a small country estate, he'd be able to live life on his own terms, while the rest of us would be encumbered by titles and obligations. I imagine the Duke will have something to say about the terms he will live on now.'

'You should send him a note to let him know you are in London. He can probably get away long enough to meet you for tea.'

'Or something stronger. That's assuming the butler at Farisdeen House doesn't look at the seal on the letter, recognise the Comeryn crest, and throw my note into the fire.'

'There is that possibility,' his mother agreed with a smile.

Conversation halted for a moment as the butler entered with their tea and his mother occupied herself fixing them each a cup.

After taking several sips, Crispin shook his head. 'Alex, a *duke*. I still have trouble getting my mind around that news! Any other shocking revelations from your morning session with Lady Richardson?'

'Well, there was something about…about Miss Cranmore.'

His irritation with his father immediately reviving, he said, 'Whatever it is, I hope you don't feel you must share it with the Earl. He had no reason to rip into you about her. Only to him does it not appear ridiculous that he could on one hand push me to court the girl and on the other forbid his daughter to associate with her.'

'To be fair, if Miss Cranmore does not succeed

in marrying into the gentry, an association with her won't do Maggie any good during her presentation next year.'

'So, you would deem her unworthy too?' he asked hotly.

His mother raised her eyebrows at his impassioned tone. 'I don't think you are quite as indifferent to the lady as you previously indicated.'

'I like and admire her. In looks, talent and charm she is far superior to most of the gently born females I've encountered.'

'Then... I'm not sure what you will want to do about this news.'

'What news?'

She sighed. 'I know my son, so of course I don't believe a word of this. But whispers are going around that you had an assignation with her in the maze at Norwalk House on the afternoon of Lady Norwalk's garden party. That the two of you were discovered practically *in flagrante delicto*.'

'That's absurd!' Crispin cried, setting his cup down with a clatter. 'Who is repeating such calumnies?'

'You know how rumours are. Someone heard a whisper from someone who knows someone who talked with the person who supposedly discovered you. No names revealed, of course, except for those of the scandalous couple. But there are also rumours that you were not the only one with whom she had a tryst in the shrubbery. That she met other men as well, and is no better than a lightskirt.'

Crispin sat stock-still, reviewing in his mind the episode in the maze. Neither he nor Hoddleston had made any attempt to keep their voices low when he confronted the Baron after rescuing Marcella. Their argument might well have been overheard—leading someone to believe *something* had happened. Indeed, she had wanted to speedily leave the maze, so that they could be seen mingling with the group gathering on the lawn. She'd expressed the hope that no one had overheard or glimpsed her struggle with Hoddleston.

'It is a bold-faced lie, isn't it?' his mother asked.

'I did walk in the maze with her. The rest is total invention,' he confirmed. 'So...how do I refute it?'

'You were seen going into the maze? Oh, that is unfortunate.' His mother shook her head. 'That's the thing about rumours. One can't really refute them. Especially as you are known to have been walking there with her. If you try to deny the story, half the listeners will believe you must be guilty, or you wouldn't lower yourself to comment on such an absurd tale. If you say nothing, others will believe it must be true since you didn't deny it. Generally, it's best to ignore scandal. You have the luxury of saying nothing and emerging unscathed, since few would be foolish enough to challenge the word of a d'Aubignon. Unfortunately, that will not help Miss Cranmore. A lady's reputation is so fragile! Especially someone like her, who does not have a powerful family to protect her.'

'So she is disgraced, no matter what happens next?' he asked angrily.

'Her reputation is tarnished regardless, though she could be saved from utter ruin if she received a proposal of marriage. Not, of course, with the rumour being entirely untrue, from you! Sadly, though, with such a vicious story circulating, it's unlikely any other gentleman will offer for her now. I'm afraid her best option is to quietly leave society and look to marry elsewhere.'

Marcella didn't wish to marry anyone anyway. But the idea that her sterling character would be so unfairly besmirched made him furious. There was only one way to save her from that...give her a powerful family to protect her.

After watching him for a moment, his mother said, 'Surely you're not considering marrying her, are you? You told me you were quite set against it!'

'I'm quite set against marriage in general. But what if someone who disliked the family started such a rumour about Maggie? Would you not want the gentleman with whom her name had been linked to do the honourable thing? Even if neither of them were guilty of any transgression? And please, do not insult me or her by noting that since Miss Cranmore isn't a lady born, the rules of honour don't extend to addressing the wrong done to her.'

'So you are considering wedding her,' his mother said wonderingly.

'Since I've only just heard this, I'm not sure yet what I mean to do. But I shall certainly not stand by and let her suffer from that venal man's machinations.'

'You mean you know who is behind this?' his mother asked, shocked.

'I know exactly who's responsible.' In a few brief sentences, Crispin related to his mother the incidents that had occurred with Lord Hoddleston. The Baron's disdain for Miss Cranmore's origins balanced by his need for her dowry and his certainty that Crispin would sooner or later abandon her, leaving her no alternative but to accept his hand.

'In this despicable act, he believes he's found the perfect way to punish her for rebuffing her. Destroying her reputation to guarantee I drop her, with no one left in the *ton* willing to marry her but him. What the varmint doesn't understand is that she won't have him on any terms. She never planned to marry into the gentry to begin with.'

'Never planned—then why embark on a Season?'

'It's complicated. I'll explain more when I can. I know I'm not at fault, but I can't tolerate letting Hoddleston get away with ruining the reputation of an innocent woman—a woman whom I respect and admire. I don't know whether she'll have me or not, but I'm going to have to make her an offer.'

His mother stared at him. 'You're certain of that?'

Crispin sat for a minute, his mind working feverishly. He'd been ever more drawn to her, despite not resolving his reservations about matrimony—particularly to a woman he fervently wished to have as happy a family life after marriage as she had before. But Hoddleston's despicable trick had swept away everything else.

He'd promised to protect her. And the only thing that would protect her now was a wedding.

'Yes,' he said slowly. 'I'm certain. Loath as I am to gratify my father.'

His mother smiled. 'At least your sister will be ecstatic. She likes Miss Cranmore very much. Which, if you esteem her and she has won over a cynic like my daughter, makes me believe I will like her, too.'

She leaned over to press his hand. 'Just make sure, if you choose to follow the dictates of honour, there's at least a fair chance that choice will make you happy.'

And that was the crux of the matter. He might have been creeping down the road towards resolving that tricky question, but he was nowhere close to the end yet.

Despite what his mother said, he didn't really have a choice. He'd known from the beginning if anything compromising occurred between them, he would have to offer for her. He'd always worried it would be he himself who would do the compromising.

Instead, that slug Hoddleston had taken care of it for him.

'You're going to be sorry you did this, Dellamont,' the Baron had said in the maze as he'd wiped the blood off his lip.

But Crispin couldn't regret protecting her.

Had Marcella heard the rumours yet? he wondered suddenly.

It was too late in the afternoon now to stop at Lady Arlsley's. With the ball to prepare for, her sponsor would likely not be receiving callers anyway. Unless some malicious 'well-meaning' friend felt compelled to stop by and chat with

Lady Arlsley, Marcella would walk into the Thaxford ballroom tonight completely unaware of what she would have to face.

Should he try to write and warn her? But he'd never called on her at her parents' home and wasn't sure of the exact address.

He'd just have to arrive at the ball early, ready to support and protect her.

Later that evening, garbed in her flattering new gown, Marcella followed Lady Arlsley up the stairs at Thaxford House, pausing outside the ballroom with the guests waiting to be presented to their hostess. As they halted, several people turned to stare at them, leaning to whisper to their companions before turning away.

Several of them Marcella knew slightly, but none met her gaze or offered greetings. Which puzzled her a little, but as she wasn't intimately acquainted with any of them, she dismissed the oddity.

Her hostess, Lady Thaxford, was noticeably cool when she greeted Marcella. However, as a marquess's wife, she probably shared Lady Arlsley's opinion that the lowly Miss Cranmore didn't belong in her ballroom. Shrugging off the snub, Marcella told herself such attitudes were precisely why she would be thrilled to be quitting society in little more than a week.

Although she hadn't revealed that intention to Lady Arlsley yet.

As they walked through the ballroom, the strangeness continued. Almost everyone they passed looked over at her and then away, not meeting her eyes before immediately turning to whisper to their companions.

By the time they reached the other side of the ballroom, Lady Arlsley, a genial smile fixed on her face as she nodded to several in the group gathered there, leaned close to Marcella and said in an urgent undertone, 'What have you done?'

'Nothing that I am aware of,' Marcella replied—before the guilty memories recurred. Nothing, except kiss Crispin in Lady Arlsley's garden, and then kiss him again, even more passionately, on the tavern terrace.

Though it was possible that another servant besides Mary—who would never have spoken of it to anyone—might have been gazing out a window and overseen them in the town-house garden, she was certain they had been unobserved on the terrace.

'You must have done something,' Lady Arlsley replied, anger in her voice. 'Even my friends shied away from speaking with me as we entered. And you must have heard the murmur of voices, seen the interested gazes following us as we crossed the room. As soon as an escort appears for you,

I shall corner Lady Anderson in the card room. This is intolerable!'

Or rather, only typical behaviour on the part of the *ton* towards an interloper like her, Marcella thought, recalling the Earl of Comeryn's fury at discovering his daughter had been riding with her.

Was his anger, conveyed to his many acquaintances and friends, the reason behind the sudden chill?

The orchestra began tuning up, gentlemen walking over to invite ladies to dance, but no one approached Marcella. Even her widower, who'd half-heartedly continued his attentions despite obviously feeling as long as she was pursed by an earl's heir, his chances of winning her hand were slim, turned away without acknowledging her when she saw him and smiled.

Something had definitely happened. But she had no idea what.

Lady Arlsley fiddled at her side, clearly frustrated at having to remain with her rather than darting off to find her friend. Once the first dance began with Marcella still standing unclaimed, the older woman turned to her and snapped, 'Follow me. Since you failed to secure a partner, you can accompany me to the card room.'

Not that she ever expected to truly enjoy these entertainments, aside from the two dances and associated conversation she was able to share with Dellamont, but Marcella was pleased with her pretty new gown and had been looking forward to the evening with mild enthusiasm. That dissipated as she followed her irate sponsor around the edge of the ballroom and into the card room.

In even more dramatic fashion than the ballroom, as soon as the card players looked up to see who the newcomers were, the low hum of voices in the room faded—and everyone stared.

'I do wish you would not bring that *person* in here, Lady Arlsley,' a viscount's wife said. 'We do not appreciate having someone of her ilk mingling among us.'

Lady Arlsley stopped short, two rosy spots of embarrassment appearing on her cheeks, while Marcella, though mystified, was otherwise unmoved. She even pitied her sponsor a bit, since that lady quailed before that evidence of this group's disapproval. Marcella didn't care one whit what they thought of her.

Before a sputtering Lady Arlsley could come up with a reply, Marcella felt a touch at her elbow. 'Miss Cranmore, here you are!' Dellamont said, bowing to her and her sponsor. 'I've been looking all over the ballroom for you. Since we've missed the beginning of the dance, perhaps you will stroll with me. If you will permit, Lady Arlsley?'

Any faces that hadn't already been turned their way swivelled towards them at the sound of Crispin's voice echoing through the silent room. Marcella noted astonishment on some faces, dropped jaws on others.

What in blazes has happened? she wondered.

Goggling at him, still incapable of speech, Lady Arlsley nodded at Dellamont. Offering her his arm, the Viscount said, in a voice guaranteed to penetrate to every corner of the room, 'Thank you for doing me the *honour*, Miss Cranmore.' And led her away.

'So what is it? Have I been identified as a carrier of the plague?' Marcella joked as Crispin walked her, not back into the ballroom, but into an anteroom that was being set up for refreshments. Proceeding with her to the windows, out of the way and out of earshot of the servants busily filling the tables with trays of food and drinks, he said, 'I'm sorry I'm late. I had intended to arrive before you, but two carriages collided on the street, and the horses from one had to be cut from their traces—' Breaking off, he sighed. 'I would have spared you that episode in the card room.'

'So you do know what's afoot. Thank heaven! Tell me, please.'

Quickly he related the rumours about them. 'I told my mother they were a complete fabrication, and asked how we could go about refuting them. She said…there was no effective way.'

'Well, that's typical! Hoddleston attacks me and *I'm* the hussy. Am I allowed to call him out?'

'Are you a good shot?'

'Tolerable.'

'That's a match I'd like to see,' he said, the serious expression on his face lightening. 'But no, you can't. Even I am not allowed to call him out, despite the slur to my name, since acknowledging the story is the same as confirming it. "No smoke without fire, etc."'

'Then what are we to do?'

'That's what we need to determine, and I don't intend to discuss it with a ballroom of people, already morbidly curious, sneaking about trying to overhear us. Will you go to Lady Arlsley's tomorrow?'

'If my ruin is as complete as it appears, yes I will. To tell her I am leaving society, which will come as a huge relief to her, I am sure.'

'Don't tell her anything yet. Not until after we talk. For tonight, I intend to dance my two dances with you, escort you in for some refreshment, chat with you, and then recommend to Lady Arlsley that you make your exit.'

He stared down at her for a moment. 'You are…at ease, aren't you? You don't appear nearly as upset by the news as I feared you might be.'

'Oh, I'm upset. I should like to wring Hoddleston's neck. Or rather—what would be a suitable equivalent? Perhaps march him at pistol point through Hyde Park with him wearing only his nether garments? But as for the opinions of the assembled multitude here tonight?' She snapped her fingers. 'I care less than that what they think of me. Though I am pained anyone could be stupid enough to imagine you would behave so badly.'

'Everyone loves a scandal and believes no one is above it.'

'Everyone believes a girl who tries to rise above her station deserves whatever she gets,' Marcella said. 'There are probably many who believe I enticed you into the shrubbery to tempt you with my body and try to force you into marrying me. They will probably applaud you for refusing.'

'We'll talk about that later. I'm just relieved that you aren't more distressed.'

'Not me. No screaming or swooning, remember?'

'I do. So,' he said, tilting up her chin and grinning at her, 'would you tempt me with your body?'

His disturbing news had distracted her for a time, but at his teasing words, her awareness of him returned in a rush, sending a tingle of sensation sweeping across her skin. She was very conscious of his tempting mouth just above hers, and how easily she could pull his face down to kiss him. 'Could I?'

'In a heartbeat.'

She might easily kiss him, but since she'd already been the cause of besmirching his reputation, she should probably refrain from creating any more scandal. 'Then we'd better go back into the ballroom.'

Chapter Sixteen

❧

The next afternoon, Marcella wrapped her arms around herself as she paced the town house garden to avoid any further discussion with her sponsor, marking time until she could expect Crispin to arrive.

On the carriage ride home last night, Lady Arlsley had been alternately upset and relieved. 'Dellamont's attentions kept us from disaster, bless him,' she exclaimed after the vehicle set off from Thaxford House. 'With him failing to repudiate you, no one is sure whether to believe the rumours or not. After all, society couldn't imagine Dellamont would continue to pay attention to girl socially so far beneath him if he'd already had her.'

To which Marcella replied with asperity, 'I'm pleased you have so much faith in my virtue.'

Glaring at her, Lady Arlsley demanded, 'Well,

are the rumours true? Did you give yourself to Dellamont? Or to any other man?'

Disgusted, Marcella replied, 'I shall not dignify those vulgar questions with an answer.'

A night's repose had left her sponsor still upset and uncertain. Marcella had barely handed Mary her pelisse when Lady Arlsley began questioning her again, and when she still refused to disclose any further details, cried, 'You ungrateful chit! Don't you realise that your disgrace threatens my good name as well?'

She'd not been able to refrain from snapping back, 'If you had bothered to accompany us on the garden walk, you would know nothing happened. But you may rest easy on one score. I expect Dellamont to call this afternoon. I don't wish to speak with anyone else, however, so I will await him in the garden.'

Stomping out of the parlour, she'd called for Mary to bring back her pelisse and escaped the house.

Would Crispin find a way to get them out of this imbroglio? He was very clever, and he knew the workings of society much better than she did. Although she was truly not concerned about her own reputation, she hated that anyone might believe he had acted so badly. Despite what anyone thought, she refused to feel embarrassed or ashamed because a vicious, venal man had tried to ruin her.

Nor had she any interest in trying to defend herself. In her opinion, their best course of action was to follow through on her original plan: let her bid Lady Arlsley goodbye this very afternoon, and terminate a presentation she'd never wanted.

What would his suggestion be?

After pacing through several circuits around the park, she heard her name called, and looked up to find him striding towards her.

Her pleasure at seeing him softened the edge of her disgruntlement. She went to meet him, happy to give him her hand to kiss. 'You must trust me,' he said, smiling down at her. 'You've not even stationed Mary here to keep watch over us.'

'But I'm already a ruined woman, remember?' she said wryly. 'Therefore I have no reputation to protect. Jesting aside, Mary does trust you. She credits you with ensuring I came to no harm when I attended the Stephenson lecture.'

'Which is my object today. To make sure no one does you any harm. Including that bastard Hoddleston, whom I wish even more fervently than you that I could call out. However satisfying that would be, it's not an effective solution.'

'Have you come up with something that would be?'

'There is really only one remedy.' Before she

realised what he intended, he dropped down to one knee. 'Marcella Cranmore, will you do me the great honour of becoming my wife?'

She froze, strong emotions clashing within once her shocked brain made sense of his words.

Fury that there was no way to counter Hoddleston's vile accusations. Awe and admiration for a sterling character that was willing to protect hers, regardless of the cost. And a deep, dangerous desire to disregard all the good reasons she should refuse and accept the hand of this exceptional man.

So difficult was that temptation to resist, she blurted out the first response that came to her lips once she forbade herself to say 'yes'.

'I thought you were offering an escape, not a trap! Please, Crispin, get up.'

He laughed as he rose to his feet. 'I'm not sure I shouldn't be highly insulted that you consider my heartfelt declaration a trap.'

Pressing on to keep temptation at bay, she said, 'I told you long ago that I didn't care one bit about my reputation among the *ton*. My family knows my true character, so once I leave society for ever, their opinion will not affect me. As long as what Lady Arlsley told me is true—that you would suffer no lasting harm from the scandal. Feeling pettish at thinking herself a victim in this, she said whenever a scandal happens, the blame is always laid on the woman. That when you are ready to wed, the competition to snag a future earl will erase any doubts about marrying you this affair might have created in the minds of eligible ladies or their mamas.'

He nodded. 'Completely unfair, but that's the way of the world. My reputation might be temporarily tarnished, but the gilded coronet in my future will soon restore its lustre.'

'Then, though I'm immensely touched that you have made me an offer, there's really no need.' To remind herself as much as Crispin, she continued, 'Neither of us should be forced into marriage before we are ready. Certainly not at the behest of a dissolute like Hoddleston! It should be our choice when and how we wed.'

Finally allowing herself to voice the question for which she really needed an answer, she added, 'Unless…unless you've experienced a change of heart since we last spoke about the matter of marriage?'

She held her breath, but after a moment, shaking his head, he looked away. 'No, not really. But I can't abide having a dissolute like Hoddleston ruin your good name.'

A stab of disappointment struck her. Summoning up what she hoped was a breezy smile to mask the pain, she said, 'He can't ruin it. Not where it matters to me, in my world. It's unlikely anyone there will ever hear any tales of what supposedly happened at Norwalk House, and those who know me wouldn't believe it if they did hear anything.' She laughed shortly. 'They would be more likely to attribute it to the right place, the arrogant venality of aristocrats who look down on everyone else. So, no more talk of a declaration. You are sure this will not harm you permanently?'

'Other than with my father, no. He'll probably believe the rumours and be furious that I put temporary pleasure over acquiring filthy lucre.'

'Surely not,' she protested, once again pained that he believed his own father could think so poorly of him.

Crispin shrugged. 'Maybe not, but I wouldn't be surprised if he did. In any case, he'll be incensed that I didn't secure your dowry, regardless of the scandal.'

'Since we are both agreed on not wishing to be forced into marriage, shall we keep to our original purpose? Leave society now, with you departing for places unknown for a safe interval. After which we may meet again later, as…as dear friends and colleagues?'

He studied her face, and for a moment, she thought he meant to say something—that on second thought, he'd changed his mind? That he wanted to explore the possibility of becoming something more than friends?

But when he did speak, with a wry smile, he said, 'I suppose that means you are refusing my proposal.'

Surprising how much it hurt to agree, but somehow she managed to summon a smile. 'I suppose it does.'

'You are sure?'

Once she had been completely sure. Now, unsettled and facing the prospect of his imminent departure from her life, she wasn't sure at all. But he, it appeared, entertained no doubts about continuing simply as friends. Which settled the matter.

'I think I must be.'

Dellamont blew out a breath, which Marcella could only interpret as relief. 'Part of me feels I should insist, in order to save your good name. But another part knows I must honour your choice.'

Which was really his choice, too, else he would have pressed her harder. Declare his affections had become so engaged, he could now seriously consider the possibility of wedding her.

That he did not was an omission that required her to refuse him under any circumstances. Even though the mixture of dread and distress she now felt made her fear that despite her best efforts, she'd somehow allowed her own emotions to become too engaged.

'Then honour my choice. To maintain our

friendship, trust and mutual admiration in a relationship that progresses at the pace we choose.'

'That is truly what you prefer?' When she nodded, he said, 'Then we will make it so.'

She would have to be content with that. She *would* be content with that, she vowed to herself.

'With my supposed reputation in tatters, I see no point in going through the final week I'd expected to remain in society. I might as well make my exit now.'

'You don't want to face down the disapproving hordes before you go? Not let it appear they have forced you out?'

'I'm normally a fighter, but that fight would have no point. My staying wouldn't change any opinions. To most of society, I'm now not merely low-born and ill bred, I'm a low-born, ill-bred lightskirt. Leaving will save Lady Arlsley further embarrassment. I can return to Papa telling him that I have done what was asked of me and the situation is now truly intolerable.'

'Very well, then. If that is what you wish, that is what we will do.'

What she'd really wish was for him not to leave her. But that was impossible, so she had better stiffen her spine, curtail further foolish imagining, and face the facts. 'You will leave immediately, too? Before the Earl learns of your intention, and tries to take you—or your poor mother—to task?'

'Yes. I'll escort Mama back to Montwell Glen as soon as she can make ready, to ensure the Earl can't abuse her, at least not until his initial anger cools. And leave on my explorations from there.'

'Then I suppose this is goodbye,' she said, steeling herself to say the words aloud.

'But we haven't had time to figure out how or when we will meet again.'

'You intend to be out of London for a good while. Call at Papa's office, if you wish, when you return, and see if we are still in London. We can figure out something then.'

Once again, she hoped he would protest and insist that they pin down now a definite time to meet again. But that sudden upswing of hope plummeted just as quickly when, after staring into the distance, at last he nodded. 'Yes. I suppose you are right. We can figure it out…later.'

This really would be goodbye, then. The pain that lanced through her was sharp enough, she just barely kept herself from wincing. Putting a hand at her chest to ease it, she made herself smile.

'I've kept you long enough. But you must let me thank you again. I've enjoyed our bargain far more than I ever imagined I would. I'll be grateful to you for gifting me with the Stephenson lecture for the rest of my days.'

'It will be a treasured memory for me, too.'

He couldn't treasure their time together as much as she had, or he wouldn't be letting her send him away.

But she was being foolish. Did she really want him to press her, when marrying him would mean endless repetitions of the snubs she'd received at the ball last night? Murmurs of the scandal might fade for a man, but never for the woman involved. Did she want to let herself suffer the indignity of having her friendship forbidden to others, like the Earl had forbidden it to Lady Margaret?

Lose for ever even a nodding proximity to the engineering world?

Austin's gentle affection would soothe the ache left in the wake of Dellamont's departure. If she could groom their long attachment into a deeper bond, secure and safe where she belonged, her distress would ease and her enthusiasm for their shared future revive.

She just needed to sever her ties to Crispin before the pain cut any deeper.

So she stood, wooden, uttering the appropriate courtesies, curtsying to his bow. Then he was gone, the garden suddenly duller, chillier, as if all brightness and colour had been stripped from it.

Not able to prevent herself, she hurried over to the garden wall. Peeking through the gate, she watched as a few moments later he descended the front entry steps, fitted his beaver hat on his head, and walked off to collect his phaeton. Without a backward glance.

Angrily she swiped at tears she vowed she would not shed.

There was no reason to feel despondent. Lord Dellamont—she would no longer think of him as 'Crispin'—had made no secret from the first that he didn't wish to marry. Obviously, nothing they had shared had given him enough reason to change his mind. If she'd thought he'd proposed because he actually wanted her...she might have given in to temptation and accepted.

But his offer had clearly been made only out of duty. Returning the refusal he hoped for and expected had been the only prudent thing to do.

It was time to cauterise the raw edges of her bleeding heart, end this chapter and move on to the next phase of her life.

After giving herself a few more minutes to settle her uncertain emotions, Marcella returned to the drawing room, which fortunately at the moment was empty of callers.

'I asked Dellamont to stay for tea, but he refused,' Lady Arlsley said as she entered. 'I had hoped you had reached an...understanding.'

'If you are asking whether or not I'm going to marry him, the answer is "no".'

Alarm flared in Lady Arlsley's eyes. 'At the least, assure me that he is not going to drop you, or you are truly ruined!'

'Let me just say that you have nothing further to worry about.' Before Marcella could inform her sponsor that her onerous chaperonage duties were over, the butler appeared at the door.

'Lord Hoddleston has arrived, asking to speak with Miss Cranmore.'

'Saints be praised!' Lady Arlsley exclaimed. 'Perhaps you do have one option left. Show him in, Mannering.'

'Should you not ask whether I wish to see *him*?' Marcella asked as the butler bowed himself out to do his mistress's bidding.

'That's of no importance,' her sponsor snapped back. 'We may salvage something from this disaster yet.'

If Marcella had had any doubts about who had started the rumours, Hoddleston's appearing today, probably to gloat over his accomplishment, dispelled them. He was about to discover that she hadn't just been making idle claims when she vowed she'd never consider his suit, she thought, pressing her lips together in determination.

The Baron walked in and made them an extravagant bow. 'Good day, ladies. You are looking lovely, but a bit...pale, Miss Cranmore. As I can well imagine, after suffering such a distressing evening.'

'You certainly contrived to make it so,' Marcella said acidly. 'In any event, it may prove to be a relief.'

'Perhaps you would allow me a moment alone to speak with your charge, Lady Arlsley?'

'There is no need for her to leave,' Marcella countered. 'There is nothing we have to say that can't be said in front of her.'

'Tender moments shouldn't have...outside witnesses, my dear,' he said with a pointed glance that she knew was a reminder of the episode in the maze. 'You can hardly be unaware that I conceived a constant affection for you almost from the first time I met you, Miss Cranmore. That regard was...shaken by the disaster that has sullied your reputation, but ultimately could not destroy it. I would have some privacy to—'

'A constant affection for my dowry, you mean,' Marcella interrupted. 'And I will never be your "dear". As I have told you on several occasions, I will not marry you. I wouldn't consider your suit when Lord Dellamont was paying his attentions, and I am no more interested in them now that society has deemed me an outcast. As I have also advised you numerous times, you will have to find relief for your monetary difficulties elsewhere. I should even think you would be relieved to look elsewhere. You never truly wanted to give your proud and ancient name to a "jumped-up cit's granddaughter who doesn't know her place". Now, I believe there is nothing further to be said. Good day, Lord Hoddleston.'

His falsely tender smile fading, Hoddleston cried, 'You think you can just *dismiss* me? Do you still harbour illusions that Dellamont will come riding in like some medieval knight to rescue his lady? But of course, I'm forgetting. How could I expect someone of your background to understand the workings of the *ton*? Let me point out the stark truth. Dellamont will never offer *his* name to a woman who has disgraced herself.'

'That's not quite accurate. *You* disgraced me. I shall no longer be attending Lady Arlsley's at-homes, so you needn't call again. Must I summon the butler to escort you out?'

Marcella stared at him, her coldly implacable gaze never wavering.

At length, Hoddleston looked away. 'I can see myself out, thank you. Good day, Lady Arlsley. As for you, Miss Cranmore—'

'I believe the conventional response is good-bye. For ever, Lord Hoddleston.' Giving him the barest of curtsies, she turned her back on him and walked over to the window.

Lady Arlsley waited only until the door closed behind Lord Hoddleston before exploding, 'Are you out of your mind? You just dismissed your last and only chance to your salvage your reputation!'

'It wasn't my only chance. As it happens, Lord Dellamont also made me offer this morning—he being an honourable gentleman who did not wish to see my name sullied by false and malicious rumours. Which, as I believe his appearance here just confirmed, were orchestrated by Lord Hoddleston. When I told the Baron repeatedly that I'd never accept him, he always replied that he would wait until after Dellamont rejected me and see what my answer would be then. I suppose he grew tired of waiting, or perhaps his financial difficulties grew too pressing. So he tried to engineer that result himself by manufacturing those rumours. He has such a low opinion of me, he was certain the scandal would drive Dellamont away, leaving me with no other option but to marry him.'

'Nor do you have any,' Lady Arlsley retorted. 'Don't you realise that, you stupid girl?'

'I have the option I intended to choose from the moment this charade of a Season began. We can both congratulate ourselves on having done our duty. I fulfilled my mother's wish by embarking on this enterprise, you fulfilled your duty to your husband by taking on the onerous task of presenting me. I know you find it incomprehensible, but

I never had any intention of wedding a society gentleman. So, you see, your fears of being held responsible for my being raised above my station have been unfounded from the start. I thank you for your hospitality, however grudgingly given. But I think we can both admit to being relieved that we shall not have to meet again. I can see myself out. Goodbye for ever to you, too, Lady Arlsley.'

Given the efforts her sponsor had expended on her behalf, it probably would have been polite to allow the woman a chance to reply. Marcella walked out of the room leaving the Baron's wife still gaping at her in shock.

Collecting Mary, whom she wasn't surprised to find waiting outside the reception room door with her bonnet and pelisse, Marcella hurried out the entry and down the front steps. There was a grim satisfaction in having had an opportunity to tell off Lord Hoddleston, but beyond that, she felt…nothing.

Her family's affection, and she hoped Austin's, would help fill the chilly void. She should probably go first to Papa's office, give him a sanitised version of what had happened, and let him break the news to her mother that she was ending her Season. Mama was certain to be disappointed and sorrowful at how what she'd imagined would be an exciting and glamorous adventure had turned out.

As she walked to the hackney stand, Marcella smiled sadly. She'd thought her time in society might be a lark, sometimes amusing, more often frustrating and distasteful. But she'd never imagined when she abandoned the *ton* that she'd be leaving behind a store of her most precious experiences...and far too much of her heart.

Chapter Seventeen

L̲ater that evening, Marcella walked into the parlour at her father's house in Tavistock Square and sat down at the pianoforte. She'd had a long talk with her father in his office, trying to sound matter of fact, but fearing he might have sensed how close she was to tears. He'd given her a hug, told her if she were ready to end her foray into society, of course he would support her and reconcile her mother to that decision.

He must have broken the news to her mother before dinner, for Mama's eyes had been suspiciously red when she appeared for the meal. Still numb, her hands automatically going through the ritual of taking out music, Marcella thought that playing would help to soothe her as well as her disappointed mother. Even better, it would bring to a halt the flood of questions Mama kept asking about why she wished to end her Season so abruptly.

She must focus now on returning to life as it was before Dellamont. But time spent with him had created such a glittering, exciting, energising interlude, she wasn't sure how to recover 'normal'. When what was once 'normal' now looked so dispiritingly dull.

Would he call for her at her father's office—in a week, a month, ever?

How was she to walk into the storeroom without recalling their marvellous adventure? Go to Hatchard's for a new book, without remembering their discussion about the restrictions placed on educating women, when he'd surprised her with his willingness to listen and learn more? Ride in the park without thinking about the talks they'd shared, the merriment of her chats and his races with Lady Margaret?

Even playing tonight reminded her of the duet they'd performed at the Dellaney musicale and how he'd rescued her from Lord Hoddleston.

She'd hoped they might find a way to play duets again. Her Season had been curtailed before that could happen.

Suddenly she realised it would be almost impossible to recover her former self if she remained in London. She needed to get away, to scenes not imprinted with the heightened excitement of him walking beside her, far from places like Berkeley Square and Hyde Park and the elegant town houses of Mayfair where around each corner, her spirits might leap at the possibility of encountering him.

She needed to get away and forget that time when the sun had shone brighter, the colours of the world appeared more vivid, and every discussion more lively, because she'd shared it with him.

She didn't dare think about kisses.

After she finished the piece, she said, 'Mama, can we go visit Grandda? I've been missing him.'

After giving her a quick, concerned glance, her father said, 'An excellent idea. I know the events of the Season can be…exhausting.'

'They were. I find myself yearning for the serenity of the gardens at Faircastle House, the sea air and long rides through the countryside with Grandda.'

'What do you think, my dear?' her father asked her mother. 'I shall need to remain in London for a while longer but I could join you there soon. Have you had your fill of buying dresses, taking tea and gossiping with friends?'

'I should miss you terribly if we go on without you, but I always love to see my da,' her mother replied.

'Good.' With a sympathetic glance at Marcella, he said, 'Let's make plans tomorrow to send you on your way.'

Marcella jumped up from the bench and went

over to give each parent a hug, dangerously near tears. They'd always supported and loved her, as they were now. Their love would be enough.

Away from here, away from memories of *him*, she would find tranquillity again.

After leaving Lady Arlsley's home on Upper Brook Street, Crispin had headed for the nearby hackney stand, intending to engage a jarvey to take him to Portman Square. He needed to warn his mother of the outcome of his meeting with Marcella and let her know he'd stand ready to escort her and his sister back to Montwell Glen as soon as they could prepare to leave.

But unsettled by their final interview, once he reached the stand, he changed his mind. A brisk walk would help soothe him and let him ponder what he should do next.

He first debated whether or not to seek out his sire and let him know he was ending his participation in the Season. But a moment's reflection succeeded in convincing him that having an interview with the Earl would just subject him to abuse for no good purpose, since whatever harassment Comeryn meted out would not change his intentions. He'd pen a note instead.

He smiled grimly. His lack of deference in not waiting to have an in-person meeting before his departure was certain to make the Earl even more furious. But he'd deal with the repercussions of that decision the next time he was forced to meet the man.

Where would he go, after he left his family at Montwell Glen?

His immediate impulse was to return to London and pay a visit to Richard Cranmore's office, seek out Marcella and cobble together those plans for continuing their friendship that the scandal had not given them time to arrange.

He'd found it distressingly hard to leave her in the garden at Lady Arlsley's, once he realised that this was to be the last meeting of their bargain. A sudden but final end to all the rides, dances, talks and adventures he'd enjoyed so much over the last month. He'd several times checked his steps, driven to return to the garden—and do what?

She was determined to leave society, and after the way she'd been treated, he couldn't blame her. He couldn't in good faith try to persuade her to delay a little longer. With the bitter taste that had to have been left in her mouth after having her character unfairly maligned, her determination to marry her engineer must be stronger than ever. Small wonder she hadn't hesitated to refuse his offer.

For which he was relieved. Wasn't he?

As he'd told his mother, his instinctive aversion

to marriage hadn't changed. But Marcella was... different from any other female he'd ever met. Over the course of their association, he'd come to believe it was possible she'd had as congenial and happy a domestic life as she'd described. He'd seen through her that a family needn't necessarily be a source of constant strife and turmoil.

He had to admit that he liked her more than he'd ever liked any female. Her lack of interest in attracting a husband allowed him to relax around her in a way he could not around conventional, marriage-minded young ladies. She was as easy to talk with as his male friends, never resorting to the coy, attention-seeking mannerisms he found annoying in other single females.

Most striking, unlike any of his friends, she was both interested in and knowledgeable about the railway enterprises that fascinated him. With her, he'd been able to talk at length about his passion for them and his visions for their future, a passion and a vision she shared.

Indeed, he thought with a grin, she possessed much more technical expertise and was probably more intelligent than he was. In addition to her keen intellect and wide-ranging interests, her sunny, optimistic personality and subtle humour made her a delight to be around.

And then there was her physical loveliness, which sharpened every sense, igniting a simmering passion that kept him always at a knife's edge of desire.

In short, being with her made him feel more energised, more alive, and more engaged than he could remember being with any of his other friends. Spending time with her magnified his enjoyment of whatever activity they shared.

It wasn't until this moment, contemplating for the first time what he would be doing, with whom he'd be spending time now that their bargain had ended, that he fully realised how deeply she'd woven her way into his life. How much his enjoyment of the things they'd experienced had been heightened by her interest and expertise and by being able to share those experiences with her.

She'd taught him about more than railways. Recalling the discussion they'd begun at Hatchard's, he now had a much greater appreciation for the difficulties faced by women whose intellectual development was hemmed in on every side by restrictions on where and how much females could study and what they could do with the fruits of their education. How frustrating and discouraging it must be for an erudite woman to have her future limited to marrying, bearing children and running a household.

She'd opened his eyes, too, to how deep and wide the sense of inherent superiority ran in those born into the gentry. Anger stirred again as he recalled the slights to which she had been subjected. She, who in beauty and intelligence was far superior to any of the gently born women he knew.

How was he to fill the gap in his life that would be left by her loss?

He had no answer to that question.

You could have married her, a little voice whispered. *If you'd been more persuasive, added kisses to your plea, she might have given in and accepted. You could have had the stimulation of her friendship every day, the privilege of making love to her every night.*

That possibility sent a bolt of excitement through him before the old familiar doubts recurred. He knew he had more in common with her than his parents did with each other, but he was still uneasy about committing to something as long-term as marriage. He hadn't been successful as a son to either his mother or his father—how could he be sure of being successful as a husband? The thought of dragging down that sunny personality, making her unhappy, was intolerable.

There was also the matter of her not wanting to become a viscount's wife. The slights and condescension she'd endured were real. How could he ask her to subject herself to that for a lifetime?

He had no answer to those questions either.

Exasperated, he reminded himself that he'd

been fine on his own before he met her. After a period of time adjusting to not having her engaging companionship, he'd be fine again.

But all this contemplation was not easing the leaden ache in his gut.

He stopped short, realising in his abstraction he'd covered the distance from Lady Arlsley's town house to Portman Square in record time. Taking a deep breath, he told himself he'd cease agonising about the end of their adventure and concentrate instead, once he'd seen his mother and sister, on packing up and getting ready to escort them out of London.

Ten days later, Crispin sat in his bedchamber at Montwell Glen, preparing to embark on his next exploratory investment journey. He'd brought with him from London copies of several bills that had been submitted to Parliament for pending railway ventures. Most interesting to him was the London & Southampton, a prospectus for which had been submitted as early as 1831, then several times revised before being submitted as the bill now expected to pass in the current Parliamentary session. Following its most recent survey, he would ride south from London through Wimbledon, Weybridge, Woking Common, Farnborough, Basingstoke, and Winchester to the terminus at Southampton. The addition of docking facilities at the port city and the need to arrange transport from the London terminus at Nine Oaks Station gave an additional element of novelty to the venture.

He was talking with Haines about what needed to be packed in his travelling kit when a footman brought up a letter. Recognising with delight his friend Alex Cheverton's sloping script—grinning at the ducal seal that closed the missive—he broke it and read through the short letter before laying it back on the desk in astonishment.

He'd been shocked to discover his old friend was now heir to a duke. He was even more shocked that Alex had written to invite him to Edge Hall, the property he'd long managed for the Duke of Farisdeen, to attend his wedding in a week's time.

He shook his head in disbelief. Granted, he hadn't seen his friend since late February, but how in that time had Alex managed to fall in love and decide to marry?

Then, if one met an extraordinary person, forming an attachment didn't require years.

Pushing the image of Marcella Cranmore out of mind, Crispin pulled stationary out of his desk and began writing his acceptance.

He couldn't wait to meet his old friend and harass him about his great destiny.

He was even more curious to meet the woman

who had tempted this self-proclaimed confirmed bachelor to marry.

His investment trip could wait. First, he needed to get himself to Sussex and bear witness as Alex, one of his closest friends, got himself married.

A week later, Crispin joined Gregory Lattimar, who'd arrived the previous evening after the long journey from Northumberland, in the parlour at Edge Hall, awaiting the arrival of the bridegroom who had gone to the kitchens to check on preparations for the wedding feast to be offered on the estate grounds after the ceremony to his friends, neighbours and tenants.

Crispin went over to clap Lattimar on the back. 'Recovered from your journey? That was one long ride.'

'It was,' Lattimar acknowledged. 'But I had to do whatever was necessary to arrive on time. I wouldn't miss witnessing Alex get leg-shackled for the world.'

'Do you know anything about the bride? Or their courtship? When we last met in February, unless I was too dense or drunk to remember, I don't recall Alex saying anything about his partiality for any lady.'

'He didn't mention a thing,' Lattimar confirmed. 'When I first received the invitation, if I hadn't recognised Alex's handwriting on the note, I would have thought you sent it as a joke.'

'Is she a bride recommended by the Duke?' Crispin asked.

'I don't know much about her, except my mother told me she's the daughter of the Duke's librarian. Which means she couldn't have been recommended by him, since Farisdeen would have wanted a much richer and higher-born bride for his heir. Also, if she's the daughter of the Duke's librarian, Alex must have known her for a long time. I understand the librarian, an antiquities scholar, has been in residence at Edge Hall since well before Alex started here as estate manager.'

'Friends to lovers?' Crispin suggested.

'Maybe. When next we are all together in London, we must pry the story out of him. With all the family milling around last night, there was no opportunity to draw him aside for private discussion, and he'll certainly be too busy during the wedding and reception today.'

And afterwards, he won't linger, too impatient to take his bride away and begin the honeymoon, Crispin thought. As he would be, if he were leaving his wedding reception to claim Marcella Cranmore as his bride.

'Can't blame him for being impatient,' Lattimar was saying. 'Lovely, isn't she, his Miss Sudderfeld? I understand she's a scholar, too, like her father. I would never have expected Alex to fall for a bluestocking.'

'One can never predict who will engage one's mind and touch one's heart.' How could he have predicted he would become so attached to a railway engineer's daughter that he still felt like a gaping hole had been ripped in his life since he left her?

Then Alex walked in to join them, such a smile of joy on his face, Crispin could have no doubt that the choice of bride had been his alone. After quizzing him for a few minutes on the outrage of having taken this momentous step without a single consultation with his oldest friends—who could hardly be of much help in making the decision, Alex protested, as both were unmarried and determined to remain that way—it was time to escort the bridegroom to church to meet his bride.

Crispin had been sceptical of Alex's sudden desire to marry. At first he'd attributed it to the Duke's desire, after losing his own unmarried and childless son, to see his new heir wedding and begetting without delay. But the glow of happiness in Alex's eyes had convinced him this wedding was entirely his friend's idea. That he was wholeheartedly, completely committed to his lady.

It was, in fact, the reason he'd decided to marry at once, Alex confided to them on the way to the church. With the Duke pressing more 'suitable' candidates on him, he wanted to convince his lady, who had no desire to become a duchess, to wed him before the Duke entangled him with someone else and the lady he treasured could find more excuses to refuse him.

No desire to be a duchess. Alex's Jocelyn sounded even more like Marcella, Crispin thought, suppressing a smile.

'Was Farisdeen finally reconciled to your choice?' Lattimar asked.

'I don't know,' Alex admitted. 'We haven't spoken since I announced my intention to marry Jocelyn. She's not the bride he would have chosen for me, of course. But I'll have no other. He may not support us, but eventually I persuaded him not to oppose me.'

Crispin and Lattimar exchanged glances. There had to be an interesting story behind that bland statement. But since they were arriving at the church, the telling of it would have to wait for another day.

'Aren't you nervous? Marriage is so...permanent,' Crispin couldn't keep from asking as they descended from the carriage and approached the church.

'Nervous? No, impatient!' Alex said with grin.

Crispin noted the evidence of his impatience on his friend's face as they walked into the church,

Alex's body tensing in anticipation. He heard the bridegroom's long, slow intake of breath as they waited by altar and saw the bride enter the church on her father's arm.

She was lovely, but it was his friend's face that Crispin watched. Alex, the solid, hard-working, serious man. His small family estate provided only a modest income, but when at Oxford, he'd never shown any inclination to go on drunken sprees or dally with the ladies, as so many undergraduates did. Level-headed, down to earth— Crispin would have said Alex didn't have a romantic bone in his body.

But the rapture on his face as his bride came down the aisle, the answering delight on the face of his bride, who never took her gaze from him as she walked over to take his hand at the altar, was the expression of a man completely and totally in love.

Of course, Alex had not suffered through the childhood Crispin had. Still, he seemed to believe marital happiness was possible. Marcella certainly did. Was he wrong to let her go so easily?

He felt a niggle of envy. If he could bring himself to wrestle past the demons of his childhood, would he open himself to such rapture by claiming Marcella?

A deep longing tightened his chest, sending an aching sadness through his body. Suddenly he wanted more than anything to see Marcella, talk with her. Perhaps, despite her reservations about marrying an aristocrat and his deep-seated worry that marriage would be the death of serenity and his fears about his ability to make happiness last, maybe he should explore the possibility of being more than just friends with her.

He already knew her bright spirit and lively mind would keep him entertained and engaged. Her beauty struck a deep chord of response in him, so that he couldn't imagine ever tiring of making love to her.

Why shy away from trying to claim what Alex had found?

Then and there, he decided before he went on his exploratory journey to Southampton, he would return to London and seek out Marcella Cranmore.

Chapter Eighteen

Meanwhile, in her grandfather's handsome manor house outside Tynemouth, Marcella and her mother were receiving her father, who had just returned from London. After hugs and greetings all around, they settled in the bright afternoon sunlight of the family parlour for a convivial tea to catch up on the news.

Marcella felt her dull spirits brighten just seeing her father, which would allow her to once again talk with him about the work she loved. Along with asking about the progress of the surveys filed to move forward towards construction of the Great Western and the projects her father was considering taking on next, she asked him, 'Did Lord Dellamont happen to call at the office?'

She thought she'd kept her tone casual, but her father gave her a penetrating glance before replying, 'No, I haven't seen the Viscount since our solicitor told me he'd come to invest. Were you expecting him to drop by?'

'When I saw him last before leaving London, he said he might,' she replied, hoping she'd managed to keep the disappointment from her voice.

She couldn't have expected him to have called yet, she tried to rally herself. It had been hardly more than a fortnight since their final meeting in Lady Arlsley's garden. Probably he had only just finished settling his mother and sister back in the country. With his father remaining in London to attend Parliament, he wouldn't have wanted to come by the city before heading out on his exploring venture.

She realised she'd lost the thread of the conversation and looked up to see her father's gaze on her, his expression concerned. He angled his head in unspoken question; she gave hers a little shake in response to tell him she was fine.

After her mother finished relating the tale of her expedition to Newcastle to order new hangings and furniture for the guest bedrooms, which she felt had grown rather shabby, her father said, 'Austin is finishing up details at the office, but will journey down to join us tomorrow.' Turning to Marcella, he added, 'I hoped you would be glad to see him.'

Austin, here tomorrow. A small spark of warmth

penetrated her chilled dullness. 'Of course. I'm always glad to see him.'

'Good.' He opened his lips as if to say more, then closed them, leaving it at that.

Did Papa know more than he was revealing about her old friend's intentions?

The following afternoon, Marcella was once again in the sunny back parlour, trying to keep her wandering attention on her book. Her parents had driven over to take tea with neighbours they'd not seen for several months, but she was not in the mood to be cheery for company—or to be asked how she'd enjoyed her latest stay in London.

She looked up to find the maid at the door. 'Mr Gilling has arrived, miss. I told him Mr and Mrs Cranmore was out but you was at home. Do you want to receive him?'

Talking with Austin was sure to relieve her dreariness. In any event, it was time to discover whether her debut had in fact prompted him to see her in a new light. Determine whether taking their long friendship to a different level was even possible.

'Of course. Please show him in, see that his usual room is prepared, and bring us some tea.'

After curtsying, the maid went back out. Marcella put down her book, trying to recapture some enthusiasm. Today she might uncover the key to her future.

'Marcella!' Gilling said, walking in a moment later to return the hug she gave him. 'You are looking lovely! Sunny as this room in that charming yellow gown.'

She must have made some progress in getting him to see her as a woman. She couldn't recall Austin ever commenting on her wardrobe before. 'You are looking fine as well. How did you leave things in London?'

'Work is going forward on the specifications for the Great Western. Already we've had enquiries at the office for the firm to potentially survey, and even contract to construct, several other pending projects. With the boom in railway construction just beginning, I don't think we will be lacking for business any time soon.'

'Father will be delighted. He prefers to remain busy.'

'How are you doing? Did you enjoy your time in London? I… I was surprised that you left so soon. I've heard the London Season lasts until summer.'

'It does, but I'd had enough. They…weren't very nice to me,' she admitted, trying to put the best face on it.

Austin frowned. 'I was afraid that might be the case, based on the way some of the aristocratic investors treat us when they come to the office. As if we were lackeys, rather than trained professionals, and should be thrilled they condescend to have us make money for them. I'm so glad the prospect of being styled "my lady" didn't turn your head. That is, you're not still intent on marrying a gentleman?'

'I was never intent on it. I only went into society to please Mama.'

'I guess you really have grown up, if you'll no longer let your mother make your choices for you. I didn't want to stand in your way if marrying into the gentry was what you truly wanted, but…well, it was a shock to know you were entertaining suitors and contemplating marriage.'

They paused for a moment as the maid brought in the tea service, Marcella waiting to reply until after she'd fixed them each a cup.

'I'm not the little girl you teased and comforted any more,' she said, picking back up the threads of the conversation.

'You are no less dear to me. Even more precious, actually. I… I know you could look much higher for a husband than a chief engineering assistant, but if you could consider it, I'd be humbled and grateful for ever if you would consent to be my wife.'

There it was…the declaration she'd hoped for,

dreamed about since she'd turned sixteen, put up her hair and let down her skirts.

So why didn't she feel more excited?

There was the important matter of her place in the office, she told herself. 'It would be good to go on as we have before—with a few changes, of course,' she added, blushing when she thought of the intimacies she would have to allow him as her husband. 'I could help you in the office, just as I've helped Father.'

Frowning, Gilling gave a negative shake of his head. 'Don't misunderstand; I admire and respect your father. But I've always felt he…took advantage of you a bit. I could understand, right after he lost your brother, that it was comforting to keep you close. But he should long ago have sent you out of that masculine sphere in which you do not belong. What would happen if any investors thought you took any actual part in the business? I know you are clever, but the bald truth is that our work would be devalued and we'd soon lose customers. Aside from the potential to discourage clients, even with you there just to pour tea, I always worried one of those arrogant aristocrats would not treat you with the respect they should. Nor is there any reason for you to trouble your pretty head calculating figures.'

Her hopes, which had risen slightly at his initial proposal, slumped again. 'I enjoy calculating figures.'

'To be sure, your work at the office occupied time. Time you were never one to fritter away shopping or gossiping with. For which I admire you! But once we married, with a household of your own to run, you'd be fully occupied. And after a time, I hope you would be as thrilled as I would be to welcome children of our own into it. They would certainly keep you even busier.'

'You would not need or want me to help outside the home?' she asked, wanting to make his position perfectly clear.

'You could make a significant contribution as hostess, as I've seen you do for your father when he entertains business associates. I'm not sure yet, I've only had a few discussions with friends, but if my career goes well enough, I might one day be interested in standing for Parliament. Clever and charming as you are, you'd make an excellent political hostess. So you see, you'll have much to keep you occupied and support me in your sphere, while I carry on in mine.'

He took her limp hand in his. 'Our marriage would be a good bargain. I've been fond of you since you were an engaging child. But I was struck to the core when I finally realised you are now a beautiful young woman. I know you've always been fond of me as well. We can take that bedrock of affection and build on it to create a truly deep and satisfying marriage. I'll deem it a privilege to take care of you and would cherish you and our children for the rest of our days. I know your parents would approve of our union, which I know is important to you.'

'What of my working with Father?'

Gilling smiled. 'Despite knowing you were making your debut, in many ways I believe your father still thinks of you as the little girl he welcomed into his office to console him after the death of his son. Once you are actually married, I'm sure he will realise it's no longer appropriate for you to work with him. Besides, some fine day, he'll be ready to retire. He will want grandchildren to play with in his declining years.'

She'd wondered what Gilling saw as the proper place for his wife, and now she knew. He wanted a conventional woman who occupied herself with conventional duties. If she accepted him, he would probably speak with her father and try to persuade him to no longer allow her to consult with him in the office.

Her one escape from exile to domestic life would be playing hostess to engineers over dinners, where she might encourage them to talk about their projects.

Would that be enough?

She was surprised to find her doubts about the

answer to that question even stronger than they had been before her aborted Season.

But with her entire life and future suspended in the balance, she shouldn't give him a hasty reply. This matter of marriage deserved long, careful thought.

She squeezed the hand she held and looked up, seeing hope and eagerness in his eyes. 'You have long been dear to me as well, and I am honoured and flattered by your proposal. But if you will permit, I'd like some time to think it over. As a child, I dreamed for years that you would ask for my hand when I grew up. But now that you've made that childhood fantasy a reality, I want to respond for the right reasons.'

'Of course. Take all time you need. I'm already delighted you have given me hope, rather than just refused me outright for my presumption.'

'I would never consider you presumptuous! Who has better right to ask for my hand than the man who has helped and supported my whole family for years? I won't keep you waiting long, I promise.'

Just then, she heard voices in the hallway. 'That must be Mama and Papa returning. Shall we... say nothing of this just yet?'

'Of course not. I won't speak of it until you give me permission.'

'They will be delighted to see you.'

Those were the last private words they had time to exchange before the parlour door opened and her parents walked in, her mother coming over to give Gilling a hug, her father shaking his hand. 'I'll turn the tea tray over to you, Mama, and go let Grandda know Austin has arrived.'

'Yes, see if you can persuade him to join us— and on your way out, find Nancy and have her tell Cook we'll need another pot of tea. You'll be staying with us, won't you, Austin?'

'I've already told Nancy to make sure his room is ready,' Marcella assured her.

'Excellent. Do sit, Austin,' her mother said, indicating a spot on the sofa beside her. 'Tell us what was going on in London when you left.'

After curtsying to the group, Marcella made her escape.

She didn't really need to consult Grandfather, who though he liked Gilling, wasn't much interested in callers, especially one whom he'd see at dinner tonight anyway. But she didn't think she could sit in the parlour and make polite conversation when the imperative to make a decision pressed like a leaden weight against her chest.

She didn't intend to dawdle and debate it for weeks. For Gilling's sake and her own, she wanted to review what she knew and what she felt and make her decision quickly.

A decision on which her whole future hinged.

She found the maid, ordered more tea, and popped in to inform her grandfather of the new arrival. He replied, as she'd expected, that he would let her parents have tea with him and then meet the young man at dinner later.

After giving him a kiss, she left her grandfather's study…but couldn't bring herself to rejoin the group in the parlour.

Instead, she grabbed a wrap and walked out the back door into the extensive gardens.

Usually walking the pathways bordered with exuberant blooms—nodding daffodils in shades of white, gold and yellow, vivid purple crocuses, and the pale stripes of early tulips—lifted her spirits and eased whatever anxiety troubled her. Today, the garden was not working its usual magic.

Perhaps because the decision she had to make was so crucial.

Perhaps because she was so uncertain what the right decision should be.

It was clear now that Austin wanted a strictly conventional wife, and would work to persuade Father to relegate her to the household as soon as they married. Could she find a man more amenable than Austin to her carrying on her work?

Where would she find such a man? Don her forbidden men's clothing again, slip into a meeting of the Institution of Civil Engineers, and conduct a survey of the members?

Despite the wry smile envisioning that tactic engendered—and the pang of sorrow as she remembered her splendid adventure, making her miss even more the exceptional man who'd made it possible—pursuing that option was impossible.

She supposed she could reject Austin, continue working with her father, and encourage Papa to bring home other single engineers. Over wine and dinner, try to eke out their opinions on the matter of educated women and their roles. If she received encouraging answers from any of them, try to attract their amorous interest.

But that course of action was unlikely to produce many suitable prospects, the process would be time-consuming, and most men would hold the same views Austin did. Along the way, if she rejected Austin, her concerned parents would be pressing ever harder for her to choose someone else to love and protect their dear daughter.

Which brought her back to the central question. She'd long cared for Austin. She was pretty sure they could turn their decade-long affection into a warm and congenial bond to last through the years.

A bond that would be warm, safe…and unexciting. A relationship that offered her the prospect of becoming a wife and mother, and she'd long wanted more than those.

After doubt and instability were thrown into her life by her father's deep grief over her brother's death, Austin had been the one person who made her feel safe, wanted, *enough*, when she hadn't been enough to ease her father's sadness. But her desires now went beyond the yearnings of a ten-year-old.

What she'd always felt for her father's assistant, she now realised, was the hero worship of a child for the attractive older man who'd indulged and comforted her in a time of great loss, and been a steady help to her family through the years.

But compared to what she now felt for Dellamont—well, there was no comparison.

The idea of spending time with Austin didn't fill her with the thrill of anticipation she'd felt when she'd known she would be seeing Crispin. She'd never experienced with her father's assistant the simmering awareness of him as a man, of herself as a woman, that she felt with Dellamont. She didn't lie awake at night dreaming of kissing Gilling or feeling his hands caressing her body, as she so often had and still did with Crispin.

With the Viscount, she hadn't had to hide her love for and expertise in mathematics or her desire to work in the engineering world. He'd admired, even seemed proud of her for it. Though admittedly she'd manoeuvred him into doing it, he'd even gone out of his way to allow her, for one afternoon, to become an active part of that world.

Don't live without passion, the Viscount had advised. Not that she found Austin in any way repellent, but the idea of kissing him didn't send fingers of fire licking along her veins as it did when she remembered kissing Crispin. She could imagine giving herself to the Viscount with enthusiasm, a melting heat spiralling from her very centre as she recalled the caress of his tongue on hers.

If she were truly honest, when she envisioned the man she wished she could invite to share her life and her bed, the face that appeared was... Crispin's.

Which meant that as she'd feared and secretly long suspected, she truly had fallen in love with Crispin d'Aubignon.

How could she have committed such a colossal blunder?

Should she have refused him that day in Lady Arlsley's garden?

But marrying him was impossible. As appealing as the man was, he was the wrong man from the wrong world. Her travesty of a Season had demonstrated that she would never be accepted as a part of his. And if she entered it anyway, ostracised and alone, she would lose all of hers.

There'd be no more working at the engineering office. She would probably have to limit her visits with her parents and grandparents, if she were permitted to visit them at all. She'd certainly not be able to entertain them at the Earl's house.

More important than any other consideration, though, was that having witnessed all her life the tender love her parents shared, she knew she could not marry anyone who offered her less than the all-consuming love she now realised she felt for Crispin.

Crispin, who had a deep aversion to marriage and would enter wedlock most unwillingly.

Even if the shock of emptiness after their abrupt parting made him, too, realise what they felt for each other was love, would he be able to overcome his instinctive resistance to marriage and offer his whole heart? She didn't believe he saw her only as a novelty to toy with, as Lord Hoddleston had always claimed, but could she hold his affection over the long term? Or with his bitter experience of domestic life, was he doomed to feel constrained by marital bonds, to eventually lose interest in the strange, unconventional woman he'd wed, and go on to pursue other ladies?

Fidelity in marriage was not a virtue valued in his world. It was absolutely required by her.

So...she couldn't marry Dellamont, who had made an offer only because his honour required it. Though she was sure he liked her and he'd admitted outright that she attracted him, he hadn't added to his proposal, as Austin had, even a modest claim of deep fondness.

Knowing now how she truly felt about him, she wasn't sure she could meet him again as a friend, if he should show up again at her father's office.

But one thing she did know for sure. She couldn't marry Austin Gilling.

Some time tonight or tomorrow, she would have to tell him so.

Chapter Nineteen

〰〰〰

The day after celebrating Alex and Jocelyn's nuptials, Crispin had set off from Edge Hall to return to London. Tempted as he was to ride straight through, in addition to arriving mud-spattered and weary, it would be far too late to call at Cranmore's office. Better to break the journey—and mull over strategy on the way.

But perhaps that hadn't been the best approach, since after two days of hard riding, Crispin arrived back at his rooms in Jasmin Street not just weary, but conflicted.

While watching joy on the face of his friend as he took the hand of the lady he made his wife, he'd been inspired with the courage to reach for the same happiness himself. And though by now he was certain the emotion he felt for Marcella was fully deserving of the description 'love', he was not truly certain whether he dared repeat his proposal.

He had no illusions that asking her to wed him wouldn't mean asking her to leave her world for one that had already demonstrated it could treat her with indifference at best, cruelty and condescension at worst. Was it really fair to ask her to take that risk—for him?

More fundamentally, she had grown up in a happy home and expected the eventual marriage she made to provide the same tranquillity and delight. A tranquil home filled with congenial spouses and children was something he knew nothing about. Could they weather the inevitable disagreements caused by the difference in their backgrounds, upbringings and expectations of life? Hang on to the excitement and joy that made their association thus far so wondrous?

But when he thought of being with her, he saw not the dissimilar background, but all the similarities in interests, outlook and goals. Besides, though society at large might never fully accept her, he didn't intend to spend much time among the *ton*. He had no doubt that his closest friends would embrace her, and she would enjoy participating in the activities and interests of their unconventional wives and families.

Though he wasn't sure he could make her happy, when he thought again of his initial goal of wedding a conventional *ton* maiden who would ask nothing more from him than eventually becoming a countess, with the right to rule over his establishment and raise his children, it suddenly occurred to him that by doing that, he might well fall into his father's destructive pattern.

Not that he would ever treat a lady with the disdain and lack of respect his mother endured from his father. But he though he wasn't sure he could guarantee Marcella happiness for a lifetime, he realised that he would be in great danger of guaranteeing he made a conventional, submissive wife *un*happy. Because sooner or later, he would begin resenting her...because she wasn't Marcella.

The unique, unusual, talented woman he really wanted.

There was nothing for it, then. He would have to risk his whole heart, despite the devastation that could occur if it all ended badly. Offer his heart, and hope that independent, unconventional Marcella Cranmore would accept the challenge of wedding him.

Two mornings later, fired with an enthusiasm underpinned by terror, Crispin woke before dawn. After dressing with care, he presented himself at Richard Cranmore's office at the earliest hour he could expect anyone to be manning a desk.

To his frustration and disappointment, he found attached to the door a note indicating the office was closed for two weeks and requesting anyone interested in contacting the firm to post a letter, or pay a return call when the engineer returned from Newcastle.

Stumped, Crispin retrieved his horse and went to ride in the park while he decided what to do next. Waiting another two weeks was unacceptable.

Had the whole family returned to Newcastle—where he recalled Marcella saying her father had another office and her grandfather a country estate?

Turning his horse back towards the gate before he'd completed one circuit, Crispin headed for his club where he could find a good breakfast and a copy of Debrett's.

He needed to discover the location of the country estate of Sir Thomas Webbingdon and hope the whole family had indeed gone there.

Several days later, Crispin rode into the pleasant coastal town of Tynemouth. He'd stopped first at Cranmore's office in Newcastle, exerting some charm and using his standing as an investor to induce the clerk to reveal that although his employer was not in the office, he could be found at the home of his father-in-law, Faircastle House, which was located near the coast just north of Tynemouth.

Crispin covered the ten miles in good time,

found the posting inn at Tynemouth the helpful employee had recommended, and enjoyed a fine dinner in the taproom. Despite the impatience that made him fume at yet another day's delay, there was no point presenting himself at Sir Thomas's house after dark and uninvited.

He would bathe, dress in clean garments, and ride out from Tynemouth tomorrow.

Would he find Marcella there? It seemed now like an eternity since he'd last seen her. A long, lonely, unfulfilling void he never wished to be stranded in again. Whatever it took, he must convince Marcella to marry him.

The next day, after waking again before dawn, Crispin waited as long as he could stand it before riding out to Faircastle House. After handing over his horse to the servant who saw him approach, he walked up to rap on the front door.

The maid who conveyed him to a pleasant reception room said she would inform Miss Marcella that he had asked to see her.

He wished somehow he could have come upon her unannounced. He worried that, forewarned of his presence, she might try to have him sent away. He didn't intend to leave until he had asked her face to face how she felt about him and whether or not she thought they might have a future.

* * *

After pacing back and forth for several minutes, the sound of the opening door had him looking up, his pulse stampeding and a shock going through him as he saw her dearly missed face. He found himself in front of her, bowing, without having any conscious memory of crossing the room.

For a moment, they simply stared at each other, Crispin drinking in every detail of her lovely form, supremely conscious of that familiar surge of desire at her nearness. With difficulty, he restrained himself from seizing her and pulling her into his arms.

'Lord Dellamont, what a surprise!' she said, her eyes seeming to rove over him with as much hunger as his were inspecting her. 'Are you investigating potential investments in the area?'

'Nothing to do with railways.'

'Then why are you here?' she asked, motioning him to towards the sofa.

Too nervous to sit, he said, 'I think you know why I'm here.'

'After discovering that my family had left London, you came here to…investigate continuing our friendship?'

'I want much more than that now. It's my dearest hope that perhaps you now want that, too.'

In his rosy imaginings, at this point, she threw

herself into his arms and declared she'd come to realise she loved him, too. Instead, unsmiling, with a sudden reserve that sent a wave of panic through him, she said, 'If I understand your meaning, you are envisioning something more formal and…permanent?'

Swallowing hard, he nodded.

'If that is true, then what has changed? I seem to recall you were determined to avoid wedlock.'

'I was opposed to wedlock in general. But when I think about spending my life with you, all I see is…joy. Joy and enthusiasm and a richness I'd never experienced until I started sharing the things that matter most to me with you. A joy and richness that, like a lackwit, I didn't fully appreciate until we parted.'

'So this time, you come to me motivated by more than just honour?'

'When I proposed before, although my heart was urging me to it even then, I was not quite able to push myself to offer you a full commitment. I've told you what kind of childhood I had. Fights, arguments, constant brangling. How could I let myself in for that? With no experience of anything else, how could I guarantee I would not revert to that pattern and drag you down into it? So I resisted, even though I knew you were different. That we shared more interests and were more in harmony than I've ever been with anyone else, even my closest friends. At first, suffering through the chill and despondency of leaving you, I tried to tell myself it would get better. That after I began to forget the delight of being with you almost daily, I'd become my old self again. Be content in my solitude again.'

'But you weren't.'

'No. The misery just got worse.'

She nodded. 'I told myself the same thing. But the sense of loss and hopelessness didn't abate for me either. No matter how much I tried to tell myself that marrying an aristocrat, cutting myself off from my background and any association with the engineering world, would mean only heartache.'

'So…you would now be willing to face that?'

'I might be…for a man who could offer his whole heart. Just as I would be willing to offer mine.'

'I had to come back to you, Marcella, but I can't claim there's no longer any risk. That I am certain I can make you happy for a lifetime.'

'No one can claim that. We must make our own happiness, together. By weathering whatever comes, good fortune or ill. As my parents did. It could have destroyed them when they lost my brother and my mother was unable to bear another son. But they drew together, accepted it, neither blaming the other, and went on. Never forgetting the loss. But not letting the tragedy master them.'

'That's the kind of bond I would like to have, too. With you.'

She smiled then. 'Good.'

His confidence increased at that encouragement, but before he could drop to his knees and deliver the proposal he'd come to offer, she held out a hand, halting him.

'Then before you say anything more, you need to speak with someone else.'

'Ah, yes. Do it properly this time. Ask your father for permission to address you.'

'No, better to ask my grandda. The one whose wealth propelled us to make our first bargain should approve the possibility of a new one. I'll take you to him.'

She led him upstairs, then knocked at a door. 'Grandda, are you busy?'

'Never too busy to see my little lass,' the reply came before the door opened.

A tall, grey-haired man with his granddaughter's bright green eyes stood on the threshold, his smile fading when he spied Crispin. Noting the powerful build, weathered face and shrewd expression, Crispin could easily believe this man, who'd begun as a boy wrestling coal from the bowels of earth, had persevered to invent and market machines that had earned him wealth and title.

'Who is this young man?' he demanded.

'Grandda, may I introduce Crispin d'Aubignon, Viscount Dellamont. My grandfather, Sir Thomas Webbingdon.'

Noting Marcella had introduced *him* to her grandfather, rather than the higher title to the lesser one, Crispin suppressed a smile. The Earl would have been livid at being accorded lower status. The introduction just confirmed to him in what exceptional regard Marcella held Sir Thomas.

The entrepreneur waved them into the room and towards chairs placed in front of his desk. The dark-panelled library was full of books, the desk littered with papers that indicated Sir Thomas was still fully engaged in business enterprises. A fire burned low on the hearth where a mantel clock ticked, and from the large window on the side wall, Crispin caught a distant view of the sea.

'What would a viscount be wanting with my granddaughter?' the man's gruff question recalled him.

'I want your permission to ask her to marry me.'

Sir Thomas frowned. 'Why should I grant ye her hand? She weren't happy in London. My fault, I shouldn't have supported her ma in sending her there. From my own dealings, I know how yer kind treat those not born among them. Ye would ask her to go back to that?'

'Have you told him about the bargain?' Crispin asked her.

'No,' she said, blushing. 'You tell him.'

After nodding to her, he turned to Sir Thomas. 'I don't normally attend London society. My father pushed me to court the "Factory Heiress" for her dowry. I wasn't inclined to comply, but if I agreed, the Earl promised to allow my mother, whom he usually isolates in the country, to remain in London and participate in the Season she loves. At the time, I had no idea that your granddaughter, who impressed me very much when I met her in Bristol, was in fact the "Factory Heiress".'

'I was very impressed with him, too,' Marcella broke in to say.

Smiling at that tribute, Crispin continued, 'At my first ball, I was astonished to encounter Marcella. After we chatted and discovered we had both become embroiled in society to honour the wishes of family, we made a pact. I would pretend to court her, placating my father and allowing my mother time in London. While my courting her would discourage fortune hunters and dissuade the malicious from slighting her. No one would wish to offend a lady who might one day be a countess. We agreed we'd maintain the deception for a month or so, then part as friends and return to our former lives.'

'I heard yer father the Earl has been struggling with decreased income from agricultural properties.'

Crispin shrugged. 'I've been making other investments, so I will not be as dependent on income from land. The wealth of the future will come from other sources.' He smiled. 'As you well know, sir.'

Sir Thomas nodded. 'I've heard about yer investments. Men can lose everything counting on foolishness, but ye seem to have a good head on yer shoulders. Ye've made sound decisions.'

Crispin looked up, surprised. Had this captain of industry investigated *him*?

As if to confirm that, Sir Thomas continued, 'I may be an old man, but I still have my finger on the pulse of what's happening. I'm no nob neither, but I have eyes and ears that let me know what's happening in society. So I know this bargain of yourn didn't protect Marcella.'

Her face paling, Marcella looked at her grandfather, stricken. 'You...you know why I left?'

'Don't ye be going all sad-eyed, lass. I know what was said about ye was foul rubbish.' Turning to Crispin, frowning, he accused, 'Ye did nothing to rescue her good name.'

'Don't think that fact doesn't gall me still! I

couldn't call the bounder out. That would only confirm the rumours. I did ask your granddaughter to marry me, but she refused.'

'Did she now?' Addressing Marcella, he said, 'Why are ye bringing him here now, if ye refused him once, missy?'

'Because he only asked me out of honour.'

Her grandfather nodded. 'A good enough reason for a gentleman. But honour wasn't enough for ye?'

'No.' She looked over at Crispin. 'He must ask out of love. And promise me everything.'

Her grandfather smiled at that before his face hardened. 'I looked into this baron who tried to ruin ye. Bought up all his debts, called them in. Given the option of debtors' prison or resettling abroad, he was encouraged to take the trip overseas. Before leaving, he's to publish an account in all the London newspapers, confessing he made up the story to discredit the heiress so he might get her dowry once she had no choice left but to marry him. Then he'll be gone from England and can trouble ye both no more.'

The old man looked at Crispin, a twinkle in his eyes. 'Ye see, there are advantages to not being born a gentleman. Ye don't have to play by their rules.'

'Bravo, sir! Thank you for doing what I could not.'

'But what about society? I'm not a green 'un, to

believe some print in the newspapers will remove all the taint from my granddaughter's name.'

'Don't think she'll be isolated. In lieu of the *ton*, I can offer Marcella the society of a small group of good friends who will accept and welcome her. Friends whom I think she will find interesting, who will appreciate her exceptional talents. One just married a woman who is a translator of ancient Greek. Another friend's younger brother wed a woman who runs a boarding school for disadvantaged girls, and his sister is a good friend of one of Marcella's schoolmates from Miss Axminster's.'

'Remember I told you about Emma Henley, how kind she was to me?' Marcella asked.

'Ah, that odd female and her friends who weren't interested in tittle-tattle about suitors, claiming they didn't want to marry and would be reformers instead?'

'Yes, those are the ones.'

'Silly women. Girls must marry. Need husbands to protect them.'

'Maybe for now, Grandda,' Marcella argued. 'But not for always. Forging new paths, one day women will be able to carve their own futures, independent of men.'

'That day isn't here yet, lass,' he said, shaking a finger at her. 'So, you think ye will be accepted and happy with these friends of Dellamont's?'

'I think they sound wonderful and intriguing.'

'But what her about duties as a countess?' Webbingdon turned to ask Crisipin. 'I understand she'll be expected to attend court, go to balls and all those fancy to-dos she so dislikes.'

Crispin shrugged. 'She'll be a countess. She can do whatever she wants.'

Sir Thomas laughed. 'I'm beginning to think I like ye, lad. As for you, missy, ye didn't want him before. Do ye think now he will make ye happy?'

'I think now he's all I ever wanted,' she said softly.

Crispin felt such a soaring rise of hope, he almost didn't hear her grandfather's next words.

'If he's an earl's son he don't need your dowry. Will he still marry ye without it?'

'Grandda!' Marcella protested, her face going scarlet.

'Keep the dowry. *She* is all I want.' He turned to face Marcella. 'All I'll ever want.'

Sir Thomas's expression softened. 'Better go ask her then, lad. And that dowry? I expect ye can have that, too—if she says yes.'

Her hand on his arm, Crispin walked with Marcella out to the garden. 'This way,' she said, linking her fingers with his and leading him down a path bordered by great swathes of early tulips and stands of daffodil and crocus. 'Walk with me in the place I love most.'

'It's beautiful here. I understand why you love it.'

'Grandda loved it first. This garden was the main reason he bought this house. He could have had newer, larger, fancier manors in Tynemouth or in Newcastle itself. But he was captivated by this place, the distant whisper of the sea, the hint of salt in the air, and the extensive gardens. Working in the mines, in blackness stinking of coal, Grandda vowed when he made his fortune, he would surround himself with light, colour, and fresh air. And he did.'

She stopped by a bench surrounded by a great intertwined mass of rambling roses, not yet in bloom. Crispin could hear the distant roar of the surf, while sharp salt-scented air filled his head.

'You would not have agreed to hear me out if your grandfather had forbidden it?' he asked as he urged her to a seat.

'I'm not sure,' she admitted. 'I love him so dearly it would break my heart to be estranged from him. But it would wound my soul to be estranged from you. I thought being distanced from my family, being forced to deal with your world, would be impossible. But now, I think I can bear anything but losing you.'

Crispin swallowed hard, hearing in those words

that he had truly been forgiven. For not continuing to press his suit the first time. For wounding her by accepting her refusal so easily and going off to leave her alone.

Placing her arm on the bench, Marcella gazed around her with fondness. 'I always feel like the sea air is blowing away worries and cares.'

'What worries and cares is it blowing away today?'

'You are here. I have no more worries.'

'While I have just one. You did refuse me before, you know. But I shall do it properly this time, not just make you a hasty bow in the middle of a garden path.'

Clasping her hand, he went down on one knee. 'Marcella Cranmore, I love you more than I ever thought it possible to love anyone. My delight and inspiration, will you risk your future and marry me?'

'Leave my former life without regrets? Even face eventually becoming a countess?'

'Remember the part about weathering hardships together? I'll have to be an earl, after all. We can help each other through it.'

'I can even weather leaving Papa and the office. Which I would have eventually lost anyway, since Papa will some day retire and Gilling didn't want me there.'

Alarm jolted through Crispin. 'You…spoke with him?'

'Yes. He made me an offer, actually. But he wanted me to be a conventional wife, and I just couldn't. Besides, that soul-searching time alone taught me to see the difference between my childhood affection for him, and what I felt for you.'

'Affection, but not passion?' he guessed.

'Not for him.'

'Thank heaven,' he said, breathing out a sigh that made her laugh. 'But since you've still not relieved my anxiety by saying "yes", let me add one more inducement. It might not be appropriate for my wife to work in an engineer's office, but I would like her to work in a similar capacity—as my engineering advisor. I have only a rudimentary grasp of the mathematical principles involved in constructing sound and safe bridges, tunnels and viaducts. I watched you at Stephenson's lecture. It was clear you understood everything, even the most technical discussion. I want you to accompany me when I go out to inspect railway ventures. Ride the routes with me, look at the technical drawings and decide on the efficiency and feasibility of what's being planned. It won't be like running your own engineering office, I know—'

Face alight, she threw her arms around him, interrupting, 'It will be wonderful! You'll let me be a real advisor, reading diagrams, calculating angles and slope? Doing all but overseeing actual construction?'

Crispin grinned. 'I haven't yet figured out a way for you to do that.'

'Yes, yes and a thousand times, yes! I love you to distraction and I will marry you, my darling Crispin!'

'One "yes" will do nicely.'

Then he pulled her into his arms, pouring his relief and passion into a kiss that promised all the delights to come, for as long as both should live.

* * * * *

MILLS & BOON

Coming next month

THE HIGHLANDER'S INCONVENIENT BRIDE
Terri Brisbin

'When is Sheena expected to arrive?'

He thought he had time to truly accustom himself to marrying the one woman he could not abide. He thought he could ease into the decision and ready himself to be, at the least, tolerant of her. From the broad smile that spread over his father's face, Robbie knew that his hopes in this were for naught.

'On the morrow. A messenger arrived with word of her approach.'

Time was up for him and any thoughts he had of avoiding this. He knew his duty to his clan.

Robbie nodded to his parents and walked away. So many thoughts and questions filled his mind that he simply left the keep and headed to the yard next to the stables. The last time he'd seen Sheena she was training her father's newest colt. Unmindful of the danger, she had mounted the horse before it would tolerate a saddle or bridle of any kind and she rode the almost wild horse through the village and back to the keep, with her hair flowing out behind her, loose and wild, making her look like some heathen goddess of old. Incandescent with joy, she faltered when their gazes met and he saw her eyes were filled with only loathing.

And, as in every moment he'd ever shared with her

or any time he watched her, she never did as she'd been told to do. She broke her father's rules, damn the consequences. She disregarded her mother's lessons on correct behaviour and her warnings about a proper upbringing for a young woman who would be a wife to and mother of chieftains or their sons.

Soon, too soon, she would ride into Achnacarry and become his problem. She would need to grow up and change to be the wife of the future chieftain. She would need to become a mature woman who understood her place and fulfilled her duties. She could no longer be the hoyden who ran wild and followed her own path.

Surely, Sheena MacLerie would try to obey her father and mother by carrying out her duties.

Yet, even as he hoped, he knew differently for he'd seen the true Sheena MacLerie and understood what was headed in their direction. She was ill prepared for the role of being a laird's wife. Robbie knew all that and more to a certainty and his stomach roiled in anticipation of her arrival.

On the morrow.

Continue reading
THE HIGHLANDER'S INCONVENIENT BRIDE
Terri Brisbin

Available next month
www.millsandboon.co.uk

COMING SOON!

We really hope you enjoyed reading this book.
If you're looking for more romance, be sure to
head to the shops when new books are
available on

Thursday 22nd July

To see which titles are coming soon, please visit
millsandboon.co.uk/nextmonth

LET'S TALK
Romance

For exclusive extracts, competitions
and special offers, find us online: